≡ HEROINES OF WWI ≡

A PICTURE of HOPE

LIZ TOLSMA

BARBOUR
PUBLISHING

DEDICATION

To Jonalyn, my beautiful, precious treasure from God. While there are still many in this world who would deem your life unworthy, you are most special to us. There is nothing unworthy about your joy, your laughter, your kindness, your loving spirit, or your hardworking attitude. How empty our lives would be without you. Even if the world overlooks you, Dad and I never will. And neither will God.

———— ≋ ————

IMPORTANT NOTE TO READERS

Throughout the book, I use the term *"Mongoloid"* for children with Down syndrome. While the word carries negative connotations today and is not used, it is period correct for 1944. As a mom of a child with an intellectual disability, I'm highly sensitive to any derogatory terms used for people with special needs and did not come to my decision to use Mongoloid lightly; however, I did want to be true to the times. You will see that the characters in the book have nothing but love and compassion for the children with Down syndrome and do not use the term in a demeaning way. My intention is not to offend but to inform in a historically accurate way.

I shall betray tomorrow, not today.
Today, pull out my fingernails,
I shall not betray.
You do not know the limits of my courage,
I, I do.
You are five hands, harsh and full of rings,
Wearing hob-nailed boots.
I shall betray tomorrow, not today.
I need the night to make up my mind.
I need at least one night,
To disown, to abjure, to betray.
To disown my friends,
To abjure bread and wine,
To betray life,
To die.
I shall betray tomorrow, not today.
The file is under the windowpane.
The file is not meant for the window bars,
The file is not meant for the executioner,
The file is for my own wrists.
Today, I have nothing to say,
I shall betray tomorrow.

—"I Shall Betray Tomorrow" by Marianne Cohn, c. 1943

⚏ CHAPTER ONE ⚏

Monday, May 22, 1944
Normandy, France

"Shh." Jean-Paul Breslau peered over his shoulder at the group of men he was leading through the western French bocage and into a small patch of trees. Overhead, scattered clouds allowed only a few dots of starlight and a thin stream of moonlight to illuminate their way through the stands of beeches, the earth fragrant with a recent rain.

But they were making too much noise, stomping through the woods, speaking in more than a whisper, even laughing. The Nazis were smart. On to them. They knew the resistance, the Maquis, was busy working in this area.

American planes were supposed to drop much-needed supplies and arms in this area tonight. Of all the various resistance efforts Jean-Paul had been involved in over the past several years, these parachute drops were the most dangerous. The Germans heard the low-flying planes. They spotted the white silks as they floated to the ground in the pale light.

Especially here in Normandy, mostly farmland, there was little area in which to hide.

Tonight his skin prickled more than ever. Maybe because Henri had fortified himself with a good deal of cognac before they'd set off. Jean-Paul shouldn't have allowed him to come, but they needed every able body to lift the boxes and get rid of any evidence of a drop before the Germans discovered the spot.

"No one's about." Henri spoke in a normal tone of voice, though he did slightly slur his words.

Jean-Paul turned and shushed him again. "Don't get us killed."

"No problem there, boss."

Henri was always the troublemaker. The least trustworthy of them all. But Yves had taken sick and Gerard's wife was about to give birth. Jean-Paul's hands had been tied. "Stay here. You can be the lookout."

"Suits me." Henri slumped against a tree while Jean-Paul, Luc, and Pierre slipped deeper into the woods. It remained to be seen if Henri would even stay conscious much less be an effective lookout. His state of inebriation made a risky mission even more dangerous.

The ground underneath Jean-Paul's feet rumbled, setting off a rumbling in his chest. The American planes were close. He and his men had to hurry to make it to the clearing in time for the drop. He motioned his companions forward.

Even in the dark he knew these woods like the back of his hand. Ever since he was a small child, he'd played in this thicket, inventing games about pirates and robbers and the American cowboys he'd seen in the cinema.

Never in his life had he dreamed that in his own backyard he'd have more adventure than he could handle.

They stumbled to the edge of the tree line as the plane zoomed overhead. He gazed up when the cargo bay opened, and the box attached to the chute floated to the ground.

It struck with a thud, the chute drifting over it almost like snow. Jean-Paul and the others hurried forward.

A moment later, light flooded the field from all directions. "*Halten sie.*"

Jean-Paul's body went cold. He blinked against the brilliance that burned his eyes. Though he couldn't make out any shapes, there must be a ring of Germans around them.

And in front of their enemy was all the evidence they needed to shoot Jean-Paul and his compatriots on the spot. No questions asked. His breath caught in his throat, cutting off oxygen to his lungs.

One man dressed in a brown uniform with tall black boots stepped from behind the light and into the center of the ring, clutching a rifle that he trained straight on Jean-Paul's heart.

Jean-Paul raised his hands.

"What is it we have here?" The Nazi spoke perfect French.

Jean-Paul couldn't pretend not to understand him. "My friends and I were out for a walk when we saw a low-flying plane. We decided to investigate."

"Is that so? And you expect me to believe it?"

"*Oui*, for that is the truth. Imagine my surprise when the plane dropped this box."

"I'm sure it puzzled you a great deal." Though Jean-Paul couldn't make out the man's face, there was no mistaking that he was tall and broad. A well-honed German prepared to fight.

Two more Nazis stepped from the shadows. Who knew how many soldiers there were around them. Perhaps more hiding among the trees.

If only he hadn't left Henri behind. Then they would have four to fight these Germans. Even so, no matter how many of them there were, they were unarmed. It was too dangerous to carry weapons in case they got picked up.

Like now.

But a few guns would have given them a chance to get away.

A burst of anti-aircraft fire filled the sky, pounding against Jean-Paul's eardrums. A brief whistle. Then a loud bang, and a large fireball lit the night.

Non, non. They had gotten the plane. Those poor Americans had no chance of survival.

"I know what's running through your mind, Jean-Paul."

He whipped around to discover Henri sauntering into the clearing, the glow of a cigarette brightening as he took a drag.

"Too bad about the Americans going down. At least their death was swift."

"Henri? You're part of them?" Too many of his countrymen were collaborators. Too few were maquisards, resistance fighters.

"You underestimated me, *mon ami*. I'm not the slow, stupid man you think I am. And yet, knowing so little about my background, you took me into your circle and told me all your secrets. Even as we speak, homes are being raided and the remainder of the group arrested."

Jean-Paul had trusted the wrong man, and now it would exact a high price. His life didn't matter, but others had wives and children who needed them.

"I told you not to allow him into our inner circle." The harsh whisper came from Pierre on Jean-Paul's left. "What a fool you were."

"We all were."

"What's going to happen to my parents?" Venom filled Pierre's shouted whisper.

And to Jean-Paul's mother. But he couldn't dwell on that. They had a problem right in front of them. "Don't say anything more, Pierre." Thankfully, Luc had the good sense to stay quiet.

This is where their training came in. If they didn't open their mouths, they couldn't incriminate themselves.

Henri swung around and came nose to nose with Jean-Paul. "Let Pierre talk all he wants. We don't need confessions. I have all the information they need."

"Are they paying you?"

Jean-Paul's hasty question got him a slap on the side of his head from Henri, multiplying the stars in the sky. "That's enough from you."

"I hope it's enough for you. Will it bring you everything you've ever dreamed of? Can you live with yourself and the blood that's on your hands?"

Henri sucker punched Jean-Paul in the stomach. His breath rushed out, doubling him over.

"I said enough. No more talking. Not from any of you." He turned to the Germans. "Come and get them. And there's sure to be a nice gift for you inside the box as well. Now it's time to deal with these traitors."

Jean-Paul fell to his knees.

His carelessness was going to cost many people their lives.

Including his own.

Wednesday, May 31, 1944

"But Eisenhower won't hear of it." Martha Klein sat at the bar of the Dorchester Hotel in London and swirled the honey-gold liquid in her glass which glittered underneath the lights. Piano music flitted from the baby grand in the corner of the lounge.

Having seen too often what drink did to both men and women and the monsters it could turn them into, Nellie Wilkerson nursed her sugarless cup of coffee. "We can't let the military brass stop us from being on the ground to cover the invasion of France."

"But what can we do?" Frances Cannes, on Nellie's left, held the delicate stem of her wineglass between her fingers. "If the military won't let us in, there's no other way. It's not like we can take a commercial flight to Paris."

Martha laughed, but Nellie bit the inside of her lip. She hadn't fought her way here, overcoming hurdles and busting through roadblocks, to be stymied now. The biggest story of the war, maybe of her entire life, was about to unfold.

There was no way she was going to be kept cooped up in a London hotel room, no matter how luxurious it might be, while the men got the stories, the bylines, and the recognition.

Martha sobered, at least until she had a little more alcohol in her system. "If I don't miss my bet, you, Miss Wilkerson, have an idea up your sleeve."

If only she did. "We can't just give up. I'm going to write to the military authorities again. Even Eisenhower must listen to Mamie from time to time. And you know how persuasive I can be."

Frances jiggled her foot, shaking Nellie's chair along with her own. "We've already written him and used every argument we could think of to get him to relent. I'm afraid he's dug in his heels."

Nellie scraped back her stool and stood. "Where's your intrepid spirit? No wonder men don't take us seriously. Not when we throw up our hands and return to our kitchens as soon as they deny us something. I know neither of you is like that."

Martha downed the last swig and also came to her feet. "You're right, Nellie. We can't give up without a fight. If our boys did that, think where we'd be now."

Frances, still clasping her wine, stood in solidarity with them. "Exactly. One way or another, we have to convince the men in charge to let us report this invasion as well."

That was more like it. Nellie could write the letter alone and make the plea herself, but it would carry more weight and have a better chance of making an impact if three of them signed it.

Half an hour later, they huddled over a table in the hotel's lobby, a lush Oriental rug covering the marble floor under their feet, red columns and tall potted palms alternating against the sides of the long room. Nellie ground her pen into the paper with the last period. "There. What do you think?"

Frances leaned back in the sage-green stuffed chair and sighed. "Read it to us one more time. But I think we're there."

Nellie held up the paper so the light from the tall lamp behind her illuminated the words. " 'Dear Esteemed General Eisenhower.' "

"I like that." Martha nodded so that her platinum-blond curls bobbed. "Butter him up from the very beginning."

"You don't think it's too over the top?" Nellie asked. The last thing they wanted to do was come off like whining, begging, nagging women.

"It's perfect." Martha waved for Nellie to continue.

" 'As we write this letter in a hotel lobby in London, the buzz around us is about the imminent Allied invasion of France. Several hundred of our male journalistic counterparts possess press passes and have secured spots on ships to take them across the English Channel. However, because we are women, we have been denied this same privilege.

" 'We ask you to right this wrong immediately and to allow us to be included in the expeditionary force. We are well aware of the risk and the danger that such an assignment poses but are willing to put ourselves in harm's way in order to report on the landing.

" 'You may well ask why would we want to do this? It is not for the fame or the fortune that we seek permission to go along with the troops to France. On the contrary, we are requesting this of you to benefit the American public.

" 'Many wives, mothers, and sisters have sent their beloved husbands, sons, and brothers across the ocean to fight for their freedom. Every day, they wonder and worry. What is happening? Are their boys safe?

" 'When word reaches them of the invasion, their worry will only increase tenfold. Because the newspaper reports of the battle will be read by these women, who better to write about it than women?

" 'We will not resort to begging for your permission or call in favors to win us spots with the male journalists. All we ask is that you, sir, consider this. The hearts of the American women long to know, but they cannot know for themselves. Their eyes long to see, but they cannot see for themselves. Their ears long to hear, but they cannot hear for themselves.

" 'Allow us to be their eyes and ears. Allow us to tell them what they desperately need to know—that America is winning their war and that their husbands, their sons, and their brothers will return to them triumphant.'"

If that didn't stir General Eisenhower to action, nothing would.

Somehow, someway, Nellie was going to be with the forces when they landed in France.

≋ CHAPTER TWO ≋

Tuesday, June 6, 1944

Nine thirty-two in the morning. That time would be seared into Nellie's memory forever. Journalists from the United States, Canada, and other parts of the world sat around several radios in the Dorchester lobby, waiting. Holding their collective breath.

All morning long, the skies above London had been busy, the hum of bombers filling the air, a giant swarm of bees buzzing overhead.

Each and every one of them knew the planned invasion had begun. Those fortunate enough to have been allowed to embed with the troops must already be there, witnessing what Nellie prayed was the turning point of the war.

And here she sat in London.

But then 9:32 rolled around. John Snagge, in the usual understated British fashion, announced the official word to the world.

Allied boots were trodding French sand.

That was all the information he gave. Nellie clenched her teeth until her jaw ached. They needed more details. How were the landings going? What kind of resistance were they meeting?

How many casualties?

She paced from one end of the marble lobby to the other, quite some distance. There had to be more. Her eyes ached to see it for herself.

Frances and Martha weren't around. At least, Nellie couldn't spy them from the crowd.

The air was close and heavy with blue cigarette smoke, choking her. Without returning to her room for her coat, she stepped into the raw, cold English morning. With this fog, it was surprising they had gotten planes off the ground and ships across the channel.

However they had managed it, they'd done it. Bully for them. That sounded sarcastic, even in her thoughts. Arms chilled, she wandered the streets for a while. Some sat in cafés, pinned against radios, awaiting more word. How agonizing if you knew a loved one was in the fray.

She wandered past Hyde Park and stopped near the Stanhope Gate and the Cavalry Memorial. This statue, constructed of guns captured in the Great War, had snagged her attention during her time at the Dorchester. St. George rode on horseback, treading over the dreaded dragon.

Ironic that it was sculpted just twenty years ago to commemorate the end of one war. The "war to end all wars" so many had said. Yet here they were again. The ever-present drone of aircraft continued, mixing with the little bit of motor traffic there was on the street.

She made her way down Constitution Hill, which separated Green Park and Buckingham Palace Garden, lush and verdant with the wet, late-spring weather plaguing the city.

Moments later, she stood in front of the palace where King George and his family resided. The entire royal household had been so brave throughout the war, never cowering, never running away, never shirking their duty. Princess Elizabeth even recently enlisted as a mechanic and driver in the Auxiliary Territorial Service.

If not for the Royal Standard flying over the palace, it might have been empty for all she knew. A group of soldiers huddled outside the gate. Officials came and went, but that was it. No crowds today. No cheering, even though they had news to celebrate.

That news came at too high a price.

She wandered a bit more, through Trafalgar Square, named for a victory in the Napoleonic Wars. If the Allies managed to win, perhaps London would one day erect a statue in commemoration of this victory. High on a Corinthian column, Admiral Nelson overlooked the scene.

Nothing extraordinary was happening here. The action was across the channel. That was where she should be. She sighed and turned toward the hotel. If only she could be at the docks when the wounded returned.

Now, that was an idea. She restrained herself from sprinting all the way back to the hotel. Once there, she changed into a pair of pants, a crisp white blouse, and a leather bomber jacket. Her poor mother would be having apoplexy about her choice of clothing, but it was much more practical for reporting. After packing a bag in case she couldn't make the last train back to London that night, she purchased a ticket and boarded the train to Southampton.

By the time she arrived, night was falling. With her pack slung over her shoulder, she made her way to the docks.

They swarmed with activity, ships coming and going, many Landing Ship, Tanks—LSTs—converted into floating hospitals, bringing to English shores those who had been lucky enough to survive the battle but unlucky enough to suffer wounds. Some of the injuries were grisly, the litters stained red with blood. She turned away at the sight of mangled legs and open abdomens.

Farther down the dock was a large ship, perhaps one that had once carried passengers. In contrast to the gray transport vehicles, this one was painted all white with red crosses on its twin smokestacks and along its side.

A hospital ship. The *Prague*.

Like a flash from an incendiary bomb, an idea struck her. This could be her chance to get close to the fighting.

In the middle of the chaos, she approached the plank leading to the ship. Maybe no one would notice.

But someone did.

"Excuse me, ma'am." A military policeman in a brown uniform and a brown and orange hat approached her. "Where are you going?"

"I'm with the press." She flashed her pass quickly, so he couldn't see that she didn't have war correspondent credentials. "I'm here to interview some of the nurses."

Probably busy with a thousand other tasks today, he didn't check too closely before he waved her away and turned his attention to another landing craft approaching, loaded with more wounded.

What kind of beating had the Allies taken?

She made her way across the deck where great cans labeled WHOLE BLOOD sat, then climbed below deck where scores of bunks had been made with crisp white sheets, gray wool blankets, and fluffed pillows.

Not long after boarding, she ran into a nurse, so young she must have just graduated from school, her uniform snowy white, her cap in place. "Can I help you?" Her voice held an unmistakable Midwestern twang.

If she told the woman she was a journalist, she would have to leave before the ship departed. But if she was a little bit more vague… "I'm horribly late, as you can tell, and I need to find my uniform so I can get to work."

"You are rather late. We've finished about all the work already."

"I'll make it up to you. If I can just change."

"Of course. Let me show you around. I'm Doris Lattimore. And you are?"

"Nellie Wilkerson."

"Welcome aboard."

Doris led Nellie on a thorough tour of the ship, including where all the supplies were stored, where the canteen was, and where the operating theater was located. Once finished with that, she found a bunk and a uniform for Nellie.

By the time she had slipped out of her pants and bomber jacket and into the dress, the ship's engines roared to life, and the floating hospital was underway, headed for France. Just where Nellie longed to be.

———— ≈ ————

Unable to sleep in the narrow bunk on the rollicking ship, Nellie climbed to the deck. Not that she'd be able to see anything, but perhaps some fresh air would be good.

She had wrapped her bomber jacket around herself, and it was a good thing she had. Even though she stood against the wall, the rain drove at her and the wind howled around her. Ah, this was the adventure she had craved. She lifted her face to the rain and allowed it to pelt her.

Goose bumps rose on her arms, and she shivered. If she was going to be a good war correspondent, she couldn't be afraid of the elements. She couldn't complain if she was cold, wet, or hungry. The boys out there fighting for her freedom weren't complaining, so she wouldn't either.

This was the perfect night to test her mettle. Could she meet whatever she was facing head on and without fear?

The *without fear* part was hard. Who knew what awaited her? She'd been afraid one horrible night so long ago, and evil had triumphed. She couldn't allow that terror to control her again or stop her from doing what was right.

At last, shivering so hard her teeth rattled in her head, she turned back inside. A few of the British crew moved about. The American medical staff slept. And they said the English were the unflappable ones.

By the time she was showered and dressed, the new day had begun. She and Doris and a few of the other nurses she had spent some time with last night ate breakfast together. No one questioned her presence on board the ship.

A British crewman entered the dining room. "We're nearing the coast."

France.

At last.

Nellie left her tray on the table and followed a group of women to the deck. She couldn't stifle the gasp that rose in her throat at the sight before her.

As far as the eye could see, boats of various sizes and descriptions clogged the water, worse than any New York City rush-hour traffic jam. The smaller boats with square fronts zipped around between shore and the large vessels, sending salty sea spray in front of them.

Here and there came the flash of large guns shooting over the cliffs beyond the shore. Overhead came the drone of airplanes, the sight of them masked by the low-hanging clouds. Adding to the noise were the frequent booms of detonated mines.

Detonated by equipment. Detonated by men who didn't stand a chance of surviving such a blast.

Nellie moved to the rail and clutched it. What a scene, like nothing she could have imagined. Barrage balloons floated over the shore like gray elephants dancing in the wind.

And then she made the mistake of glancing down at the choppy sea. Gray sacks floated in the choppy waters. She squinted. No, those weren't sacks at all. They were soldiers, floating facedown in the water, their heavy packs pulling them below the waves.

A day in the water had left them bloated, their arms and legs dangling in the sea.

Nellie turned away. Breakfast hadn't been a good idea.

But she didn't have a chance to dwell on that, because the first

Landing Craft Transport, or LCT, pulled alongside the *Prague*. The open, rectangular box bumped against the *Prague*'s side. Crewmen came aside Nellie on the deck and lowered what might pass for open coffins. The soldiers on the landing craft filled the boxes with the wounded, and the men manning the ropes hoisted them aboard the *Prague*.

Nellie stepped back so the real nurses could triage the injured. The very first brought up was a German who shouted what sounded like curses at the top of his lungs. Though they attempted to subdue him, he fought them off, even though blood oozed from a bandaged head wound.

Nellie pushed her way through. "Shh. They are here to help you." Though she didn't speak German, her soft words whispered into his ear must have been enough to soothe him.

He gazed at her with wide eyes, startling in their blueness, and she nodded and smiled at him.

As if everything would be all right. But would it?

More and more men were hauled on board, and Nellie lost sight of the German soldier. She lifted a quick prayer for his healing before heading off to bring water and blankets to the wounded and to offer them a word of encouragement.

It wasn't long before the metallic stench of blood filled her nostrils, overpowering even the saltiness of the water beneath her.

All day she worked, with only short breaks to relieve herself. Doris was at her side most of the time. Because she was supposed to be a nurse, Nellie had hidden her camera and didn't snap any photographs. But the images were imprinted on her mind.

Her white uniform was now stained with blood, as were her hands and even her shoes. She'd never be able to wash it off, even if she scrubbed her hands until they were chapped.

At one point, with hunger gnawing at her stomach, she sent several cabin boys to make some sandwiches so they wouldn't faint from lack of food. Never had roast beef tasted so good. Even the glass of water she drank was the best she'd ever had.

Still the wounded came, filling up bed after bed. Those winter-white sheets were now stained crimson. When she got a few minutes, Nellie changed from her dress into her much more comfortable and practical pants and jacket. The coat was baggy enough that she managed to tuck her camera underneath it.

At about ten in the evening, as the sun dipped to the horizon behind them, Nellie, Doris, and some orderlies and other medical staff climbed into one of the coffin-like boxes, lowered themselves onto an LCT, and set off for the beach to collect more wounded.

Nellie turned to Doris, spray from the waves coating her lips with salt. "How can there be any more survivors this long after the battle?"

Doris gazed at her with wide eyes. "They just don't stop coming. When I signed up for this, I never imagined it would be quite so intense. So. . .so brutal. Is this what men do to each other?"

"Unfortunately, yes." Nellie had seen it firsthand. Even her father was tainted by evil. Hatred for other men. There was so little good in this world. But that was why she needed to be here, getting these stories. So that they might plant in the hearts of men the hope of evil being defeated once and for all.

"I don't know how I'm going to make it until Germany falls. If it falls. I saw plenty in my nurse's training. Nothing like this. How are you managing to stay so calm?"

At least Doris hadn't realized that she wasn't a real medical professional. "I don't know. We have jobs to do. We just do them. After the war, we'll have time to think about our experiences."

The LCT approached the shore and beached itself. Its front ramp fell open, allowing Nellie to stroll onto dry land. But this place where children had played in the sand, families had picnicked, and young lovers had bathed in the sun was no more. Abandoned tanks and trucks littered the place. Red flares lent the entire scene an eerie glow.

Doris clicked her tongue. "Look at this beach. It's amazing anyone survived."

Nellie surveyed the scene the best she could. "It must have been horrific."

She, Doris, and the others moved up a marked path, one that had been cleared of landmines. As they left Omaha Beach, the scene changed. Sand gave way to grass, sweet and fresh and summery, a reminder that what was destroyed could be built again.

And so it would have to be for the village there. Either the retreating Germans or the advancing Allies—likely a little of both—had reduced Vierville-sur-Mer to rubble. Just days ago, it had been a charming town.

Now the handful of residents paid a steep price for their liberation.

All night long, they tended to the wounded and loaded the LCT over and over again with patients to be transported to England. Nellie didn't even have time to be tired or hungry.

By dawn, Nellie's backpack heavy and her eyelids heavier, the *Prague* was filled once again to capacity with wounded. She and Doris sat against the stone wall of what had been the village's church, waiting for their turn on the LCT.

Nellie had no intention of returning to the *Prague* though. This was her opportunity to tell the women at home the story of the invasion and the Allies' progress. She had a chance to be their eyes and ears. To show them just what their boys were fighting for. And dying for.

Her stomach churned as the deception she'd been living the past day turned bitter on her tongue. "I have something to confess."

Doris drank from her canteen. "What?"

"I'm not a nurse."

Doris sputtered, sat up straight, and stared at Nellie. "What do you mean? You've been working with us this entire time."

"Only getting water and blankets and the like. I didn't dispense any medication or anything. I'm a photographer for the *Chicago Tribune*. Eisenhower refused to allow any women journalists in France. I hadn't planned on stowing away, but it just worked out. No one questioned me."

"And so you snuck on board?"

"I'm sorry for deceiving you, but I'm not sorry for being here. I hope I was helpful to you."

"I guess you were." Doris sighed. "You worked as hard as any of us."

"So you're not mad?"

"I'm steamed. But I kind of understand. If they hadn't allowed nurses here, I would have done whatever I had to do to get on that ship."

Nellie released a pent-up breath. "I do have a favor to ask."

"And that is?"

"I'm going to slip away and join the American troops. My work here isn't finished. It hasn't even started. I haven't snapped a single photograph. Please, don't say anything to the others when you get back."

"It's going to get you and maybe even me into a big pot of hot water if they find out how you got here."

"I'm so sorry about that." Nellie touched Doris's hand. "I hope you don't get reprimanded because of me. You didn't know who I was or what I was planning on doing."

"Will you be okay? It's dangerous here."

"I'll be fine. And thank you. When you get home, write to me at the *Tribune*. I'd like to make this up to you. You're a swell gal."

"You'd better get going before I change my mind."

Nellie stood, hugged Doris, and slipped into the hull of the church and out the other side. While the medical staff was still about, she hid among the gravestones in the churchyard. Doris's voice carried on the light breeze, though Nellie couldn't make out the words. At last, the footsteps of her companions faded away. Still she crouched behind a large, weathered stone with an angel perched atop it.

An hour or so passed before she crept toward the beach as the *Prague* set sail for Southampton.

Without her.

The time had come for her to get to work.

⧨ CHAPTER THREE ⧨

Thursday, June 8, 1944

The cold dankness of the prison cell seeped into Jean-Paul's bones. He'd sat here for how many days? And how many more would he endure before his end came?

So far, there had been no interrogations. No beatings. No torture. Nothing. Just emptiness. And perhaps that was the worst torture of all. Insanity would set in. By then he'd be so starved for any type of human contact, he would tell the Germans everything he knew.

Then again, with Henri turned against them, there was no need for that.

How could Jean-Paul have been so stupid? In these uncertain times, you didn't dare trust anyone. Not a soul. Not even your own mother. Because you never knew who was working on the Nazis' side.

Shouldn't he, of all people, know that?

But because Henri was the friend of a friend, Jean-Paul had allowed him into the innermost circle without many questions. He had proven himself. Until now.

The perfect German operative.

Jean-Paul rested his aching, feverishly hot body against the chilly stone wall and closed his eyes. For a long time, he poured his heart out to God. He spoke to his *Père* about his loneliness, about his fright, about his remorse. He prayed for his men's safety and that of his mother.

At some point, he must have fallen asleep, because a great commotion outside his door woke him with a start. It took him a few minutes to get his bearings before he sprang to his feet, and when he did, the world spun and threatened to topple him. What was going on? Ignoring the dizziness, he scuffled to the cell's door.

"They're here! They're here!" a man shouted from down the hall.

Jean-Paul stretched until his nose stuck out of the little barred square opening high in the door. "Who? Who is it?"

"The Brits, Americans, Canadians. They've landed here in Normandy."

"Normandy?" Another voice rose above the din. "Why here?"

It was genius, really. "Because the Germans were expecting them in Calais. This is the best news we could receive."

His neighbor concurred. "They have to be moving this way. Has anyone seen our captors today?"

A chorus of no's rang out.

A cheer went up from the prisoners.

"This is it, men. They've bugged out. We're free." The original speaker's proclamation was full of glee.

Someone else laughed. "I don't feel very free."

Merci, Lord. Merci.

Many long hours passed. No food or water came. Jean-Paul's stomach rumbled, and his tongue stuck to the roof of his mouth. Chills racked his body. When would the villagers remember the prison? Was there anyone left here at all?

The thin sliver of light that poked through the small square in his door dimmed. By the time a door creaked open, darkness had fallen. Keys jangled.

"I'm *Père* Charles." The voice was older, warbling. "You're safe. I'll release you. Just let me figure out these keys and locks." With maddening slowness, he scraped the key in a lock. Quite some time went by before the door clicked open.

"Give me those, *Père*. I'll let the rest of the boys out." One of the freed prisoners set to work and sped up the process.

A few minutes later the door to Jean-Paul's cell swung open, and he staggered out, inhaling a lungful of urine-scented air.

The old man—a priest, given his dark clothes and dingy white collar—stood to the side as men rushed out of their cells, slapping each other on the back. Jean-Paul turned to the man of God. "*Père*, why are the Germans gone? What has happened?"

"Our allies have arrived at last. They stormed the beaches two, almost three days ago, not far from here. The Nazis, may they bear the full force of God's wrath, abandoned the town ahead of their arrival. It's been a bloody few days. Many men on both sides have lost their lives."

"But this area is liberated?"

"I haven't seen a British or American soldier yet, but neither have I run into a German since early this morning. So I suppose our little village and the area around it are free."

Though it took much of the energy he had left, Jean-Paul couldn't stop the grin from lifting the corners of his mouth. He joined his fellow inmates, all now released, in a rousing refrain of "La Marseillaise," his country's national anthem, one he hadn't been able to sing for four long years.

Oh, how good and cleansing for the soul. Luc was there too, his clothes hanging on him, his face pale, but nothing a good bed and a few warm meals wouldn't fix.

Luc came and hugged Jean-Paul. "Can you believe it? When those Germans surrounded us, I thought that was it. I was pretty sure I would never see my family again. But somehow, someway, we made it."

"God's grace. Nothing more."

"I say it was a stroke of luck. Great timing. If we were going to get arrested, it happened in the right place at the right moment."

"Let's get out of here." Jean-Paul pumped his fist in the air.

The men cheered. Several shouted something about going to the pub for a drink. For Jean-Paul, a good wash up and a soft bed would do.

In the distance, artillery fire sounded. He rushed to the prison's door, along with several other men, all crowding the opening to see what was going on.

Several planes roared overhead. German or Allied? Impossible to tell. In any case, they didn't bother this tiny hamlet. But the western sky glowed red. Out there, away from this quiet-for-now corner of France, a battle raged. One for life or death. One that would determine the fate of the free world for many long years to come.

How could he stand here thinking about his own comfort when so many—both civilian and military—remained in peril? Despite the chills and fierce headache that racked him, he had to get back to work. Right away.

He spun around to find Luc, but the spinning didn't stop even though he did. He leaned against the doorframe to halt the crazy tilt of the world.

It didn't work.

Luc caught him as he slid to the floor.

———— ≈ ————

Friday, June 9, 1944

Nothing made sense to Jean-Paul. Sometimes people were shooting at him. He couldn't see them, but their bullets hit his chest with ferocious pain. Sometimes his mother sang to him, the words of a French lullaby on her lips. Sometimes the weather was hot. Sometimes it was cold.

Most of the time, however, there was darkness. Nothing but deepest darkness. A hole he couldn't crawl out of. One that threatened to consume him.

With all of his might, he resisted. Fought against it.

It exhausted him.

Darkness again.

But then came a sliver of light. The tiniest bits infiltrated the blackness that had overcome him. He clung to it. Worked to enlarge it. And he managed to do so until he blinked in the sunlight streaming through a spotless window.

But he didn't recognize this place. What was it? Why was he here? He moved around. He was in bed.

Ah, yes, he'd taken a fever at the prison. That must be why he didn't have the strength to lift himself to sit.

Just then, the door opened and a young woman with flowing black hair entered. He recognized her from the photos Luc showed him of his wife. "Josephine." Jean-Paul croaked out the word.

"*Oui.* It's nice to meet you at last. And good to see that you are awake. You had us worried."

"Luc?"

"He's fine. He brought you here in the middle of the night and then left again. It was quite the feat for him to get you here, weak as he was from prison, but he managed somehow. He's back to work, even though we've been liberated."

"I have to go." But when he pooled his strength and sat up, the world did that crazy spinning thing again. He slumped against the pillows.

"It's going to take you a while to regain your strength."

"But all the work we have to do. We're expecting more drops, there are still Jews in hiding that need ration cards, and there are more children to be slipped across the Swiss border."

"Luc, I'm sure, is carrying on. You're more good to him well than passing out and raging with fever."

He slumped his shoulders.

"Good. I'm glad to see that you agree with me and have resigned yourself to staying here."

"You have too much practice with Luc."

She laughed, pure music. Luc was one very blessed man. "I'll be back with some broth. Vegetable only, but it should fortify you." She turned to leave.

"Josephine?"

She gazed over her shoulder. "*Oui?*"

"*Merci.* I owe you a great debt."

"When you get back to things, just keep my husband alive. That is all I ask."

With the Germans on the run, that would become increasingly difficult.

The early morning sun had just streaked the eastern sky pink when Nellie left the LCT she had been forced to sleep in. Toward the end of the day yesterday, she had at last managed to meet up with a group of American soldiers. But they didn't have a tent for her, necessitating her stay on the boat.

Thankfully, at least to this point, the commander hadn't demanded her credentials. He did mumble something about women and combat and oil and water, but she paid little heed to it.

She would show them that women deserved to be here. She'd take a photograph that would show them all.

After stretching and yawning and forcing herself to come awake, she made her way to the beach.

Omaha Beach.

The place where, mere days ago, a fierce battle had been fought. And won. But at a great price.

Right now, she was the only one up. Where days ago, men had swarmed this place and the sound of gunfire had filled the air, now all was peace. Gulls soared overhead, their cries breaking the dawn's stillness.

The sunlight cast its rays over the dunes behind Nellie, reaching its fingers to illuminate the scene. Today, here alone, not busy with finding wounded and getting them evacuated, she had more time to contemplate the scene in front of her.

Czech hedgehogs, metal I-beams that stuck out of the water at low tide and that were meant to rip open the bottom of boats at high tide, stood in a row, curving around the beach. Stuck and wounded landing craft and trucks lined the sand.

And men slept on the beach. Not the sleep of the weary, but the eternal sleep of the slain. The stench of rotting flesh overpowered the brine of the salt water.

This is what war did. It scarred the landscape, yes, but so much more than that. It ripped men's bodies apart, their blood staining the ground red, their lives ebbing away, given to protect and preserve their country.

Why did men do this to each other? Why was there so much hatred?

Another scene, one from her childhood, attempted to push its way into her brain. *Not here. Not now.* This wasn't the time or the place to dwell on that. But it was so similar. Men who hated other men and killed them.

What she had witnessed twenty years ago didn't make sense. What she was witnessing today didn't either.

She shivered but not because she was chilled. Well, in a way she was. The scene before her eyes would seep into her bones and the coldness of it would remain with her forever. She would never be able to shake it.

As she withdrew her camera from its case, she kept reminding herself that she could do this. She had to do this. For a while, she occupied herself with surveying the scene with a detached, professional eye, studying the angle of the light, deciding which shots to capture.

She waded into the water, the wetness seeping through her boots and her socks, to photograph the Czech hedgehogs, making sure to highlight the long string of them buffeted by the waters of the English Channel. Then she turned to a square truck stuck in the sand and lined up the shot. She pushed the shutter. At that moment, she spied a dead soldier behind the steering wheel.

For a brief time, she closed her eyes to erase the image from her brain. How would she ever develop this film?

Someone touched her shoulder, and she startled, hand to her heart.

"Sorry, Nellie. Didn't mean to scare you so." The American soldier, Clarence Mills, was so thin, it was almost unbelievable that he managed to carry the pack he had on his back. He was one of the first she'd met yesterday and he was one of the few here who had compassion for her situation and did what he could to provide for her. Last night he'd brought her something to eat and some blankets to make a bed in the LCT.

She dismissed his concern. "I guess I was engrossed in my work."

"It's hard to comprehend, isn't it? All these men are gone."

"I was thinking the same thing."

"War is ugly. And here you are, trying to make it pretty."

"Photographs don't always have to be pretty. Sometimes they tell a story. That's what I want mine to do. Tell the story of this war so the world knows what is going on and so our children and grandchildren and all those who come after us will never forget what happened on this beach or in these fields."

She and Clarence made their way up the embankment, stopping every few minutes so she could capture another image for those who were and those who were to come. When they reached the cliffs, she gazed upward at the German bunkers, their now-silent guns still trained on the beach below.

No wonder so many men died in the waves and on the sand. "Help me up here, Clarence."

He scrambled ahead of her, then lent her a hand up the cliff to one of the concrete monstrosities. She ducked into the bunker, the shady dankness of it deepening the chill in her core. As she crawled forward, the rough concrete scraped her hands. A narrow slit peered over the water and the land.

She positioned her camera and snapped several pictures. What a view. Perhaps this would help the Americans understand better what happened on this beach and on the beaches up and down the Normandy coast. How so many young men gave their short lives to preserve the freedom of those they loved.

She couldn't allow herself to grow nostalgic about what they were calling D-Day. So far, the Allies had advanced only a few miles into the French countryside. Hundreds more stood between them and Berlin. So many obstacles still to overcome.

So many more lives yet to be lost.

Once she had all the pictures she wanted, or at least all she could stomach to take, she and Clarence strolled to the military camp in silence. What could one say after experiencing such horror? Nearby, troops continued to dig graves. What a monumental task lay in front of them.

She would somehow have to find a courier to return the undeveloped film to London for processing and publication. That task consumed most of the morning and proved to be futile. She couldn't ask the member of the Army Pictorial Service to send it with his. In fact, she steered well clear of him. If word got back that she was here, she could be in some serious trouble.

"Hello? Nellie?"

The high-pitched, almost boyish voice could come from none other than Clarence.

Behind him, commotion stirred in the camp. Men scurried to and fro. Tents came down. Jeeps roared on the muddy, makeshift road. "What's going on?"

"Time to move out. We leave in an hour."

An hour and they would be gone? "Where am I supposed to go? I'm not attached to this unit. I'm pretty much out here on my own."

"Oh, doll, I never thought about that. Let me see what I can do. I can't leave a lady alone."

With that, he strode away to continue his preparations.

Nellie stared after Clarence, the carnage she'd witnessed on the beach still fresh in her mind. Would he even make it home alive? Would any of them?

The chill from earlier in the day returned.

About thirty minutes later, Clarence came back with a Jeep and a few rations for her. "Don't tell anyone. I managed to finagle my way behind the wheel of this baby. Climb aboard. We'll have to take some back roads so none of the officers see me with a pretty dame like you, but it'll be an adventure."

With some food in her stomach, Nellie settled into the Jeep with Clarence and they took off. She'd tied a scarf around her head, and it was a good thing she had. If they were in the States, he would receive a speeding ticket for sure. "Hey, watch out for my equipment." Her camera banged against her chest. She'd refused to allow him to take it from her when he loaded her duffel bag.

He shouted so she could hear him. "I heard reports from up ahead that there are troops clogging the roads to the nearby villages. I'm going to enjoy driving at this speed for as long as I can."

"Just be careful. If the *Tribune* gets wind about any accidents involving their expensive camera, they will not be happy. They might even court-martial you." Who knew if this was true or not, but it sounded good.

Clarence slowed down a bit but not enough for Nellie's liking. She clung to the edge of the seat with one hand and her scarf with the other as he zipped along the wet, slimy road.

Up ahead, the lane curved. Clarence didn't let up on the gas.

"Watch out!"

Her warning came too late. The Jeep skidded on the slippery road. The back end fishtailed. For what seemed like minutes, Nellie's heart stopped beating.

The Jeep tipped onto its side, sending her crashing into Clarence. Then into a hedge.

And the world stilled.

Except for the hiss of the radiator.

Time ticked away as Nellie lay there. After a few moments she struggled to pull herself over to the young soldier, the bush's sharp branches snagging on her pants and in her hair.

Pain zipped through her neck. "Ugh."

Clarence didn't move.

"Hey, are you okay?"

He didn't answer her.

"Clarence. Come on. That's enough kidding around." Any second he would jump up and laugh at her for being so gullible. Right? Right?

But he didn't.

She managed to come to a half stand.

Holding her breath, she dared a peek at Clarence.

He was so pale, lying there on the ground. Blood seeped from underneath his head.

"Clarence!"

No, no. This couldn't be happening. Not to him. He'd survived the beaches for it to come to an end like this? No. It couldn't be.

She struggled out of the hedge and into the road. But no one was around.

She turned back to him. "Don't do this. You can't do this." She had to do something, but what? Oh, if only she had taken a first-aid class. The bleeding. She had to stop the bleeding. She yanked her scarf from her head and wrapped it around Clarence's.

Little good that did. Blood soaked through the silk in no time.

Now what? She glanced at her white shirt. Well, it had been white at one time. By now, it was pretty dirty. But she had no other options.

She slid off her bomber jacket and then her blouse. If Mama could see her in the middle of the French countryside in nothing but her brassiere, she'd have a fit. Especially since God had been bountiful to Nellie in that category. Good thing Mama wasn't here.

As fast as possible, she slipped back into her jacket, ripped her shirt into strips, and wrapped them around Clarence's head. Even as she did so, she brushed his skin. His very cold skin.

It had to be because, even though still in the Jeep, he was lying on the ground. That was why he was losing body heat. With all of her might, she lifted him and cradled him close in an attempt to warm him.

"Mama used to tell me the story about the time it snowed in Mississippi. She was just a little girl. Golly, but it was cold then. She and her brothers and sisters and her friends played outside as long as they could stand it in nothing but their thin coats and bare legs.

"But she said when they went inside, her mama had fixed a very, very special treat. She'd mixed a little cocoa with some milk and heated it on the stove. Mama said it was the best thing she'd ever had, because it warmed you from the inside out.

"So you think about that, Clarence. How hot chocolate warms you from the inside out. And you get nice and toasty now, you hear?"

Even as she spoke the words, tears trickled down her cheeks.

Because even though she willed life back into the young man, the fact was that his soul had taken flight.

⋛ CHAPTER FOUR ⋛

Saturday, June 10, 1944

"*Merci* for everything you've done for me, Josephine. I appreciate it so much." Jean-Paul stood in front of the cottage she shared with Luc, the musical laughter of their children in the yard drifting their way. Reminding him of all he and the maquisards fought for. At least the Germans hadn't found her and exacted their revenge on her as they had promised when they'd arrested Jean-Paul, Luc, and the others.

"As I told you before, the one thing you can do to pay me back for my nursing care is to watch out for my husband. You must be sure he comes back to me." Her dark eyes bore into him.

"You're worse than any drill sergeant in the army." He gave her a light nudge in an attempt to keep the atmosphere from becoming too heavy.

"I mean it, Jean-Paul." She pulled her full lips into a frown. "I need my husband to return to me whole. We've known each other our entire lives. Without him, I have nothing. *S'il vous plaît*. Take care of him."

"I can't make promises during war. I don't even know where he is or if I'll be able to reconnect with him."

She teared up. Jean-Paul bit the inside of his cheek, an ache in his heart for this woman. But sacrifices were oftentimes required. This was one of those times.

"For my children."

"I will do everything in my power."

She kissed his cheeks, her own damp. "*Merci.* May God go with you."

"And may He be with you, whatever may come."

Without a glance back, mostly to maintain his composure, Jean-Paul strode down the brick walk to the road that ran in front of Luc and Josephine's stone cottage set among a riot of flowers. The sweet odor of roses and lavender soothed him. Slowed the thudding of his heart.

Because Henri had compromised their operations, Jean-Paul might have a difficult time locating his group. They couldn't stay where they'd been, but hopefully they had remained in the same area.

Before long he reached the edge of town. Farmland and the peace of the bocage stretched before him. Here and there, a few sheep grazed on the green summer grass. The muddy road was rutted and the lawn between the street and the hedge was trampled. Yesterday, Allied troops had marched through this vicinity, off to fight more battles and free more of his countrymen.

But there was still so much work to do. So many lived in fear yet. How long before the troops got bogged down as they had during the Great War?

Just because the enemy had been driven from this small slice of France didn't mean the Maquis could let up on their efforts to save those who continued to live under Nazi tyranny.

And the fighting remained fierce in this area. All night, he'd lain in bed, the *prr-prr-prr* of the machine guns and the rumbling booms of artillery fire keeping him awake. It could be that the Allies had been pushed back.

He turned onto a different road, one that would lead him farther into Normandy, an area where he might locate the rest of his group. Here, the road wasn't as rutted. The walking was easier. What a good thing. He hadn't gone but a few kilometers, and already he was breathing hard, and his knees were weak. Soon he would have to stop and rest.

Up ahead, the road curved. A pair of tire tracks, the only ones visible, were deep, then they wriggled all over the place. Despite his fatigue, Jean-Paul picked up his pace and rounded the bend.

There. A brown-green Jeep lay on its side. A woman with dark brown hair that curled at her shoulders stood beside it covering her face with her hands, her shoulders shaking.

He approached her with caution. "*Excusez-moi, madame?*"

"Oh, *s'il vous plaît,* help us. He's dead. I've been with him all night." With this proclamation, a fresh round of tears streamed down her face. Her French bore the marks of a deep American accent.

Jean-Paul dropped his rucksack and went to the Jeep. Inside was a fair-haired, very young man. He leaned over and felt for a pulse, the man's skin cold. There was no heartbeat. "*Je suis désolé.*" He studied her from the tips of her muddy combat boots to the top of her mussed brown hair. "I am afraid you're right. Your friend is dead."

She wiped her eyes with the sleeve of her leather jacket, smearing a streak of mud across her face. All that served to do was add to her appearance of vulnerability.

"Where were you going?"

"I'm a photojournalist with the *Chicago Tribune.*"

Ah, so she was taking photographs of the fighting for a newspaper in the United States.

"Can you help me?" Her voice was thin.

What was a woman doing alone in the middle of a foreign country? She should have stayed with the unit she'd been attached to. Who knew when the Germans might return?

"Come with me, *madame*, and I will help you." At this point, he didn't know how, but he would.

"But we can't leave him here."

Jean-Paul glanced around. While he had falsified papers that should pass muster if the Germans might happen by, hers certainly wouldn't. Her press credentials would do her little good. In fact, they would endanger her. "We can do nothing for him."

"But he should have a proper burial."

"*C'est impossible.* We must go. I don't know who might come. Now, *madame.* We must get off the road before someone sees us."

"I can't."

The rumble of trucks filled the air. There was as good a chance that they were German as they were Allied.

He grabbed her by the wrist.

She fought him off and worked to collect her spilled film and muddy camera. This one wouldn't be deterred. He scooped up an armload of film and his backpack.

The trucks closed in.

"Now, *madame*, now. We must hurry. They will come and take you."

With his free hand, he pushed aside the branches of the privet hedge and motioned her through. She glanced behind for a last time, then slipped through the bush. He did the same. Staying low, he pulled her away from the road, all the time praying that the trucks would pass the wrecked Jeep without a second glance.

The screech of brakes sounded just in front of them.

Doors creaked open and boots splashed into the muddy water.

Then came the sound of German voices.

———— ≋ ————

As Nellie and the Frenchman huddled behind the hedgerow, the damp seeping through her pants, the guttural flow of the German language surrounded them. Her heart thrummed in her chest. Just two days into her stint in France, and she'd already had enough adventure to last her the rest of her life.

The small amount of German she'd heard here and there over the years didn't do her any good in deciphering what the soldiers were saying. With one eye closed, she managed to peep through the leafy bushes and catch a glimpse of the three olive-clad Nazis. Two were tall and trim, one short and muscular. All of them leaned over Clarence's body.

When the short one kicked Clarence, she stifled her cry. Could they show no compassion for the dead? He was unable to harm them in any way. But no, darkness surrounded them, like darkness surrounded all men. Love was a precious commodity in all too short supply.

For a moment, she closed her eyes and clenched her hands. Then she willed herself to peek once more. One of the tall soldiers, weapon clutched in his hand, crouched over Clarence and touched the improvised bandage around his head.

Now they must be talking about how someone else must have been here tending to his wounds. The tall one who remained standing gestured to the surrounding countryside as he barked at the shorter man. Probably ordering him to comb the area for whoever had been with Clarence.

What were she and the Frenchman going to do? There was little place to hide. The hedgerow did nothing to provide them cover.

As soon as the German set about searching, he would discover them. Beyond this, there were only open fields.

She gazed at the man beside her, widening her eyes and shrugging her shoulders in question.

He pointed to a tree a few yards from them. She hadn't noticed it before, so intent was she on what was happening in front of her. He put his finger to his lips, then gestured for her to follow him.

Staying low, they waddled toward the tree as fast as possible. Once they reached it, the Frenchman pulled her to the back side of it. He flattened himself against it and pressed her to himself until not a sliver of paper would have passed between them.

In any other circumstance, she would have slapped the man. But they needed to make themselves as invisible as possible. Surely, though, he must be able to feel the pounding of her heart. She worked to breathe as shallowly and infrequently as she could.

Beside them, the branches rustled as the German poked his rifle through the bush and parted it. He moved ever closer to them. The crackle of the leaves under his feet was now on the other side of the tree as he circled it.

Nellie and the Frenchman inched their way around the tree, keeping low so the other Germans wouldn't see them over the hedgerow. Now the rustling came from where they had been standing a moment before.

Seconds later, the tall German shouted to his men. The doors of their truck cracked open and shut, their engine roared, and after a few minutes, it faded in the distance.

With a whoosh, Nellie released her breath. Still, the Frenchman clung to her. "You can let go of me now."

"Hush." His whisper in her ear sent a shiver slithering down her back.

For several more minutes, they stood without moving, without speaking. Was he holding her for pleasure? The Germans were gone. They were alone now. Only the robin chirping in the tree above them broke the stillness.

Finally he released his grip on her, and she stepped away.

"I had to make sure they were gone and were not going to come back." No light shone in his dark eyes. He was serious. And he'd known what he was doing.

Well then, it was long past time for introductions. "I am Nellie Wilkerson. I work for the *Chicago Tribune* in the United States." Her cheeks warmed. She'd already told him who she worked for.

Now a small smile graced his thin lips. "It is very nice to meet you. And my name is Jean-Paul Breslau. I am, as you can tell, from France."

"Paris?" This assignment might be her chance to visit the City of Light, to stand in front of the Eiffel Tour and drink coffee in a café along the Champs-Élysées. What a dream come true that would be.

"*Non.* A small town that you have never heard of before. Now, we must find where you are supposed to be."

"You would help me?"

"Of course. I could never leave a woman alone, especially not in the middle of a war. It is very dangerous, and you do not know where you're going."

She nodded. "That's true. You must be from around here if you do."

He sized her up. "At least you're dressed for walking. That's good. Come, now. The troops did not take this road. I think I know which one they would have used. I don't understand why you were driving this way."

"Clarence, the young man who died…" Her voice cracked, and she cleared her throat. "He was supposed to be driving me to the front lines. I think he was having a little fun and wanted to see the sights. Though I don't know how he could have seen any at the speed he was traveling."

At that, Jean-Paul raised one dark, bushy eyebrow. "Are you hurt? Can you walk?"

Fine time for him to be asking this after he'd dragged her through the bushes and held her against a tree. She smoothed down her hair and picked out a couple of twigs in doing so. "I'm fine. But if you give me directions, I can find my own way. I insist."

"Absolutely not."

≣ CHAPTER FIVE ≣

For the rest of the morning, Nellie, who had given in to Jean-Paul, trudged beside him, even as the sun beat on their heads. Each patch of farmland was demarked with hedgerows. When the sun was overhead, they knocked on a farmhouse door. Jean-Paul spoke to the farmer's wife, his rapid-fire French enough to give Nellie a headache. Yes, it was a beautiful language and one she understood, but right now, it reminded her of a machine gun.

Too many horrific images crowded their way into her brain. That horrible night when she was a child. Clarence, broken and bleeding on the side of the road. She rubbed her eyes but couldn't erase those pictures as easily.

The farmer's wife offered them some bread and cheese and a bit of water. Enough to sustain them on their journey.

Once on the road again, she couldn't help but pepper Jean-Paul with questions. "Do you know where we are?"

"Roughly. I asked the woman if she had seen the troops go by. She hadn't, but she thought they're in a village not too far from here, so that's where we're headed. It's difficult to find our way though. When they left, the Germans turned the road signs around."

Nellie couldn't hold in her chuckle. "How very clever of them."

Jean-Paul nodded. "But it won't help them. The Allies will find them. The Germans will lose the war."

"Does that make you sad?"

He halted so fast, she moved several paces ahead of him and had to turn around to face him. "Why do you ask such a question?"

"Because I don't know you. For all I know, you might be one of them."

"I would have turned you over to them then. I'm not one of them." He spat out the words. "I am loyal to my country. I might ask you the same."

"Of course I'm loyal to my country. Why wouldn't I be?"

"In war, one doesn't know."

Did one ever know? That hot Mississippi night taught her you never truly knew the deep, dark secrets someone might be hiding. So many men in her town proved themselves to be very different in the night than in the light of day.

She wiped beads of perspiration from her forehead. "Why aren't you at home? Where were you headed when you found me?"

"You ask too many questions. I don't like people who ask questions." He adjusted the rucksack's straps and marched by her.

Before she knew it, she had to jog to catch up to him. No one enjoyed interrogations, but if they were to go very far together, she had to know something about him. "Fine, then. I won't ask you anything. I will order you to tell me something about yourself."

He glanced sideways at her, that dark, narrow-eyed look back on his face. "You aren't a general to tell me what to do."

"How do you know I'm not?"

"I don't. That is why I won't answer any of your questions. If you need to know something about me, I'll tell you at that time. For now, we walk. Soon you will be back with your Americans, so there is nothing I must tell you."

They continued their march. The leather jacket didn't breathe, and Nellie was sweating underneath it. There was little she could do to remedy the situation since her shirt had been left behind. Neither could she do anything about the blisters on her heels from the new boots. She hadn't had sufficient time to break them in.

But she would never let Jean-Paul know that, the insufferable man. They must have walked miles upon miles without saying a word to each other. Every step was more unbearable than the one before. Never in her entire life had she spent so much time in someone's company without saying a word.

If all Frenchmen were like this, she would skip seeing Paris and return to England. At least there, though they may have stiff upper lips, they spoke to you.

Time wore on. They skirted a few towns with their red-tile roofs and church steeples pointing to the blue sky. For an hour or so, they rode in the back of a farmer's truck.

Every now and then, a group of planes flew overhead, some of them high, some of them low. Perhaps some of the men she'd met during her time in Britain were in the sky piloting them.

Long past the time her stomach started crying for dinner, pink streaked the sky behind them. At least now she had some idea of the direction they were headed. East was good. That was where the fighting must be. She could rejoin the troops and get some swell shots of the action.

She'd make a name for herself in the industry. No longer would she be Nellie Wilkerson from the rural South. That stain, that stigma, would be gone forever.

At last they neared another town so much like the ones they had bypassed from time to time throughout the day. Was it only yesterday morning that she had strolled on the beach? That was a lifetime ago. "Are we going to get food here? Is this where the Americans are?"

"Do you have money?"

"A little. Do you?"

"*Un peu.* Maybe enough to fill our stomachs for a while."

"Good. I'm so hungry, I could eat a horse."

There went that eyebrow shooting up again. "You eat horses?"

"Of course not. It's just an expression that means I'm very, very hungry."

"Oh. Well, we will see what we can find here. There hasn't been much food for a while. That farmer's wife didn't want to give us any at first. I had to persuade her."

"Do whatever you have to do to get us a meal."

They entered the village. Ancient stone buildings rose up on either side of them. Though it was not yet dark, the streets were quiet. How would they ever find food in such a sleepy little town?

And then a soldier rounded the corner and headed in their direction. One not in an American uniform. Even from this distance, the eagle on his hat was unmistakable.

This town was still in German hands. Somehow, they had managed to wander behind enemy lines.

Her mouth went dry, and the stomach that had growled a few

moments before now roiled. "Jean-Paul." She whispered his name.

"Let me talk to him. You stay quiet."

The Nazi approached and stopped in front of them. In a harsh tone in his harsh language, he said something to Jean-Paul, who pulled an identity booklet from his pants pocket and handed it to the soldier.

With a grunt, the Nazi handed the papers back to Jean-Paul, then turned his attention to her. She had to remind herself to breathe. The German said something to her, but she had no idea what it was.

Jean-Paul answered for her. Whatever he said, it wasn't good enough for the soldier. The two of them went back and forth for a while, Jean-Paul gesturing so wide he almost whacked her in the face.

From the venom in the Nazi's voice, it wasn't going well for Jean-Paul. Suddenly Jean-Paul kneed the soldier in the groin, grabbed Nellie by the arm, and yanked her to follow him.

"Run!"

With her camera banging against her ribs from the outside and her heart hammering against them from the inside, Nellie raced down the village's main thoroughfare behind Jean-Paul.

No one else was about.

Thank goodness the town was small, probably just a few hundred inhabitants in total, and they soon cleared it, back into the countryside, the dirt lane lined with hedgerows.

Just when Nellie's burning lungs couldn't draw in another breath and her burning legs couldn't take another step, Jean-Paul pulled to a stop. He leaned over his knees, gulping great quantities of air. He stumbled, then collapsed to the ground.

She knelt beside him. "Are you okay?"

He waved her away.

But his face was devoid of all color. She unscrewed the lid from her canteen and offered it to him, and he drank long and deep. When he handed it back, she also drank from it and then sat back. "I suppose we'd better head the other direction. Clearly, we aren't where we need to be."

The daylight was dimming and soon it would be too dark to find their way. He shook his head and voiced her fear. "We'll have to spend the night here. Tomorrow we can get our bearings and return you to the Americans."

Nellie sighed. The early-morning hours she'd spent on Omaha Beach two days ago were almost another lifetime. How could so much happen to one person in the course of thirty-six hours? "I guess we don't have much choice."

Where would they sleep, though? They couldn't return to the village. There were no homes in sight. Nothing but hedges and farm fields marked by an occasional tree. The evening breeze stirred the branches of a nearby hedge and the leaves danced. Already she'd spent one night in the open. Counting the LST, two nights.

Even after the small gust was over, the rattling of branches didn't cease. The bushes moved, but not with the air current. She nudged Jean-Paul and nodded in the direction of the movement.

He motioned for her to stay where she was. Jeepers, he didn't know her, did he? When he crept forward, she followed, her breathing rapid and irregular. What might they find behind there? Even a better question—who might find them?

Perhaps this wasn't the best idea. But just as she was about to pull him back, a round of childish giggling came from the hedgerow.

A child? Out here at night?

She pushed ahead of Jean-Paul and parted the branches.

Underneath the bush crouched a little girl, maybe about four years old, tickling her own nose with a bright red feather.

"*Fifille*. Little girl."

The child startled when Nellie called to her. Even in the softer evening light, she made out the child's flat nose, wide forehead, and teardrop-shaped eyes. She was a Mongoloid.

Just like Velma.

She must have wandered away from her home. Despite the risks, they had to return to town and find out where she belonged. She couldn't spend the night outside. Her parents must be frantic about her.

"Come here, *mon chère*." Nellie smiled and spoke in a soft voice to persuade the girl to come out. Little by little, she approached until she was able to reach out and touch the child.

The trusting soul didn't fight Nellie but allowed her to draw her from the hedge and pick her up. Nellie turned to Jean-Paul. "I don't know how much she understands. She must be lost."

In the distance, gunfire rent the stillness of the twilight. Quite a bit of it. No booming artillery, just shot after shot after shot. Every muscle in Nellie's body tensed.

Jean-Paul also stiffened. After several minutes, the guns fell quiet, and he leaned over the girl. "Are you lost? Where are your *mère* and *père*?"

She snuggled deeper into Nellie's arms.

"We have to get her home. I know it's not ideal, but we have to risk returning to the village."

"Not that one. See, there is one closer." He pointed in the opposite direction, and in the waning daylight, a church's steeple jutted heavenward, a dark silhouette against the sky. "Let's just be sure to steer clear of any Germans. And whatever you do, don't say anything."

"*Pourquoi?*"

"Why? Because you have an American accent."

"Oh." Her college study and her time in Lyon before the invasion must not have been enough to erase it.

He reached out for the child, but Nellie hung onto her. "You almost passed out after our sprint before. Conserve your strength in case we need to do it again." Together they made their way toward the village.

Though the sky was supposed to be red this time of day, it was deeper and more intense than the sun's afterglow. It was the red of fire. A large fire.

"What's going on?" Nellie's stomach clenched.

"I don't know."

They continued forward, the child still in her arms, Jean-Paul lagging behind her. As they entered the village, all was quiet. Much, much too quiet. Though curfew was approaching, there should be people out and about. Men on their way home from work. Children at play until the last possible minute.

They went a short distance farther before encountering thick black smoke. And an unutterably horrible stench.

The source of the red glow and the crackling of burning wood was unmistakable. As were the screams of horror coming from inside.

Hot, angry flames shot out the windows of the church. But where were all those who should have been fighting the blaze? The village was as deserted as an abandoned American mining town.

Except for the brown-shirted Nazis ringing the place of worship.

Jean-Paul grabbed her by the arm and pulled her back, around the corner from the church.

She attempted to break free. "We have to go help. There's no one even battling the fire. Those Germans are just standing and watching."

"No one is going to help them."

"What do you mean?" She peeked around the corner at the church. The light from the flames illuminated a woman crawling out of a window, holding an infant.

Then one of the Nazis opened fire, felling the woman before she'd gone two steps.

Nellie crumpled to the ground and was sick.

≣ CHAPTER SIX ≣

The sight in front of Jean-Paul weakened his knees more than his recent illness had. Over the past four years, he'd witnessed some awful things, so terrible, he would never be able to speak of them.

But this…

Even if he would want to talk about it someday, there were no words that would be able to fully convey the horror of what was happening in front of his eyes.

No wonder there was no one about the village. They were locked inside the church. A place of worship and love twisted into a chamber of brutality and death.

The piercing screams and cries of the villagers twisted his gut. He had to close his eyes to shut out the terror of it all. But this was an image that would forever be burned into the back of his eyelids.

More gunshots. More pleas for help from inside what should have been a sanctuary. More noxious fumes, the stench of burning flesh filling the air.

He breathed through his mouth to avoid smelling it, but it didn't diminish the taste. He gagged.

Once Nellie finished emptying her stomach, he pulled her to her feet. The little girl, her dark eyes wide in her flat face, was still in her arms. "We have to get out of here."

"We can't just leave them. There has to be something we can do."

"The Germans will only shoot us. What good can we do? The best thing is to leave and protect this child. She must have somehow gotten away from them. If they find her, they will kill her for sure. The Nazis don't care for anyone who isn't perfect."

"But—"

"Don't give them a reason to take three more lives."

She swallowed hard before following him away from the grisly scene. Gunfire erupted from time to time behind them. He couldn't allow himself to think about what that meant.

The sky, stained with flames and smoke, was bright enough to light their way. They returned to the spot where they had discovered the little girl hiding in the hedgerow. With the town unsafe, and unable to trust anyone in the vicinity, they had little choice but to spend the night in the field.

The roll of darkness spread across the land until it enveloped Nellie, Jean-Paul, and the little girl. They huddled together behind the hedgerow. Nellie's stomach growled, but she had nothing with which to fill it or anything to offer the child. Still, the girl didn't whimper. She clung to Nellie as if her life depended on it.

And it may well.

At some point the child fell asleep, her breathing regular and even. Oh, to be so young and innocent, not even realizing what had happened in her village. Probably to her family.

Nellie had once been that pure and unsullied. The world had once been a happy place, full of sunshine. People had once been good. Fathers were strong men who loved their children and sought peace for their families and their towns. Evil wasn't a word in her vocabulary or a concept she understood.

That had changed one sultry summer night, when the world of a nine-year-old girl was shattered by her very own father. He proved not to be a man of love but a man filled with hatred. Enough that he would lead a mob and take the life of an innocent man.

That hatred wasn't limited to rural or small-town Mississippi. It permeated the very ground beneath her feet. Every inch of dirt on the planet was stained with blood. With evil.

Was there any good left anywhere?

Perhaps only in the brown eyes of a Mongoloid girl.

Nellie inhaled, smoke from the church fire lingering in the air, the taste of it in her mouth churning her stomach again. She turned to Jean-Paul. "How many, do you think?"

He stared straight ahead into the darkness. "Hundreds."

She released the air she held. "So many. Why?"

"Usually it's because of something the Maquis have done, like blowing up rail lines or killing a soldier."

"Usually? You mean this isn't the first time something like this has happened?" The girl shifted in her sleep, and Nellie repositioned her aching arms.

"*Non,* it isn't." Now he faced her, his eyes blazing even in the night. "You are very naive, Mademoiselle Wilkerson, living in safety while the rest of the continent has been under the German boot for four insufferable years."

"May I remind you that London was almost pulverized during the Blitz? I can't begin to tell you how many nights I spent in the Underground fearing for my life. I've witnessed the carnage the Nazis can wreak on a country."

"But this is a scale that you haven't had to deal with. Bombs falling on cities are very bad, I agree. They leave destruction and snuff out innocent lives. But the rounding up of innocent civilians and burning them alive is unspeakable."

She couldn't disagree with him. The horror she'd witnessed today was beyond what she'd experienced in London. And that was indescribable. Evil heaped upon evil.

"What do we do now?"

"I suggest you get a few hours of sleep. I'll hold the child for a while, if you'd like. First thing in the morning, I'll scope out the village and make sure the Nazis are gone. My guess is they will be. They don't often stay around once they've done their dirty deeds."

"What about the girl?" Since they'd found her, she hadn't spoken a single word. Even though they had asked her what her name was, she hadn't answered. Perhaps she couldn't. How would they ever locate her relatives?

"We'll have to ask around. Someone in the vicinity is bound to know who she is."

Nellie handed the child to Jean-Paul and leaned against his broad shoulder, a steady, solid place to be. Not at all uncomfortable. In fact, a little too not uncomfortable. Still, she allowed her eyes to flutter shut.

Little good that did. Every time she drifted off, the shouts and screams from the fire melded with that night so long ago into a single nightmare. More than once, she jolted awake. At last, she took the girl back from Jean-Paul and let him sleep, his head warm on her shoulder, his hair tickling her neck.

She stared at him, even though there was little moonlight, this virtual stranger so close. Again, not unpleasant.

The loss of all those lives must not have bothered him the way it did her, because he slept well for a while, snoring in synchronicity with the little girl.

At long last, the sky brightened, though clouds hid the sunrise. Both Jean-Paul and the girl awakened. Now she did cry, big tears rolling down her dirty face. "*Maman. Maman.*"

Jean-Paul and Nellie glanced at each other. Nellie tucked a stray strand of the child's blond hair behind her ear. "We will find your *maman, mon chére.* Don't worry. Are you hungry?"

Even with what Jean-Paul had labeled her horrible accent, the girl must have understood, because she nodded and wiped the tears from her round cheeks.

"We'll find you something to eat too. Don't worry. You'll be fine. I promise you that."

The child snuggled against Nellie, content for now.

Jean-Paul rose and helped Nellie to her feet. "You shouldn't tell her that we'll find her mother. We may not be able to keep that vow."

"She needs hope. We all do." Nellie set the girl on the ground, then knelt in front of her. "What is your name?"

"*Nom?*" She pointed to herself.

Nellie nodded.

"Claire."

"*Très belle.* I like that name very much. Well, Claire, let's see if we can find some breakfast. How does that sound?"

Claire grinned. Poor little thing.

Jean-Paul headed toward town, Nellie and Claire following. He turned. "You need to stay put. If I go alone, I can stay low. The two of you tagging along will only draw suspicion. *S'il vous plaît,* for once, do as I say. You don't want to endanger Claire, do you?"

He knew how to strike where it would hurt the most. "Of course not."

"Then wait here for me. I'll be back as soon as possible. Perhaps I'll even be able to find a little breakfast."

While Jean-Paul was gone, Nellie taught Claire how to play patty-cake. Each time they finished the verse, Claire said, "Again. Again." And so they recited it until Nellie's voice was hoarse.

Just when her vocal cords couldn't take another verse, Jean-Paul returned. "As I suspected, the Nazis are gone. They committed their despicable deed and left the area. A few people are milling about, searching for loved ones. I suggest we take Claire into town and see if anyone knows her."

He could have saved the time and allowed them to accompany him in the first place. She bit her tongue to keep the words from pushing past her lips. She took Claire's hand, and they made their way back to the village.

Yesterday at this time this was likely a bustling borough, women out buying bread, men on their way to work in the small shops that lined the main street. From outward appearances, no one would know such a horrific act was committed here.

And then they came to the church, a burned-out hull containing the ashes of hundreds of humans. The bodies of several women and children lay scattered about the churchyard, testament to the German's unwillingness to allow any to escape. Nellie pressed Claire's face into her leg so the child wouldn't see.

An elderly, heavy woman with care-worn eyes, her light hair disheveled, approached them. "They are animals." She spat on the ground.

"Did you live in this town?" Jean-Paul scanned the area.

"No one who lived here survived. Those beasts rounded up each and every one of them and murdered them. The men they took to a farm, herded them into the barns, and shot them. All of them. My husband found their bodies first thing this morning. And you see what they did here."

"Do you know this child?" Jean-Paul took Claire by the shoulder and turned her around.

The woman gasped. "Claire Dumay? Where have you been?"

Nellie put her hand on Claire's head. "We found her hiding in the hedgerow outside of town. Do you know her parents? Where can we find them?"

"Everyone knows everyone here. As for her parents, you will find her father in one of the barns and her mother's and brother's ashes in the church. Along with those of her grandmother and her aunts and cousins."

Jean-Paul stepped in front of Nellie. "Does she have any relations who could take her?"

"Not that I know of." The woman shook her head, and a curler flew out. She must not have taken much time getting ready this morning. "Most people are born here, live their lives here, and die here."

The moment hung in the air between them.

After a while, Nellie broke the silence. "What do we do with her?"

The woman turned and eyed Nellie. "You aren't from around here. Are you English?"

"*S'il vous plaît*, just tell us what is to be done."

"You know that Claire is Mongoloid. She won't have a normal life. It's best you find some institution for her. Not that there are any left after the Nazis and Vichy emptied them of the undesirables."

"There must be somewhere." Nellie almost pleaded now. Claire couldn't be left alone to fend for herself. "Could you take her in? Do you know of someone who might?"

"No one would want her, another mouth to feed and one not able to contribute. We're having a hard enough time keeping our own bellies full."

"I'm begging you."

The woman shook her head, another curler flying out. "I can't help you." She turned to leave, then spun around. "My sister told me of a convent in L'asile. Apparently, they have taken in children who are like Claire. Perhaps they can help you."

"*Merci. Merci beaucoup.*" Nellie lifted Claire and kissed her cheek. "I'm sorry we didn't find—" She skipped saying the word so it didn't send the girl into another fit of tears—"but we will find you a wonderful place to stay."

Jean-Paul cleared his throat. "You do know where L'asile is, don't you?"

"I assume it's not far from here. The woman said people stay here all their lives."

"It's east of here."

"Toward the Germans."

"A good deal east of here."

Nellie furrowed her brow. "How far is a good deal?"

"Three to four hours by car. East of Paris."

"That will take us deeper into Nazi-held territory."

"Exactly. And it won't be easy to travel with Claire. Her very looks put her in peril."

"Oh." Nellie deflated. "Then what's to be done?"

"Perhaps we can find a way to get her with you west to the Allies and then to England."

"Whatever we do is risky, though, isn't it?"

"*Oui*. Very much so." Jean-Paul stroked his round chin and hemmed and hawed for a few minutes. "Instead of taking her into the heart of the fighting, I think it would be better if we take her to the convent. The sisters will protect her. Then we'll see about getting you where you belong."

Nellie's shutter finger itched. She'd had such grand plans when she arrived here, so much work to do documenting the war. Who knew how long it would take for her to reconnect with the Allies and get her film out.

Then Claire tugged on her thumb. When Nellie gave her attention, Claire gestured to be picked up.

So much like Velma. Only the color of their skin was different. Otherwise, they were very similar.

Nellie hadn't turned her back on Velma. She certainly wouldn't turn her back on Claire. "I think it's crazy to be talking about going east when the Allies are only a few miles west of here."

"A few miles in distance, perhaps, but a thousand miles in ability to reach them. Look at what the Germans did here."

"Exactly. If they did this to these innocent people, what might they do to Claire? To you or to me? I say we head west."

"East it is or nothing. If you decide to head toward the beaches, you and Claire will be on your own."

Heat rose in Nellie's chest. "Are you threatening to abandon us?" Then again, men had no heart. No compassion for others. They were cruel and ruthless, even when it came to innocent people.

He shook his head. "Just trying to get you to see sense. I haven't known you long, but I know you're stubborn and used to getting your own way."

"My own way? You know nothing about me. Fine. We'll go east then."

Jean-Paul grinned.

If possible, Nellie's cheeks burned even hotter. He'd tricked her into giving in to him.

"One thing before we leave." Nellie pulled her camera from the case around her neck. "Claire, you stand here." She positioned the child in front of the charred church. The cloudy day dissipated the shadows, helping with the shot.

There Claire stood, her wide lips pulled into a frown, a strand of blond hair falling over her distinctive eyes.

Nellie snapped the photograph.

And prayed it would show the world that even in the midst of evil, there was hope for survival. Hope for thriving.

⌇ CHAPTER SEVEN ⌇

No sooner had Nellie snapped the photograph of Claire in front of the church where her family perished than a French gendarme rounded the corner.

"Hey! What are you doing here? No photos. Give me that film. Now!"

Jean-Paul's heart pounded. They had to get out of here before the Vichy collaborator saw Claire. In a flash, Jean-Paul scooped up the girl, grabbed Nellie by the hand, and hightailed it away from the church and the village.

In front of him, those who had gathered to pay their respects or perhaps find out if their family members were still alive scattered. It was as if a cat had entered a room full of mice. Everyone moved in circles, in any direction that was away from the gendarme.

He had Nellie and Claire to think about. To spirit out of the area before anything happened to either one of them. No matter which direction they headed, danger lay in their path. Even toward the Allies was risky. There could be Nazis or Vichy anywhere.

Just outside of town sat a truck loaded with early summer produce. The farmer, perhaps coming from outside of the area, must have stopped for a short time, because the engine sat idling.

Then he came from the nearby farm and climbed into the truck's cab.

"Hurry." Jean-Paul urged Nellie, who did an admirable job of keeping up. He set Claire down, helped Nellie into the truck among the vegetable crates, handed Claire to her, then jumped in beside them. By the time the farmer hit the gas, they were all aboard.

"This is crazy." Nellie had to shout for him to hear. "Do we know where this truck is going?"

"I have no idea."

"Then I suggest we get off and find out." She set her mouth in a firm line. She was digging in.

"How are we going to jump off a moving truck? Do you like the idea of two broken legs? And what about Claire?" The little girl sat among the crates, not crying but not smiling either. Poor child must be so confused.

"Well then, as soon as he stops. We can't just ride forever with him. I'm sure some of my contacts in the journalism field will be able to locate whatever family Claire may have left."

"Suit yourself." He leaned against one of the crates and studied Nellie. Her brown hair just brushed her shoulders in big curls, framing her flawless face. When she smiled at Claire, her cheeks rounded. Even in men's pants and a filthy bomber jacket, her camera and its wide strap always around her neck, there was a certain softness to her.

If she weren't so hardheaded, she might even be pretty. Not a classic beauty like Jean Harlow, but pretty.

When that fire flashed in her eyes though, it was a warning to take cover. He'd discovered that in the couple of days since they'd met. She possessed spunk by the trunkful.

And then when she leaned over and whispered in Claire's ear, brushing her hand across the child's grimy face, there was a maternal quality to her. Charming. *Oui.* She was *belle.* Beautiful.

After a bumpy ride of at least four hours, the truck entered a village and slowed. Right away, the softness that had smoothed Nellie's features hardened, and the determined set of her jaw returned. "This is our chance. We go no further."

He couldn't argue the point with her. They had been traveling east, deeper into German territory. Farther away from the Allies and the protection they would offer.

The truck stopped in front of a grocer's. No sooner did it do so than Nellie hopped down and reached back for Claire. Jean-Paul handed her down and dropped to the ground himself. They merged into the shoppers and businessmen out and about.

"Time to find out where we are." Nellie approached a woman with two small children in tow. "*Excusez-moi, madame.*"

Jean-Paul yanked her back and hissed in her ear. "What are you doing? Don't call attention to yourself or Claire. Let me handle this."

She huffed but allowed him to approach the woman. When she told him where they were, he almost couldn't contain the grin that threatened to explode. He returned to Nellie. "We aren't that far from L'asile, the village where the convent is. Maybe a couple of hours on foot. Are you up for a walk?"

"Are we really?"

"God has smiled on us and brought us to the doorstep of the place we need to be."

"But what about getting to the Allies? This photograph should be developed and distributed. The world needs to know what happened at the town where Claire came from."

"This is His providence. We can't turn our backs on it, not when He has provided. I'm taking Claire to the convent. It's up to you if you want to come or not."

A tear trickled down Claire's cheek. Nellie bent down and wiped it away. "Poor thing. You've been through it, haven't you? So strong and so brave. It's important to get you to a place you'll be safe." She glanced at Jean-Paul. "She's caught in the middle, and it's not fair to her. Together, we'll take her to the convent."

As they trudged off, Jean-Paul prayed this place would be the shelter they all needed.

———— ≈ ————

The night air cooled Maria-Theresa's skin, and the wind billowed her white nightgown as she moved down the portico in the convent's courtyard. She inhaled deep and long, the pungent odors of cooking oil and incense filling her nasal passages and tickling her tongue.

She had no need of candlelight or lamplight. No worries about breaking the cursed blackout. For over seven decades, she had called this place home. By the time the Great War came here, she was already an old lady.

And now, this.

The breeze rattled last autumn's dead leaves that had never been swept away, caught in the maelstrom the courtyard created. Another reminder of a season past, a time gone that would never be recaptured. *Oui*, the world was changing, and not for the better. That the Lord should not tarry any longer was Maria-Theresa's constant prayer.

But tarry He did as war once again ravaged and scorched the land. This time, the battles were not always set on the field, but sometimes in schools and homes and churches. Even convents.

Now winded by her wanderings, she leaned against the ancient stone wall still warm from the afternoon's sun. She would not live to see the world changed. That much she knew. Her heart could not take much more of the evil that permeated to man's very marrow.

Yet the Lord didn't call her home. He must still have a purpose for her to fulfill in this life, though what that purpose could be was unknown to her. That was what she must trust in these trying times. A little while until she crossed the glittering Jordan to a celestial creation that would never be marred by war.

She pushed herself away from the wall and unpinned her hair, allowing it to cascade over her shoulders and to her waist. The wind picked up the gray strands and blew them around her face, which she lifted to the sky. Never had a man touched her silken tresses, now thinned by age. Never had a man whispered his love for her in her ear.

But what she had was enough. The job the Lord had given her had been enough. At her advanced age, He still had work for her, plenty to busy her hands and mind and make up for everything she had missed.

Because she had a heavenly Husband.

From deep inside the drafty convent, the baby wailed. Someone would hurry to quiet him because there could be no noise. No one must know of his existence. No one must know of the other child either.

As she had predicted, the crying quieted within a few moments, and silence once again covered the sleeping convent.

This is why she had come to St. Roch all those years ago, a child who had experienced too much hatred and violence in her young life. Hatred and violence that had stolen her innocence.

The refuge and solitude this place offered her was a balm to her soul. And it continued to be so. She would never have been happy out there. These walls didn't confine her.

Just the opposite.

They set her free.

Soft footfalls interrupted her musings. The rigid form of Sister Angelica approached. In the muted moonlight, Maria-Theresa could just make out her ever-present frown. What did she have to be so sour about?

"What are you doing out here at such an hour? You know the damp air is not good for you. And in your nightshift, for mercy's sake, and your hair down." She slipped her arm around Maria-Theresa's, so possessive in her manner. "Come now, let me get you back to bed."

"I'm not helpless. I enjoy coming out of that stuffy room of mine. And whoever said night air wasn't good for you never stepped out to gaze at the stars God flung across the sky."

"Very poetic of you, but you need your rest."

Maria-Theresa pulled from Angelica's grasp. "Please, Sister, I have lived twice as long as you. I know when I need rest and when I don't. My eternal sleep isn't far off. I want to enjoy every hour the Lord grants me on this earth."

Sister Angelica sighed. "We just don't want you to get sick. You know we can't bring a doctor inside, because of the children." She inhaled to say more, but the ringing of the bell at the gate interrupted her words.

Praise the Lord.

But who would come here at this time of night? Sister Raphael appeared and scurried to meet them. A stillness, a holy peace, expanded inside Maria-Theresa's chest.

Frown lines creased Sister Raphael's forehead. "What should we do?" She wrung her hands.

"Why, let them in."

The other two stared at Maria-Theresa as if she'd spoken in a foreign language.

Sister Angelica paled. "What about the children? We've admitted no one since Albert arrived."

"These who come will not do us harm."

Now the stares changed to penetrating gazes, as if they were working to determine her soundness of mind.

Sister Raphael leaned in. "How do you know? Did you see a vision?"

Maria-Theresa waved away her ridiculous words. The bell rang again, the gong chiming throughout the convent. If they didn't answer it soon, it would wake the children. "Just do as I say. I only know that we will be safe." *Non,* she couldn't explain the soft, regular beating of her heart or the steadiness of her breaths.

She just knew they needed the people who had arrived. God had sent them.

Sister Angelica was the one who snapped to attention and, head held high as always, marched to the gate. "Who are you? What do you want?" Her voice screeched like a mother bird defending her brood.

"*S'il vous plaît,* let us in." A deep voice, the words spoken in perfect French.

Maria-Theresa had been right.

Sister Angelica glared over her shoulder. Maria-Theresa gave a single nod, and her fellow nun withdrew a key from her pocket and unlatched the gate.

A man and a woman tumbled inside. The man, tall and dark, barked commands of his own. "Lock it. Lock it now and don't let anyone else in. Is that understood?" He mussed his already disheveled hair.

The woman's hazel eyes were large in her face and mud smeared her cheek. Several dark stains dotted the ill-fitting pilot's jacket she wore. She had been through an ordeal. They both had.

And the woman held a small child by the hand. Maria-Theresa studied her.

A Mongoloid. God had indeed brought their visitors to this place for a reason.

Maria-Theresa stepped forward. Who cared that she was in her nightgown, her hair loose and her feet bare? She went to the visitors and touched their arms. "You are welcome here. Your arrival is providential. Here you will find rest and peace and shelter. A place for your little one."

"Oh, she's not ours. We found her when the Nazis killed everyone in her village. They—"

She touched the woman's lips and closed her own eyes. "We do not need to know the details. God sees all, and He is the One who has brought you here in your time of need. You will be safe."

The woman continued, her voice thin and reedy, her words thick with an accent. "We don't want to bring trouble here, but we would be so grateful for a place to sleep tonight."

"You will be here longer than that. Your way won't be easy, but God will bless you. Right now, you need a meal and a hot bath and a soft bed. All of these, we can provide." Maria-Theresa opened her eyes.

Sister Raphael scowled. "This isn't a good idea, Sister. Think about. . ."

"I am. They are always in the forefront of my mind. And I believe that God has sent these for their sake. Sister Angelica, please lock the gate tight. *Monsieur, madame,* follow me, *s'il vous plaît.*"

Oui, the arrival of these two was a very good thing. God had mighty plans for them. As she led the way into the dark hall of the convent, a light flooded her.

This was God's answer to their problem.

⫶ CHAPTER EIGHT ⫶

For the moment, the nuns had left Jean-Paul, Nellie, and Claire alone in the kitchen, steaming bowls of soup on the long table in front of them. At the aroma of onions and rosemary, his mouth watered. All was silent in the spacious stone room, the fire dying in the stove the sisters had stirred up to heat their visitors' meal. Only the anemic glow from a single lantern lit the space.

The quiet, the darkness, the peace of this place, soothed him. He could relax here. After years spent with the Maquis, fighting and running, it was a strange sensation.

Across the long, heavy wood table, Nellie slumped on the hard straight-back chair. She clinked her spoon against the sturdy pottery bowl but didn't take a bite.

"What's wrong?"

She lifted her gaze to him, her face unreadable in the dim light. "I almost died twice in the past few days. Twice. The closest I came to this before was when the ship I was on to England hit a storm. And I was never in any real danger then." She pushed the bowl away, scraping it against the table.

Perhaps he had become so used to daily danger that he had become immune to it. He'd had several close escapes himself in the past couple of weeks. He sipped the fragrant offering and relished in the warmth it spread through his body. "It is something that follows us every day." A specter that haunted both his days and his nights.

"You seem unfazed. Like you've been in this position before. Have you?" She tugged down the bomber jacket. The sisters had promised her a change of clothes, not only for her but for all of them.

"We have lived with the Germans for four years now. You never get used to death. It's always around you. Every one of us knows someone who has died. On the outside, it may look like it doesn't affect us. But it does. Deep down here." He thumped his chest.

"You never answered my question."

"But I did." He resumed slurping his soup, and after she stared at him for a long while, she ate as well. If she waited for him to divulge details, she would wait for a very long time. The horrors of war were not to be spoken about. Better to tuck them far away, bury them like the garbage you bury in the yard.

They finished their dinner in silence and then washed their bowls and glasses without a word. Being in this place did that to a body. Made words unnecessary. Superfluous.

Claire yawned, wide and loud. Even though she had slept in the vegetable truck, it had been a long, hard day for the poor child. Despite her trials, she placed her trust in him and Nellie. He wouldn't have been able to do so in her position.

Outside these gates of solitude, a war raged. People died by the hundreds and thousands each day. He couldn't remain and enjoy this sanctuary longer than tonight. First, he had to deliver Nellie to the Americans, and then he had to find Luc and rejoin his men. Wherever they were.

He wiped his hands on the rough burlap towel and turned to retire to the room the sisters had made up for him when a faint mewling emanated from below them. As soon as it sounded, it died away.

Nellie came to his side. "Did you hear that?"

He nodded.

"So far they haven't said anything about any other Mongoloid children they are hiding. Could that be one of them?"

How did he answer? For whatever reason, the nuns weren't divulging yet that they had any other children here.

"Come on." Nellie tugged his arm. "It sounded like it might be downstairs. I'd like to meet them and make sure this is a good place for Claire."

He stepped in her path to block her. "Most likely a wild cat. You don't want to be bit. Leave it alone."

She drew her lips into a frown. "You and I both know that's not the case."

"Nellie, *non*. You cannot. We won't say anything about it until they do."

"Why not?"

"They have their reasons. When you hide someone, before you let anyone else in on that secret, you want to be sure they are completely trustworthy."

"But—"

He waved her away. "Let me walk you and Claire to your room. She needs to go to bed."

"I can find my way." Even in the dim light, her eyes flashed.

"Let me be a gentleman. This is France, after all." He struggled to put on his most charming smile.

She melted a little, her rigid face giving way to a slight grin. "Since you put it that way, you may."

Side by side by side, they strolled the dark, quiet corridors until they came to a heavy door at the end of the hall. "I believe this is where Sister Angelica said you would be."

Nellie nodded. "Thank you for everything you've done for me the past few days. I don't want you to think I'm ungrateful."

"I don't believe that of you. Put Claire to bed and get some rest as well. I will see you in the morning. *Bonsoir.*"

"Good night." With a soft click, she shut the door.

Jean-Paul stood in the hall and took a deep breath. Then, instead of turning to his room, he wandered down the stairs to the kitchen again. He sat at the table in the dark, his hearing heightened. Early in the occupation he learned to listen well, always alert for footsteps, vehicles, bumps in the night.

Every now and again more mewling came from below, hushed within the space of a few heartbeats. Then soft footsteps scurried up the stairs and in his direction. He stepped from the kitchen and into Sister Maria-Theresa's path.

She came to a crashing halt, almost running into him, and clutched her chest. He reached out to steady her.

"*Monsieur*, are you trying to give an old woman a heart attack?"

"My apologies. Tell me, what is going on here?"

Her dried, cracked lip trembled.

"I might be able to help you. I have. . .ways. Connections. Just share with me."

She glanced over both shoulders, then pulled him until he was bent halfway over, at her height. For several minutes, she stared into his eyes, her gaze intense, but he resisted the urge to turn away. Let her gaze into the depths of his soul. She would see that he was trustworthy.

"I believe God sent you when we needed you the most. Come with me. I will show you."

He only prayed that he would be able to help them with their hidden treasure.

———— ≋ ————

Nellie sat on the edge of the hard, narrow bed in the closet-sized room and rubbed the goose pimples off her arms. There was no fire, no brazier, nothing to warm the chill from the air. Even though it was June, these thick stone walls kept out the warmth and held in the cold.

Right across the hall, the door to the room open so Nellie could hear her, Claire slept in her own small bed piled high with blankets one of the sisters had left.

Nellie rubbed her eyes. Would she be able to get any sleep tonight, or would the horrific images she'd seen in the past few days continue to plague her? Would the ceaseless rewinding of that film in her mind ever stop?

She moved to the pitcher of water and bowl on the plain washstand and splashed her face, then wiped it with the rough white towel. Once she had folded it and returned it to its spot beside the bowl, she turned toward the bed where Sister Angelica had laid a plain black dress and a white sweater.

A wooden crucifix on the wall above the bed drew her eye. "Lord, there has been so much loss. Is there any good left in the world? Is there any hope left? No matter where I go, it follows me. Will it be my time soon?"

The thought sent another shiver through her, from head to toe.

"Please, protect us."

She slipped off her pants and bomber jacket and slid the dress over her head and shrugged into the sweater. She would have to scrub the blood from her trousers. For now, it was nice of the sisters to lend her the dress.

Still, she couldn't crawl underneath the rough blanket. Couldn't bring herself to close her eyes for the nightmares that were sure to come. Less than two weeks ago, she was in London, at one of the most luxurious hotels, enjoying a cup of tea while listening to the radio. How a life could be upended in the matter of a few days.

Drawing the borrowed sweater around herself, she exited her room. Perhaps there was some milk in the icebox. If she heated that, she might be able to sleep.

The stone floors were cool underneath her bare feet as she crept down the stairs and through the corridor. A sliver of moonlight slipped through the blackout curtains in the window at the end of the hall, just enough to illuminate two shadowy figures disappearing behind a door.

There could be no doubt as to the identity of the one. Unless one of the sisters was unusually broad and tall, it had to be Jean-Paul. The other, unless she missed her guess, was Sister Maria-Theresa, with the way she almost floated, despite her advanced age.

Where were they going? When she reached for her camera that was always around her neck, it wasn't there. She had left it in her room. After a glance at the stairs, she turned and followed Jean-Paul and Maria-Theresa down the hall.

The door they had disappeared through led to a stairwell. Here and there a light brightened the way. Since there were no windows, there wasn't a need to worry about blackout conditions.

The mewling sound from earlier was louder now. They must hide the children in the basement. She picked up her pace and came to the bottom of the steps. The noise now sounded on her left, so she turned that way.

At the end of this passage was another large, heavy door. Were all French convents like this, with their mazes of halls and corridors? There was the sound again, almost like crying. She raced for the door and flung it open. Jean-Paul and Sister Maria-Theresa stood just in front of her, blocking her view of the room.

Jean-Paul whirled around. "How did you find us?" He growled, almost like a bear.

"I followed you."

When Sister Maria-Theresa turned toward her, Nellie was able to see into the large room.

A room with a crib and a couple of beds.

Sister Maria-Theresa smiled. "God sent us these children, and now you have brought us another." Her voice had an ethereal quality.

Nellie moved to the crib. There, an infant of maybe six months or so slept. His forehead was wide, his nose flat, his lips thick. The woman from the church was right. They did hide Mongoloid children here. The baby smiled in his sleep, like he was having an enjoyable dream.

Nellie glanced at the other child, then turned to Sister Maria-Theresa. "Is he a Mongoloid too?"

Sister Maria-Theresa nodded, her gray hair still not confined in a wimple. "*Oui*. Not quite perfect enough for Hitler and the Aryan ideal. But worthy in God's sight."

"How long have they been here?"

Sister Angelica rushed over, a scowl marring her still-young face. "Those are enough questions for one night. You must leave and go to bed. Never speak to anyone about this." Her eyes held a cold, hard glint.

From what Nellie could tell, the stern nun would go to any lengths to protect these children.

What Sister Angelica didn't know was that these children stirred Nellie's heart.

Because of Velma, Nellie would never do anything to jeopardize these precious lives.

⊫ CHAPTER NINE ⊰

Monday, June 12, 1944

Before dawn had a chance to paint the sky with its watercolor brush, Jean-Paul was up, dressed, and out the gate. Now that they had safely brought Claire to the St. Roch convent, he had to find out if he could connect with anyone from the resistance. And if there was a way to get Nellie back across the lines and returned to where she belonged.

The mild, early-morning summer air smelled of dampness and fresh-cut hay and just-baked bread. Even at this early hour, it was clear it was going to be a beautiful day.

Closer to the beginning of the occupation, a man Jean-Paul knew only as Rogue lived in this area. He'd met him a time or two. The question was if this man continued to live in the area and work from here as a home base or if he had moved on or if he was even alive.

If he was here, how was Jean-Paul ever to find him?

The sun peered above the horizon, its rays tentative at first, then strengthening as the morning came on. Shopkeepers flung their shutters open and unlocked their doors.

Some time had passed since Jean-Paul had been in this village. And he'd only passed through once, to pick up some forged papers from Rogue. Going to his house was dangerous, but it was a risk Jean-Paul had to take. An older woman, a basket in her hand, wished him *bonjour*. He struggled to bring to mind the color and location of Rogue's house.

For a while, he wandered the streets. Up ahead, the sight of a brown-shirted Nazi snagged his attention. He turned down a different road and continued his search.

The town came to life more and more, but still, none of the houses were familiar. Jean-Paul scoured his memory. Ah, wait a minute. There it was, sitting in the middle of the block, its red-tiled roof so much like every other house in the village. The difference with this one was that it had red roses climbing up the brick exterior, the bush now a riot of flowers awash in the sweetest perfume.

Jean-Paul opened the gate in the little white fence and made his way to the door. He knocked and waited for an answer, gazing at the garden as he did. Rogue had always kept a neat little flower bed, but now it was overrun with weeds, almost choking out the irises whose purple and yellow buds were fanning open.

A still-muscular middle-aged man cracked the door, his icy blue-eyed stare startling Jean-Paul. "Who are you?" The man spoke German.

A flapping drew Jean-Paul's attention to the flagpole on the cottage's far corner. There hung a red flag with a midnight black swastika fluttering in the breeze. How could he have missed it?

This was no longer Rogue's house.

"I'm sorry to disturb you so early in the morning." Thank goodness his father was German, so he spoke the language without a flaw. It was one reason he had been so successful in his resistance work for four years.

"Who are you?" the man repeated, peering at him with piercing, soul-searching blue eyes.

Jean-Paul steeled himself and shuttered his face, standing tall and at attention. A knee-jerk response *Vater* had instilled in him.

"Wait a minute." The German stroked his pointed chin. "Are you the new driver I've been begging for? It's about time they finally sent you."

Before Jean-Paul could open his mouth, the man grabbed him by the arm and pulled him inside. "What's your name? I didn't get any papers, but they seem to have forgotten us in this insignificant hamlet."

Jean-Paul's mind went blank. Nothing came into it. None of his training, none of his years in the Maquis, did him a bit of good right now. "Herman Braun."

Oh, why had he blurted out that name? That was his father. If this man decided to do any investigating, he would discover that Herman Braun was a fifty-something officer in Berlin.

"Your rank?"

"*Gefreiter.*"

"Hmm. Of course they wouldn't send me anyone of a higher rank than that. Never mind. All you need to know is how to drive. Can you manage that?"

"*Ja.*"

"I'm Major Weber. I'm sure they didn't bother to inform you of that either."

"They did not." Jean-Paul could hardly squeeze the words from his pinched throat. How had he gotten himself into this mess? All this time, he'd been a leader in the Maquis. One of the best maquisards around. But when it counted, he couldn't talk himself out of a jam.

Then again, this might be an in for him, a way for him to find out what the Nazis were up to.

"Where might your uniform be? Your appearance is disgraceful and unbecoming of a Wehrmacht solider."

Jean-Paul swallowed and toed the home's hardwood floors, buying time for him to think. "I made a narrow escape from the Allies on my way here. They stripped me of my uniform, but I managed to find some clothes and get away."

Weber swore. "Those Americans and Brits are getting too close for my comfort. They likely sent you at last because we'll have to pack up and move east at a moment's notice. Come in, then."

They weren't even going to stay and fight?

Instead of the cheerful home this had been when Rogue lived here, there was now nothing more than a large, hip-height table in the middle of the living room, the top of it covered with papers. As he moved farther into the house, a glance at them told Jean-Paul that these were maps.

A gold mine of information, if he could get a moment to study them.

Weber gathered the papers together and held them close. "Your name is so familiar to me. Have we met before?"

"*Nein,* sir. It's a common enough name."

"That's true. You probably need a good breakfast."

"*Ja,* that would be very good." Though he had to find a way to get out of here and back to the convent. By now, everyone would be awake, and they would be wondering what happened to him.

He choked down the eggs and bread that the maid served. How could he be here, fraternizing with these people? He should have made an excuse and left. These were the kind of men who had killed so many, including everyone in Claire's village. They were the kind of men who wanted to kill Claire.

He managed to stuff a few slices of the still-warm loaf of bread into his jacket pocket. With extra mouths to feed, the nuns would be hard pressed to have enough food.

Though he longed to sip and savor the bitterness of his first cup of real coffee in four years, he downed it in a few throat-burning gulps before he stood. "I would like to see the conditions of the roads in the daylight, if you don't mind. And then I'll take a look at the vehicles to make sure they're in good running order." Even if he would have no idea if they were or not.

"Why rush off? You've had a difficult night. Your room is the first on the right at the top of the stairs if you'd like to get some sleep. And we have to find you a uniform."

"I don't sit still much. Always like to be on the go. And if the uniform needs to be altered, I can take it to the tailor, if you point the way."

Weber eyed him with his Aryan-perfect blue eyes. "Very well. But return here by noon. I have an appointment then, and I'd like you to drive. Heil Hitler." Weber gave the one-armed salute.

Though it killed Jean-Paul to do so, he returned the gesture and bolted out the door.

———— ≈ ————

A tug on Nellie's arm brought her out of her slumber. She rubbed her sandy eyes, blinking to come awake. It was still dark out. Why was she being awakened so early?

The tugging continued, and she peered down. There was Claire, a grin strung across her face. Nellie sat up. "*Bonjour.*"

Claire giggled and turned away.

Nellie stopped her with a touch to her back. "*Rester.* Don't go away. Come be with me for a while."

Claire climbed onto the small bed and snuggled with Nellie, like

Velma had so often done.

Nellie breathed in the fresh scent of soap. No perfumes, just cleanliness. For someone to have given her a bath, Claire must have been up for a while. Her blond hair was still wet but plaited into two long braids. "I'll sing you a song. One to get the morning off to a good start. *Frère Jacques, Frère Jacques, dormez-vous? Dormez-vous? Sonnez les matines! Sonnez les matines! Ding, dang, dong. Ding, dang, dong.*"

Claire clapped her hands as Nellie finished the song. So she sang it again. And again. And again. About the time her voice was ready to give out, Sister Angelica entered the room and scooped Claire from Nellie's lap.

Claire cried, but Sister Angelica crooned into her ear, and her tears soon turned into sunny smiles. At least in this dark place, someone was happy.

Sister Angelica sent a glare Nellie's way. "You've missed morning prayers. And breakfast is almost over."

"I'm sorry I slept so long. I must have been more tired than I thought. I'll be right down."

"See that you are." Sister Angelica, with Claire still in her arms, swept from the room.

By the time Nellie made it to the dining room, only Sister Maria-Theresa remained, a cup of what passed for coffee in front of her. The nun motioned for Nellie to take a chair and folded her gnarled hands in her lap. "You have a way with them."

All Nellie could do was nod. The lump in her throat was too large for her to speak.

"You aren't afraid of the children?"

Nellie leaned back and stared at the wizened woman. "Why would I be afraid?"

"Many don't understand them. How their minds work. How they see the world around them. When we don't understand each other, that's when hate and prejudice grow. You love someone who is like these children."

"I do."

Sister Maria-Theresa patted Nellie's hand. "And you miss her."

"*Oui.*" She couldn't say any more about Velma without blinking back tears. For someone who never cried, she'd been teary enough the past few weeks.

"Why are you here, then, and she is home? You come from America, don't you?"

Nellie sat back and worked to smooth out the wrinkles in the borrowed dress. Jean-Paul must be right about her accent. "I took Velma with me to Chicago because her mother was dead and her sister is unable to care for her, but when I was assigned to London, I had to leave her behind."

Silence fell over them. "I can see that you're torn about that. You believe you haven't done enough for her."

Nellie's soul stood naked in front of this old nun. "I think about her all the time and what life must be like for her. I found the best institution I could afford, but it's still an institution, not a loving home like she'd been used to."

"If she's not your daughter or sister, why have you taken care of her?"

"She's my best friend's sister. But from the day her father died, I pledged to take care of her. And that's what I've done. Until I boarded that ship and sailed to England." Nellie studied the well-polished table in front of her. "I abandoned her, just like everyone else did."

Sister Maria-Theresa sipped from her cup.

"And now I'm abandoning Claire. She has no one left in the world. It's only been a couple of days, but she trusts me, and I don't want to break that trust. I have a job I need to do though. Photographs that I have to get out of the country as soon as possible, ones that may make those in America who don't understand what's going on here sit up and take notice."

"Claire will be in good hands. You don't have to worry about her. Sister Angelica can be rather dour, but she loves the children and is never cross with them. Sister Raphael is as sweet a soul as they come. They'll look after your Claire."

Nellie took a piece of bread from the basket in front of her, buttered it, and bit into it.

"You're exhausted. Why don't you go get some more sleep? Sister Angelica and Sister Raphael will take the children to the garden to play soon, and then it will be nap time. Claire will be here waiting for you when you wake up."

Nellie wiped her hands on her napkin and rose. "I do have to find the Allied forces, anyone who's a friend and not a foe, so I can get back to work."

"I think maybe the Lord has something else intended for you. You do realize that we are still deep in Nazi-held territory here, don't you?"

She had been trying to push away that thought. They should have never gotten on that vegetable truck, even though it seemed to be the only way out.

"Go on, now. There will be time later to make sense of it all."

Nellie obeyed Sister Maria-Theresa's instructions and climbed the stairs to the second floor. As she made her way down the hall to her room, there was Jean-Paul. She called to him. When he didn't stop, she hurried to him and touched his elbow. "Didn't you hear me?"

He didn't turn, so she scurried in front of him and stopped his progress. "Are you ignoring me? Did I do something to make you angry?"

"*Non*, pardon me. *Bonne matinée.*"

"Good morning." She gazed into his dark, hooded eyes, then down at what he held in his hands.

The brown uniform of a Nazi with an armband bearing the swastika.

⋚ CHAPTER TEN ⋚

Blood whooshed in Jean-Paul's ears as Nellie stared at the Nazi uniform in his hand. When she'd called to him and then run in front of him, she'd dashed his hopes that he'd be able to make it back to the room without anyone noticing his presence. Of course she'd be the one to find him.

Now she turned those lovely hazel eyes on him, her narrow-eyed gaze hard and distant.

"This is not how it appears."

She blinked several times, fast. "I'm not quite sure how it appears. Where did you get that?"

"I am now a driver for Major Weber."

She stumbled backward against the smooth stone walls, flattening herself against them. "Am I your prisoner?"

He drew his eyebrows together. "My prisoner? I don't understand."

"I thought you were a maquisard, but you are a collaborator. If so, why did we hide from the Germans?"

He couldn't suppress the chuckle that built in his chest. "I'm afraid you're mistaken. I am pretending. I am no German." Well, maybe in blood but not in spirit. He'd abandoned his father's ideology long ago. Had never truly embraced it.

Now she drew her eyebrows into a V.

"I can find out secrets. Military ones. Troop positions. And I have access to a vehicle. That gives me great freedom."

At that news, her face brightened, those pink, round cheeks plumping. "Will you be able to get me back to the Americans?" She stood on her tiptoes. "Can I rejoin them today?"

"That will not help you, I'm afraid."

She huffed out a breath and once again slumped against the wall. "Oh."

"Do you think your soldiers would allow a German vehicle through? They would shoot us without question."

"Even if I told them who I was and who you were?"

"You wouldn't have the chance to open your mouth. You'd be dead before you said a word."

"Then I don't see how this new position of yours is going to help me."

"You don't trust me." Then again, in her position, he wouldn't trust himself.

She didn't break off her stare. "Can you blame me? I'm in a strange land with a war raging. I'm lost, and I'm alone. So no, I don't trust you."

"But Sister Maria-Theresa does." Without even trying, he had won the old nun's allegiance. She saw something in him, deep in his soul, something he didn't even see in himself. She had no reason for her faith in him, in a day and time when that was a precious commodity rarely given away.

But for whatever reason, it was this woman before him whose trust would be the most precious of all to him. He had no explanation for this desire. Nevertheless, it was there.

"She is too trusting. If you'll excuse me, I'd like to sleep for a while and freshen up before I work on a way to get myself back where I belong." In a flash, she disappeared behind her door, closing it with a little more force than necessary.

For a while, he stood in the hall, staring at the massive, dark door, simple, unadorned, yet effective in shutting out the world.

But the world would refuse to be shut out. He turned for his own room down the corridor from hers and slipped inside, hiding the uniform underneath the coverlet on the bed. The miracle was that the Nazis had left this convent alone for as long as they had.

Sooner or later, they would discover the secret hidden inside its ivy-covered walls.

With the Allies closing in, his guess was that it would be sooner.

Already, they had taken away a number of the nuns. It was only a matter of time before they came for the rest.

He left his room in search of Sister Maria-Theresa. Though Sister Angelica and Sister Raphael ran things around here, it was Sister Maria-Theresa who had the most insight, the most wisdom of them all. Like a butterfly drawn to a bright flower, he was drawn to her.

He discovered her in the main room, a much-read Bible in her narrow lap, her gaze intent on the words printed in it. He settled himself on the worn brown sofa across from her, the springs poking his back. They took their vow of poverty seriously here.

Sister Maria-Theresa didn't lift her gaze from her Bible. Instead, she swept her fingers over the words, as if the tips of them absorbed God's truth directly into her heart. Perhaps she couldn't even see them well but found comfort in just touching the book.

"You've been on a mission." Her words flowed from her tongue like water from a spring.

"How did you know?"

One corner of her mouth tipped up. "You didn't find what you sought."

"*Non.*"

"But God will bring a blessing from what you did discover."

"How do you know?"

Now she directed her look at him, her pale-blue eyes wide. "How do you not? No matter what comes into our lives, God uses it in the best way for us. His ways and His plan are perfect. You will learn that in the coming days, though the lesson will be difficult."

He sprang to his feet and paced the worn and faded red rug. "I don't need any hard teaching from God."

"He's already teaching you. He has been your entire life."

"My more immediate problem is what to do about Nellie. I don't know how I'm supposed to get her back to the Allies when we're a good distance behind enemy lines. We're deeper in Nazi territory than she believes we are. And even though I've found an in with the Germans, it hasn't solved her problem."

"Your work is a good work. Keep it up. As for the young woman, she is meant to be here, even though she may not know it herself. She too will see in time how all things work for good."

Jean-Paul spun on his heel and marched from the room. He'd been out of his mind to seek advice from a crazy old woman. She couldn't see the future. Like the rest of them, she had no idea what tomorrow would hold. Not ever, but especially not now. Today, this hour, this minute, could be the last of his life.

Even if it was, he would die fighting for those who couldn't fight for themselves.

He returned to his room to don his new uniform.

———— ≋ ————

Once Jean-Paul left the room and his footsteps faded down the hallway, Maria-Theresa lifted herself from her chair and hobbled to the chapel, the familiar spiciness of incense cocooning her in its embrace. This was where she came alive, where she was most at home.

Her halting steps were silent on the smooth stone tiles beneath her feet, but the long-worn wood pew creaked as she settled onto it. Her bony knees would no longer allow her to kneel, but God understood. All He asked was a humble, contrite heart.

She raised her gaze to the crucifix, the symbol a reminder of the place where Christ died, then closed her eyes.

"Mon Père, *I pour my heart out to You this day, coming only in the name of Your precious Son, asking for His forgiveness and for Your acceptance as I enter into Your presence.*

"*Holy Lord, You have brought these young people to us for a reason. I understand that and believe that, though I know not what it is. We will need help soon, won't we? I feel that in these old, tired bones. I have lived my life, and my time is short.*

"*But those little ones downstairs, they are so precious in Your sight. All three of them. You created them. You knit them together in their mothers' wombs, and You have counted each hair on their heads. The world may not love them, but You do.*

"*What is to be done, Lord? Open my eyes. Open Jean-Paul and Nellie's eyes. Prepare us for what is to come. I fear it will not be easy. I fear it will be frightening. I fear the outcome.*

"*You love us, even when the world doesn't. Jean-Paul's heart is hard. Nellie's focus is on the world. Turn them toward You and use them for whatever purpose You have ordained for them from the beginning of the world.*

"Pave the road before us. Make each crooked path straight. Prepare the way.

"More than anything, place a hedge of protection around us. Hold us in Your almighty embrace and do not let us go. Bring us through the fire of trial to the other side without a hair on our heads singed."

On stiff legs, she rose and made the difficult climb down the stairs to the nursery. How many more times would she be able to make this trek? Yet, despite the difficulty, she did so with gladness.

The children were now down for their morning naps. With silent feet she limped to the bed where Leo slept while Sister Raphael sat in a rocker and fed Albert.

Maria-Theresa brushed Leo's cheek, then leaned over the girl with golden hair. She placed her age-spotted hands on the child's silky locks and lifted her eyes to heaven. She needed no words to speak to the Father. He knew her heart and saw all.

Maria-Theresa had just glanced up when the infant gave a hearty burp. Sister Raphael placed him in his crib and came to Maria-Theresa's side. "Are you ready to return upstairs?"

"*Oui, merci.* I believe it is time for me to rest as well."

Sister Raphael looped her arm through Maria-Theresa's, and together they made the arduous climb.

"What do you make of the new arrivals?" Sister Raphael paused on the third step from the top for Maria-Theresa to catch her breath.

"They are heaven sent."

"Isn't that a bit cliché?"

"Not when it is true."

"You trust them too easily in a day when you shouldn't."

"I can see in their eyes they are dependable." Maria-Theresa nodded, indicating her readiness to continue. "I wouldn't take a chance with the children's lives."

"I know you wouldn't, but you cannot be too careful. How do you know what they're like? They are strangers. Even people we know could give us away in the blink of an eye."

"I'm aware of that. Now, if you don't mind, I'll go to my room."

Sister Raphael released her and turned toward the kitchen. Just as she was about to spin the knob to her narrow room, Maria-Theresa spied a dark flash at the end of the hall. Her eyes may not be the best anymore, but there was no mistaking it was the young American woman. "Nellie."

For a split second, she froze.

"Come here, *s'il vous plait.*"

Like a child caught filching a sweet, Nellie approached Maria-Theresa, her head down.

"Where were you going?"

Nellie lifted her gaze, strong and blazing like a winter's fire. "I have to find the Americans so I can get back to the work I came here to do."

"And you must sneak about to do that?"

She leaned closer, the odor of lye soap clinging to her. "Did you know that Jean-Paul has a Nazi uniform? He says that he got a job as a driver for them, that it would be a help to us. In the same breath, he tells me that it won't do any good in helping me get back across the lines. Doesn't that sound suspicious?"

Maria-Theresa clasped her always-trembling hands in front of her. Could it be that she had been wrong, at least about Jean-Paul? Up to this point in her life, her instincts had always been impeccable. *Père*, a member of the French gendarmes, told her that from the time she was small.

Perhaps her age was clouding her judgment. Perhaps Jean-Paul was a better actor than she gave him credit for. Perhaps she had been too trusting.

Non. She had seen the goodness in him. Had peered deep into his soul and seen what God was doing in him. Had seen what he was and what he could be. "What we observe on the outside is only a part of the true measure of a man."

"I hope you are correct, Sister. For now, I must be off." Like mist under the morning's sun, she disappeared.

And Maria-Theresa prayed once more that she hadn't been wrong about Jean-Paul.

⁝ CHAPTER ELEVEN ⁝

After a long night and morning in the darkness of the convent, the bright summer sun was a shock to Nellie's eyes. She squinted as she stepped through the nunnery's gate and onto the dirt road that ran in front of it.

How different from summer in Mississippi. There was no searing heat and humidity, no songs of sharecroppers in the fields, no hum of cicadas. In fact, the bucolic scene was so peaceful and still, it was almost difficult to believe they were in the middle of a war zone.

She lifted her camera, stepped back, and framed St. Roch in the shot, snapping with a click of the shutter. Too bad she didn't have color film. The azure sky contrasted with the ivy-covered walls and the riot of flowers in a stunning panorama.

Perhaps if she were a painter, she would be able to capture the true beauty of this place.

She shook her head. That was not what she was here for. Not even for taking photographs of charming convents in the French countryside.

She was here to cover war. Good thing Sister Maria-Theresa hadn't detained her. The old nun's gaze had bored right into Nellie's soul, as if she could see all the secrets she hid deep inside. No wonder Nellie squirmed under the woman's scrutiny.

Nevertheless, she had a job to do.

To that end, she turned her face toward the town in the distance and tromped in that direction. No need to get distracted by the beauty of this place or by the charm of the children hidden behind the rusting iron gate.

How going to a town full of the enemy would help her get back to the Allies, she had no idea. But it was a place to start. Time to get back to where she belonged.

The walk to the village didn't take long. A weight fell on her shoulders as she entered. The weight of the oppression these people had endured for four long years. She passed a woman pushing a pram and an old man tottering about, leaning on his cane.

They gave her hollow-eyed stares. In a place this small, most likely everyone knew everyone. She was a stranger. Though she gave them her warmest smile, neither one responded in kind.

Now that she was here, what was she supposed to do? Coming had been a mistake. But how else was she supposed to find her way west? Ah, up ahead was a train station, its stone facade worn by years of sun and rain, its paint peeling and neglected by years of war. A few people milled about the platform, including a group of children clad in blue shirts with blue and yellow striped scarves around their necks. A woman accompanied them, her hair teased high, round glasses a little too small for her face. Like Scouts back home, probably on their way to summer camp.

Despite the upheaval of their world, life went on in some strange way.

Perhaps she could travel by train as far as she could and then make her way the rest of the distance on foot. Though she didn't have much, she did have some money that she always kept stuffed in her brassiere. It was a trick she'd learned from her grandmother, who had always hidden cash inside her corset, claiming it was the safest place to keep it.

She wasn't wrong.

She stepped to the counter and opened her mouth to speak but caught the words on the tip of her tongue before they spilled out.

Accented words.

Words that could get her in a great deal of trouble.

The ticket taker said something to her, but she couldn't make it out over the roaring in her brain, so she shook her head and backed away. Even if she managed to find a way to ask for a ticket to the end of the line, the Germans who patrolled the station with their large dogs would ask to see her papers.

All she had were her American pass credentials.

She scurried away from the station and back into the heart of the village. The baker, wiping flour from his apron, was locking his door for the day, his shelves cleaned of all he'd had to offer. A group of children ran down the street, chasing after a scrawny black-and-white puppy.

What was she going to do? Perhaps she'd be able to use some of the money she had to bribe a farmer to drive her to the lines. From there, she'd have to figure things out. As long as she headed west, she'd be going in the right direction with a chance of getting out of this pickle.

That was the ticket. The town was too risky. She'd do better to find someone trustworthy in the country. Perhaps the nuns knew of someone who could help her.

She stepped out to cross the cobblestone road.

A Jeep's horn blared. Brakes screeched.

Just in the nick of time, she jumped backward and avoided being run over.

She met the driver's eyes. Jean-Paul. Of course she would have to run into him here. Almost literally. Swell.

No flicker of recognition sparked in his eyes, he kept them so well hooded. In fact, he shifted the vehicle into gear and inched forward. Then the brown-shirted German beside him shouted at him, and Jean-Paul braked.

The Nazi hopped from the car and made his way toward Nellie. Her heart skidded to a stop, then resumed beating in a wild, uneven gait.

Before the Nazi could reach her, Jean-Paul was in front of her in a flash.

The older man barked an order in German. Jean-Paul answered him. Back and forth they went, the officer's face reddening with each passing parley.

All Nellie could do was stand stock still and keep telling herself to inhale and exhale. After several agonizing minutes, the German stepped back to the vehicle and folded his arms in front of his barrel chest.

Jean-Paul spun to face her. "Why are you here?" His low words were sharp.

"Just—"

"Get back to the convent. It's too dangerous. He almost arrested you."

Mere seconds later, Jean-Paul and his new boss sped away.

Her throat burned.

She had been foolish. Jean-Paul had just saved her life.

———— ≋ ————

At long last, Jean-Paul managed to drop Weber at the house. When they drove to the village hall, Jean-Paul could have sworn Marianne Cohn was strolling down the street in the direction of the train station with a group of Scouts in her wake, as if she were a mother hen.

He'd only met her once, and then just for a few minutes. That was earlier in the year, when she had first teamed up with Rolande Birgy to spirit Jewish children across the border to Switzerland.

The work she did was risky, the same work as Georges Loinger and Marcel Mangel. They dressed Jewish children as Scouts, pretended they were going on holiday, and then slipped them over the border. But crossing was illegal, and Swiss authorities had been known to send Jewish refugees back into France.

Still, he had to see her. Perhaps she knew what had become of Luc and the others. Maybe she knew where Rogue or any maquisard might be working.

Word did get around. Jean-Paul and his group often contacted Rolande and Marianne and Mila Racine, before she had been arrested, to bring the Jews they were helping to safer places.

On the pretense that he needed to pick up some supplies, Jean-Paul raced toward the station and parked the Küblewagen in front of it. Marianne and the children milled about the platform, waiting for a train to carry them east.

In order to keep from startling them, he approached her from the back. Once he was directly behind her, he leaned over and whispered in her ear. "Marianne, it's me. Jean-Paul Breslau. We met earlier this year."

She turned around and glared at him, her eyes magnified by her glasses. Though she frowned, her words were soft. "What do you want with me?"

"You're taking these children on holiday?"

She nodded, producing her identity booklet, probably to make it appear like he was indeed a German soldier. "To Annemasse."

"And what word do you have on the other Scout leaders?"

"The ones you know?"

He nodded and handed her ID to her.

"Nothing. I'm surprised you're here."

"I have a situation myself that I'm taking care of."

"Watch out. A desperate German is more deadly than a hungry wolf."

Goose bumps broke out on Jean-Paul's arms. He raised his voice for the benefit of any who might be standing nearby and wondering about their hushed conversation. "Have a good trip, mademoiselle."

"*Merci.*"

His steps were slower as he returned to the Kübelwagen. If only Marianne had been able to provide him the information he needed. For now, he'd continue with the charade he'd started. Perhaps when she returned this way, she would be able to tell him more.

By the time he arrived at the convent that evening for a visit, darkness had already descended over the little hamlet, all light obfuscated by clouds and blackout curtains. Between kowtowing to Weber's demands, saving Nellie's skin, and speaking with Marianne Cohn, it had been a long day. At least he brought back a few loaves of bread he'd managed to smuggle from Weber's house, enough to help out the sisters and children.

Since he didn't have long before he needed to be back at Nazi headquarters for the evening, he deposited the bread in the kitchen and went in search of Nellie. He found her burrowed in the old stuffed chair in the main living area, her dress discarded for her now-clean pants, her legs curled underneath her. "So this is where you have been hiding."

She glanced up from the book in her lap. "I haven't been hiding."

"My apologies. What were you doing in town today?"

"Trying to find a way back to my people. Isn't that what you would do in my situation? In fact, you did say you needed to locate the Maquis yourself. To return to your people. Now you're driving for the enemy. What is going on, Jean-Paul? I don't understand.

"You said you wouldn't be able to help me, but I can't stay locked up here forever. I have a job to do. When I didn't show up with the rest of the unit, they probably went searching for me. And when they found Clarence's body and not mine, they most likely assumed the worst. My poor mother must be frantic."

"I understand. For her safety, I haven't been able to contact my mother in four years. She has no idea if I'm dead or alive. You have to believe that I'm doing all I can—for you, for the children, for myself. And that driving for the Germans is part of that."

"I don't see how."

"This is where you have to trust me."

"I'm trying." Her tone had softened a great deal. "It's hard. I'm frustrated. I've never been a sit-around-and-do-nothing kind of person."

"I can see that."

"So I'll admit that going to town today was foolish. In the past week or so, I've done a number of unwise things."

"Like sneaking into France?"

"How…?"

"Not that hard to figure out. If you were attached to a unit, they would have made sure you were with them. They wouldn't have left you alone with a reckless young man. How did you manage it?"

"General Eisenhower wasn't giving passes to any female journalists, so I went to Southampton where I heard the wounded from the beaches were being brought. An opportunity arose for me to be on a hospital ship. As we say in America, the rest is history."

"Are you out of your mind?"

"Quite possibly."

"I have to hand it to you. You're fearless. Reckless too, but definitely fearless." He blew out a breath and stepped closer to her. "Will you please be more careful from now on?"

"I'll do my best, though I make no promises."

"It's not just your life you're putting at risk. It's Claire's and the other children's and the sisters' and mine. Just think before you act."

She nodded and stood. As she left the room, she touched his bare forearm, her fingers warm and soft. "*Je suis désolé*. Truly sorry."

Once she was gone, Jean-Paul forced himself to relax the muscles in his jaw. All he could do was pray she would believe him and trust him.

Before he could turn himself down to a simmer, Sister Maria-Theresa drifted in, the ethereal quality she had lighting her like a lamp in a dark room. How could someone so old and frail have such a presence?

For a long moment, she stopped and stared at him. He squirmed under her scrutiny.

"You're troubled." A statement from her, not a question.

There was no use denying it. The old woman could see straight through him. "It's Nellie. I've only known her a few days, but she's driving me crazy. She went into town and almost got herself arrested."

"She doesn't understand. For all of the war, she's been sheltered. Even in London, while the bombings there were terrible, once they stopped falling, the people there could go about a somewhat normal life. Here, it's very different. You need to teach her."

"How?" Even though she'd said she'd try, Nellie would never listen to him. She was a headstrong woman who would never follow instructions.

Sister Maria-Theresa stood so close to him that when he bent to her level, her breath whispered across his cheek. Though small, she remained as straight as a willow. "You need to tell her."

Goose bumps broke out over his arms again. It was as if she could read his mind. "Tell her what?" His voice squeaked.

"You know. If you don't show yourself to her, how will she ever trust you?"

"How do you know I have something to tell her? Do you have some special kind of power? Are you a spiritualist?"

"Never." She grimaced. "I would never be involved in the dark arts. But when you've lived as long as I have, you learn how to read people. I can see it in your eyes, how they are haunted. I can tell by the way you hold yourself, just a little back from others, never too close to them."

Jean-Paul sucked in a breath. "I promised I would never tell anyone."

"I wouldn't want you to break a promise. But is it a vow you should have made in the first place?"

Simone, the woman he had loved, was long gone. And the vow he'd made never to speak of her was to himself.

In those long hours after he'd lost her, he found himself in church, the candles at the altar providing the only light flickering in the empty building. He had slid into the pew a broken man and poured his heart out to God. His holy presence had filled the place. And Jean-Paul.

The healing had begun there.

But to keep from returning to that deep hole he'd found himself in before he entered that church, he had promised that Simone's name would never leave his heart or cross his lips.

"Go find Nellie." Sister Maria-Theresa's voice brought him back to the present. "Tell her even a little bit."

If he did, he might break into a thousand pieces, shards of glass that could never be reconstructed.

⚊ CHAPTER TWELVE ⚊

Monday, July 3, 1944

While Sister Angelica played dolls with Claire on the floor, Nellie fed Albert, with a single pale-red curl all the hair he had. She rocked as she did so and hummed a soft tune. If Jean-Paul could see her now, he would know she wasn't all rough edges.

She kissed the infant's smooth forehead. Albert broke off from sucking and smiled. Poor little one, to be separated from his parents. To perhaps never grow up with them.

"Where did Leo and Albert come from?"

Nellie's question stopped Sister Angelica short, holding a doll in midair. After several heartbeats, Sister Angelica gave the doll to Claire. "Go tuck your baby into bed and sing her to sleep. It's time she takes a nap."

The girl hurried to comply with the directions. Sister Angelica stood and brushed a few crumbs from her habit, likely left there from earlier when she had read Claire a story while the child had a snack. Sister Angelica settled herself in the rocking chair beside Nellie. "It's better that you not know the details. Their parents were afraid for their children's lives and their own."

"I can see that they are all Mongoloid. And Jean-Paul told me the Nazis are out to kill all who are not perfect."

"Anyone Hitler deems unacceptable is being eliminated. The Jewish people, certainly, but also those who are crippled or mentally disabled.

Jehovah's Witnesses, Gypsies. There is word they go to camps and never return."

How could a man be so cruel? Her heart asked the question, but her head already had the answer. She knew. She'd seen it firsthand. This wasn't the only time in human history a great cleansing had taken place.

And it probably wouldn't be the last.

"So their parents entrusted them to you?"

"*Oui.* They believe we are better able to hide them. We have, well, our ways. But they aren't foolproof. If the children were ever discovered, they wouldn't last a minute. Even if they are found here, they wouldn't make it out of the convent gates alive. And we would also be transported to a horrible place."

"That's why they're in the basement."

"We have to keep them as silent as possible, which isn't easy with Albert and Leo. The basement is the best place to muffle the noise and keep them from prying eyes."

Nellie shivered. "Is there anything I can do to help when I leave?"

"The best thing you can do is to remain mute on this subject. Pretend like you have never been here and have never seen what you have seen."

"How long have they been with you?"

"Both Leo and Albert came here within a few days of their birth. And now, with our liberation on the horizon, we hold our breath, say our prayers that we will be able to finish the job we started, and wait."

"And if liberation never comes?"

"It will. In one way or another, it will." Sister Angelica bored her stare clean through Nellie.

Almost like she was the one chosen to liberate them.

———≈———

At the end of the day, Jean-Paul was happy to tug off the hated brown uniform and sponge off the dust and grime of the day. As he donned his simple blue pants and red checkered shirt once more, he wished he could also wash away the Nazi filth that surely must cling to him.

He had tonight off. Weber didn't need him to drive anywhere. His belly already full of German food, he headed downstairs to the nursery, an extra roll and a hunk of cheese in his pocket.

Claire was the first one to notice when he entered the room. In an instant, she was beside him, clinging to his legs. "Up, up."

"Well, you are rather demanding, aren't you?" But he grinned and lifted her into his arms.

Sister Raphael, rocking Albert in one corner of the room, laughed. "You are too lenient with her. She knows you'll give her whatever she wants."

"After what she's been through, she deserves it."

Leo was harder to win over. Jean-Paul had been working on earning the boy's trust, but now he remained on the other side of the room, intent on stacking his blocks and knocking them over.

"*Bon soir*, Leo." With Claire still grasping to his neck, he made his way to the corner. "Can you show me what you're doing?"

Without glancing up, Leo nodded and continued placing one block on top of the other. Then he pushed it down.

Jean-Paul and Claire laughed. Leo smiled and peered through his long dark lashes at Jean-Paul.

"Let me see if I can do it." He took his time stacking the blocks in a perfect tower. Though he didn't watch Leo, the prickle on his neck told him Leo watched him.

Once Jean-Paul finished, he sat back. "There. Now what do I do?"

This time, Leo gave a genuine grin. With a great amount of glee, he pushed the blocks over, and they toppled to the floor, muffled by the rug that covered the stones.

Claire clapped, and Leo and Jean-Paul joined her. As she entered the room, Nellie also applauded. "What are we so excited about?"

"Leo knocked over the tower." He infused his voice with enthusiasm. From the corner, Leo chuckled. The first time he'd gotten the boy to interact with him and show some emotion.

Nellie's eyes sparkled. "Hooray, Leo. Well done. In English, we would say *swell*."

Leo edged a little closer to Jean-Paul. Perhaps he really was making inroads with the boy.

Nellie sat crossed-legged on the other side of Jean-Paul and tipped her head. "Seems like you've made a friend."

"Seems like I have. I was beginning to think he'd never warm up to me."

"We've been here for a while. I've been trying to be patient and not push you, but you've been busy driving around town with your German friends. Will you be able to help me or not? Perhaps I could have one of the sisters purchase me a train ticket."

"That doesn't solve the problem of your American papers. As soon as the conductor comes through and asks for identification, you'll be arrested."

"I can't sit around and do nothing. Sister Maria-Theresa believes I have a different purpose for being here other than taking pictures. But I've been busy while you've been gone. I used my field developing kit, and look." She handed him an envelope.

He opened it to find several photographs inside. One was of St. Roch. There were the children. A few of the beaches of Normandy where the Allied troops had come ashore, abandoned vehicles littering the sand.

And then came one that made his breath hitch.

There stood Claire in front of the church where her family died. The light shone on her face in stark contrast to the charred hull of the church. A sad little angel in the midst of destruction and evil.

Never before had he seen anything so beautiful or poignant. The image reached into his very soul and plucked at his heartstrings. "Nellie." He breathed her name.

"It's better than I could have imagined. I knew it had potential when I took it, but it wasn't until I developed it that I saw what it truly was."

"A masterpiece."

She touched his arm, just for a moment but enough to leave a spot of warmth and a slight tingle. "Nothing iconic."

"I disagree."

"But what is more important is that I captured the entire story in one shot. And that was my intention. So that, without a single word, the world will know what Hitler is doing. And that there is hope in the midst of the evil of this world."

"You have to guard this with your life. And don't allow it to fall into the wrong hands. The Nazis prefer to hide their dirty deeds. That's why they wanted no survivors in the town." He handed it back to her.

As she slipped it into the envelope, her hands trembled. Good, he had gotten through to her. Perhaps she would be more careful from now on.

"You see now why I have to get out of German-held territory as soon as possible. The public needs to know that the rumors they've been hearing about German atrocities are true so that they will support the troops and so that more young men and women will sign up to do their part for their countries."

"Don't worry. I'm working on a plan. In the meantime, it might be a good idea if we start teaching Claire and Leo how to play hide-and-seek."

She furrowed her brow. "Why is that important?"

"I think Claire may already know. It's what saved her life. Either she got frightened when she saw the strange men come into her village, heard the screams of the women, and ran away, or else her parents taught her that if any bad men ever came, she should run under the bushes and be quiet."

"That would explain why she was there and not with the rest of her family."

"Whatever the case, it likely saved her life. And that lesson needs to be reinforced for her and taught to Leo so that if the Germans ever search the convent, they aren't scared and they know not to make a sound." He stood and reached out to help Nellie to her feet. "Ready?"

"You mean to do it now?"

"What better time to start?"

"It's still light, but it is almost the children's bedtime. The sisters would be rather sore at us for keeping them up so late."

Sister Raphael, who had been rocking Albert, shooed them out. "It's important. There is no time to waste. Have a little fun too."

So they moved to the back garden where there was a small patch of grass. Claire was already good at the game and knew what to do. Leo was a bit more of a challenge, but even he thought it was fun to find places to hide. They would have to work on getting him to be quiet.

Leo crouched behind a bush, a spot Nellie had pointed out to him. Jean-Paul walked by him to see if he would make any noise. Instead of staying put, the little boy popped out with a "Boo!"

Claire wasn't about to be left out and also jumped from her hiding place to try to scare Jean-Paul. He picked them up, one under each arm, and turned to Nellie, dimples deepening in each cheek. "What shall I do with them?"

"I think we need to tickle them."

The four of them ended up in a pile on the soft grass, a tangle of arms and legs and the sweet cacophony of laughter.

Half an hour later, when the children still had energy but Nellie and Jean-Paul were worn out, they leaned against the convent wall while Leo and Claire raced about the garden.

Nellie fanned her face. "Why do you do this?"

"What do you mean by 'this'?"

"Put your life at risk for others. If the Germans found out you were a maquisard, your life would be forfeited. Yet you continue on."

"I can't sit by while the Germans murder thousands upon thousands of innocent people." Oh, the memories that assaulted him with those words. "I've seen it with my own eyes."

She turned to him, even as dusk deepened to twilight. "You have?"

Sister Maria-Theresa said he needed to be open with her. That his vow wasn't to God but to himself. But it was a vow nonetheless. Could you break it if it had been wrong to make it in the first place? Telling Nellie might educate her. Help her see that she needed to be careful.

He inhaled a long, shaky breath. "Before the war began, when I was a university student, I met and fell in love with an incredible woman. Simone was beautiful, with hair and eyes as dark as the night. I loved her with all my heart. She was Jewish. Though my mother knew her background, I never told my father.

"When the Nazis invaded, Simone wanted me to help her go into hiding. I didn't take her seriously. I didn't take the German threat seriously, even though, because of my German father, I knew what kind of people the Nazis were.

"Soon after the Jewish laws were passed, Simone was out, just shopping to get what food she could. The Gestapo picked her up. They didn't bother to send her to a camp. Instead, they beat her to death."

Nellie touched his wrist, sending a shiver of warmth, if that was possible, up his arm and straight to his heart.

"That was almost four years ago already. My soul has healed, but that's when I got involved with the Maquis. I couldn't allow the Nazis to do to one more person what they did to my Simone."

"I'm so sorry. Thank you for telling me. I understand better now what motivates you. Why you are trying to protect me and these children."

He stared into the darkening sky. "No one deserves to die the way

Simone did. No one deserves to be murdered at all."

They stood in silence for a while longer, only the occasional giggle from one of the children breaking the silence.

Then a noise pricked Jean-Paul's ear. He stopped breathing.

Headlights swung around at the front of the convent.

Quick as a flash, he grabbed Leo and covered his mouth. Nellie did the same with Claire.

As the German rang the bell and Sister Angelica opened the gate, they slunk into the shadows.

———— ≈ ————

Nellie couldn't breathe. Did Germans have eyes in the backs of their heads? Did they multiply so they covered the entire land like a swarm of locusts?

Jean-Paul remained statue-still beside her as the Nazi at the gate continued to speak with Sister Angelica. Neither of the children squirmed or even made a peep.

Nellie kept her sight trained on Jean-Paul and her hearing attentive to what was happening at the gate. "Can you understand them?"

Though she whispered, he put his finger to his lips. Yes. Right. If she spoke, the children would believe they also could. She swallowed, even though her throat was tight.

Every muscle in her body was taut. Ready to spring into action. She'd had too many encounters with Germans already. No need to add another one. Especially after what Jean-Paul had just shared with her.

The conversation at the gate was mercifully short. In the space of a few short minutes, the speaking broke off, the gate creaked shut, and the German's vehicle roared to life and sped away.

Still, Jean-Paul didn't move. So neither did Nellie or the children. For several more minutes, they remained in position. This had turned from a game of hide-and-seek into one of freeze tag.

At last, a soft light shone from the door, and Sister Angelica slipped through it into the garden. "All is clear."

Nellie allowed herself to relax. "What did he want?"

Jean-Paul set Leo on the ground. "That was Major Weber, the officer in charge of this area. He was searching for me. I have this evening off, so I don't have to stay around their headquarters. I just had to be back there by curfew. Though why he came here, I couldn't tell you. I've been here long enough that surely he would have rung the bell long before this."

"He doesn't trust you?"

"I'm not sure. He might have just been curious as to where I go on my nights off."

"Or he might not trust you."

"Or he might not trust me."

"What are you going to do?"

"I have to leave. Go into town and be seen somewhere or another. Make up some excuse for my absence. Try to explain why someone thought I was here."

"But you'll be back?" Her heart had softened toward him. Because he'd lost the woman he'd loved, he was willing to sacrifice his life to save the lives of others. He was her touchstone in this confusing, frightening place.

Sister Angelica shook her head. "Perhaps it would be best if you stayed away. You're only going to bring trouble here if you return."

Jean-Paul took Leo by the hand and led the way inside. Only once the door had shut behind them and the bolt slid into place did he turn to them. "Sister Angelica is right. I'm leading the Nazis to the children. And to you. That's a risk I'm not willing to take. I won't be back unless I have new information. Even then, I'll do my best to get word to you without putting in an appearance."

Sister Angelica took Leo and Claire downstairs, and Jean-Paul turned to go.

"Be safe." Nellie whispered the words.

Jean-Paul glanced over his shoulder and flashed her a crooked smile. "I'll try."

CHAPTER THIRTEEN

Tuesday, July 4, 1944

"Ah good, you're awake. I thought you might sleep all morning. Especially after gallivanting around the area all night long." Weber glanced up as Jean-Paul made his way down the stairs in the Nazi headquarters. Two other men, both in similar brown uniforms, stood near Weber, staring at the drawings on the table.

Early morning sunshine streamed through the window, dust motes floating on the air. The perfume of coffee and hair cream permeated the room.

Weber pointed to a position on the map streaked with red and blue lines. "I need you to drive us to the front."

"The front? Why?"

Weber raised a gray eyebrow.

"Forgive me, sir."

The major waved Jean-Paul away. "You are aware that the Allies are now on French soil."

"Of course."

"I run the operations in this area. We need to prepare for a fight. Or to flee. And I must know how much time remains before I have to make that decision. Are you up to the job or are you too lily-livered? Or untrustworthy?"

Perhaps this was some kind of test for the Germans to discern where his true loyalties lay. "I'm up to the job, sir. Where are you planning to go, and what route are you thinking of taking?"

Weber motioned him over, and Jean-Paul's heart added a couple of extra beats every minute. This might be the chance he'd been waiting for to see the maps. Find out what the Germans were up to. "The Allies have spread out along this line."

Jean-Paul worked to keep his mouth from dropping open. They had advanced so little in the space of a few weeks? The pace was slow, but perhaps the war would be over by winter. Wouldn't that be wonderful? Still, lives hung in the balance, especially if the Germans got desperate. No telling what they would do with those they still held in the camps.

"I'd like to go to here." Weber jabbed the map. "That should give us a pretty good idea of how things are progressing."

"Yes, sir. I'll ready the Kübelwagen." Gritting his teeth, he gave the required one-armed salute, then made his way to the garage, the sun warming his head and back. The poor children who had lived in the cold convent for years. The chill must go right through to their bones, even in summer.

If only he had a way to take Nellie along with him. It would get her close. But it would also put her in a great deal of danger, having to cross that compact line of fighting again. Though how they had ever managed to get through it in the first place was a mystery.

He opened the door to the converted barn and made his way to one of the three Kübelwagens parked inside. The vehicles stood bumper to bumper down the barn's middle aisle, horse stalls on one side and cow stalls on the other. The odor of fuel overpowered whatever stench of dung might have remained.

He checked to be sure the one on the end had petrol, put the top down, then pulled it to the front of the house. Weber and his two companions slipped inside the converted Volkswagen with its spare tire on the front of the car. Within moments, they were bumping along the rutted dirt road headed northeastward.

Verdant fields edged with hedges or trees covered the undulating terrain before giving way to charming villages with brick houses and churches that had stood guard over the towns and the people's souls longer than anyone could remember.

The three Germans chatted with each other as they drove through the bocage, and Jean-Paul kept his mouth shut and his ears open.

"We must not allow the Allies to gain any more ground." The one with the big ears, Zimmer, leaned forward. "If we don't stop them soon, there will be no stopping them."

"But we will. We won't let *der Führer* down. For him, for the Fatherland, we will continue the fight until our last breath." The tall, darker-haired soldier shook his fist.

"And that might be what it will come down to." Weber slid on a pair of sunglasses.

"What do we do in the meantime?" Jean-Paul kept his eyes on the road as Zimmer asked the question.

"In the meantime, we need to finish the jobs we were given when we came here." Weber turned around to address his colleagues. "We must hunt down every Jew that we can. Ferret them out. And it's about time to liquidate that convent."

Startled, Jean-Paul spun the steering wheel and almost swerved off the road. Perhaps they hadn't been so much wary of him but had been scouting the nunnery.

"Watch it, Braun." Weber narrowed his eyes at Jean-Paul. "What kind of driver are you?"

"Sorry, sir. There was a squirrel."

Weber cursed. "Forget about the squirrel. His life is insignificant."

That was what the Nazis thought about most life. Insignificant. Unimportant. Not worthy to be lived.

Unless you were pure Aryan, you had no right to breathe.

A cloud passed over the sun, casting them in shadows. What about Claire? She was precious and happy, a joyful soul in the midst of great darkness. Whoever she touched couldn't help but smile. Was that insignificant?

What about that shy little boy, Leo, who had slipped beside Jean-Paul, finally rewarding him with his trust? In that moment, that act wasn't insignificant.

None of those children were insignificant. All of them were worthy of life and love.

But now they had prices on their heads. Large prices.

Had the Germans discovered what was happening in the convent? Had they seen the children in the garden one day or heard Albert crying as they passed? Maybe they didn't even know about the children and just wanted to be rid of those who served God rather than Hitler.

Whatever the case, the situation at the convent had grown more serious. Their game of hide-and-seek last night hadn't been for naught.

"*Ja.*" Zimmer chimed into the conversation. "Those nuns have been left alone for far too long. We took some of them away at the beginning because they refused to fly the German flag. I say we grab the rest of them. Who knows how many Jews they have aided in the past four years."

"Good." Weber gave a single nod. "I'll leave that up to the two of you to coordinate. We'll also conduct more sweeps of homes, barns, businesses, anywhere Jews could be hiding. By the time we leave—if we leave—we'll have cleansed France of every undesirable."

As the Kübelwagen bounced over a pothole, Jean-Paul's stomach lurched.

They had to evacuate the nuns and the children as soon as possible.

Or else the Nazis in the Kübelwagen with him would snuff them out like the flame of a candle.

———————≈———————

Carrying plates from the dining room table, Nellie made her way to the large kitchen and deposited them on the counter. Sister Angelica and Sister Raphael were already up to their elbows in water. Soap wasn't available, but they scrubbed the dishes and utensils hard enough that they were plenty clean.

She spun to return to the dining room for more dishes and almost ran headlong into Jean-Paul. "Golly, it's a good thing you didn't come up behind me when I had my hands full of plates, or I would have dropped them."

"*Je suis désolé.*" Dark half-moons shadowed his eyes. "I need to speak to you alone. It is very important."

And by the way his eyes bored into her, it must be. "Sure." She dried her damp hands on her pants and followed him to the empty living room, a beam of orange sunlight slanting through the window, shining on the polished coffee table.

When he settled himself into one of the armchairs beside the floor-to-ceiling fireplace, she got comfortable in the one across from him. "What is it? This sounds serious." She folded her hands to keep them from shaking.

"I'm afraid it is. I overheard a conversation while I was driving Weber and two other Germans to the front today. They had much time to talk and let their words flow freely, like men who've had too much wine. Surprising, since they are suspicious of me and where I go in my off hours."

"The Germans haven't pushed the Allies back, have they? This isn't turning into another Dunkirk?" She twisted the apron that covered her pants until it was as tight as a spring about to be sprung. She'd been in the south of England when the British troops had returned from that debacle. Bedraggled. Worn. Defeated.

She had managed to take some heart-rending photographs, enough to get a front page picture in the *Tribune*. But the cost to the British forces and to the European people had been huge.

If the invasion the Allies had just launched ended in another catastrophe, the war would be over.

Germany would win.

"*Non.* Nothing like that. I saw a map. The Allies are marching west and making some progress."

She blew out a breath and relaxed her shoulders.

He crossed and uncrossed his legs before leaning closer to her and dropping the volume of his voice. "The Germans are preparing to evacuate farther east. They know the Allies will be here in the coming days."

"That's a good thing then." Why was he so nervous?

"They won't be here soon enough. It might be a week or maybe a month. Probably closer to a month. Before they leave, they want to finish what they started here. Flush out any remaining Jews. At the beginning of the occupation, they arrested some of the nuns from this convent for refusing to fly the German flag. They want to come back and haul away the rest of the sisters."

Her gut twisted. "If they do that, they'll not only take the nuns, but they'll find the children."

"Exactly."

"We can't let them cart away the nuns. But we especially can't let them get their hands on the kids."

Precious Claire, with her golden hair and her high-voltage smile. Little Albert, with his single curl. Leo, shy but curious. All of them. Each of them precious.

As dear and as precious as June's younger sister, Velma, her dark-as-night face not unlike Claire's. After that horrible night, Nellie's friend June had never been the same. As she grew older, she flirted with plenty of men. Had her first baby at sixteen. Another followed by another father a year later. No man in the house to help her and Velma.

That was when Nellie stepped in. As soon as she graduated college, she took over Velma's care. Though Nellie had been forced to leave her at Wellspring Institute for the Mentally Challenged, and it had almost broken her heart, at least Velma was safe, not hunted like a rabid dog.

Nellie had visited her there often before coming to England. Though Velma was now a young woman, her mind had not progressed beyond that of a small child's. Each time Nellie visited her, they had so much fun coloring pictures and dressing up dolls and playing with balls.

The heartache of missing Velma was a pain that stabbed Nellie almost every day. Would Velma even remember her when she returned?

Nellie rose and paced in front of the massive fireplace. "So how do we go about saving both the nuns and the children?" She rubbed her chin, then paced some more, the tapping of her shoes on the floor the only sound in the quiet, cavernous room.

He rubbed his temples, his brow furrowed underneath his widow's peak. "I've heard of a group called *Oeuvre de Secours aux Enfants,* the Children's Aid Society. Georges Loinger and Marcel Mangel are cousins who are part of it, and I know them a little bit. I'm also familiar with several others who aren't part of that group but who do good work, including Marianne Cohn and Rolande Birgy."

"What do they do?"

"Smuggle Jewish children across the border into Switzerland. In fact, I saw Marianne with a group of children at L'asile's train station several weeks ago. It's dangerous work, but they've been successful. We need a ruse, though, a reason to be traveling with the children that won't raise the Nazis' suspicions."

So the group of children dressed like Scouts she had run into at the train station had been Jews on their way to the border. What a clever way to ensure their freedom and their survival.

She returned to her pacing. "Jewish children are a lot easier to disguise than Mongoloids. How do you suggest going about it?"

"That's going to be the trickier part." Jean-Paul took to pacing beside her.

"And you're suggesting going to Switzerland? Why do you always want to go east instead of west?"

"To go west would mean running headlong into the fighting."

"But we somehow got behind the lines without encountering any fighting."

"I'm not sure I could duplicate that feat. It's too risky, especially with the children. We can't take the chance of them getting caught in the crossfire."

She bit the inside of her cheek as she stared unseeing at the cold hearth. Only the soft ticking of a clock on the mantel broke the stillness. Even the children downstairs were quiet.

Evil, evil everywhere she turned, like a nightmare that followed her even in her waking hours. From her earliest days, she'd seen it. Been a firsthand witness to it. Now, like then, she was helpless to stop it, this locomotive barreling toward them.

She had stood by and said nothing and allowed Mr. Joe to die. She wouldn't do it again. "Then we need to find a way to get the children to Switzerland. Is it far from here?"

He fingered his open collar. The clock chimed the top of the hour. "It's not the distance that matters so much but how we are going to get them there. These children would be more conspicuous on a train than Marianne's group and the *Oeuvre de Secours aux Enfants*."

She raised an eyebrow and stared at him as he gazed beyond her. His dark eyes were as stormy as the English Channel on a winter's night. "The baby shouldn't be a problem. We can keep a blanket over his head and, if the Nazis want to check him against his identification, we can tell them he's sleeping and we don't want to disturb him. That takes care of Albert, but what about the other two? They're too old for us to disguise."

He nodded, his lips pulled into a frown once more. "I agree. The children can't hide in plain sight."

"*Non*, they can't." She bit her lip. "Even if we could conceal their faces, they might speak and give themselves away. This is going to be difficult." Then an idea hit her so hard it almost blinded her. She stopped pacing and stood in front of him. "We can take the train, but we don't have to ride in the passenger cars."

He shook his head, his pomaded hair not moving with the motion. "What do you mean?"

"There have to be boxcars that we can ride in. It's not cold, so we don't have to worry about freezing. If the Nazis find us, we either run or hide the children. We've been teaching Claire and Leo to play hide-and-seek. I think they can do it."

"Are you sure?"

When given a chance, Velma had been able to do so much. She was brighter than most people gave her credit for. "*Oui,* I am."

"And you are sure you're ready to take on such a challenge?"

She gave him the hard stare she always gave the kids back home when she had dared them to fight her. Yes, she was ready. "If not us, then who?"

———————≈———————

The three nuns in their black habits and wimples, faces drawn with exhaustion and worry, sat around the large dining room table, lights glowing from the wall sconces and from the simple chandelier above the well-used table.

Sister Angelica steepled her fingers in front of her puckered mouth. "What is this all about? You have us quite concerned."

Jean-Paul swallowed hard and focused on the women in front of him. This wouldn't be easy news for him to deliver. But he and Nellie needed their help. "Today, while I was driving some German officers around, I overheard a conversation that has serious implications for you. Before the Allies arrive here, the Germans are going to clean out the convent. Arrest you all."

Sister Raphael shook her head. "Why? We've done nothing to them."

"Because you refused to fly the flag."

"They did arrest several of our order at the beginning of the occupation, but that was so long ago." Sister Raphael wrung her hands. "Why now?"

"Because they can. That's the best explanation I can give you to a question that has no real answer. When evil lurks in the hearts of men, they have no compunctions, no conscience. They will make up excuses for their despicable behavior to soothe their minds so they can sleep at night."

Sister Angelica nodded. "All true. They are the lowest of the low. For what they've done, I hope they burn."

Sister Raphael sucked in a sharp breath. "Sister Angelica, have you no Christian charity in your heart?"

"Not for the likes of them."

Jean-Paul held up his hand. "This isn't a debate over the eternal souls of the Germans. We have little to no time left. I will do my best to stall them, but I don't know how long I, a mere driver, will be able to put them off. Nellie and I have been speaking about how to save you and the children, and we have a plan. We can't do this alone. It will take all of us to get the children to Switzerland."

He turned to Nellie beside him, and she flashed him an encouraging smile and nodded. She'd been the one to orchestrate it. All he'd done was flesh it out. He'd never met a woman with so much tenacity. She would have been a real asset to the Maquis over these past four years.

He returned his attention to the sisters. "The plan is this. We will secure false papers for all of you. Once we have those in hand, we will stow away in a boxcar on a train to Annemasse. When we arrive there, we will find the mayor, who has been sympathetic to those fleeing the Nazis, and he will help us cross the border."

"Waiting another minute is madness." Sister Angelica came to her feet. "We need to leave as soon as possible. What if the Nazis raid us before you manage to spirit us away?"

"We were hoping that there might be an area in the convent where, if need be, you can hide."

Sister Angelica nodded. "There is a place below us with a hidden passageway to the outside. I'm not sure how much good it would do us. It might provide temporary shelter if the Nazis didn't discover it. I guess it's a good thing you've been teaching the children that game. Then we only have to worry about keeping Albert quiet."

Nellie tipped her head side to side to stretch her neck. "This plan isn't perfect, and it's not guaranteed to work. The children do the best they can, but they don't always understand why they must keep quiet. All the more reason to move as fast as possible to get everyone out of here. And you, Jean-Paul, have to stall the Germans for as long as you can."

Sister Angelica fisted her hands.

As if in slow motion, Sister Maria-Theresa rose. With each centimeter she gained in height, the tension in the room subsided. Even Sister Angelica unclenched her hands.

Sister Maria-Theresa's voice was as smooth as the finest bottle of red wine. "My dear sisters, we all understand the severity of what faces us. From the time the first German boot touched French soil, our lives have been in peril. We have watched while some of our sisters from this very convent were taken away, yet to be returned to us in this life.

"We should be thankful Jean-Paul and Nellie brought us this information. Our situation would be very dire indeed if they hadn't. We would have no chance at escaping without them.

"They have asked us for our help and our cooperation so that lives may be saved. We share that common goal. We owe them our complete trust and assistance." Little by little, she returned to her seat, the room as hushed as if in the middle of prayers.

Perhaps the sisters were offering up petitions to the Almighty. They could use them now.

Sister Maria-Theresa's words brightened Nellie's eyes and plumped her cheeks with a small smile. When that happened, Jean-Paul's heart did a little dance in his chest.

What was he thinking? They had a job to do. One that would require their full attention.

"Bless you. You are one spot of goodness in this harsh world." Nellie gazed at Sister Maria-Theresa.

"That she is." Well, maybe there were two spots of goodness. These women in front of him, including Nellie, were a rare breed.

The sisters exited the room, their heads bent. Once they were gone, Nellie turned to him. "I guess we need to get those forged papers as soon as we possibly can."

"Because of my work with the Germans, I hope to be able to procure those. The problem is that my handwriting is terrible. I'm not sure I can make credible copies."

Nellie sucked in a breath. "I might be able to give it a try. I got good at forging my parents' signatures for notes from school I didn't want them to see."

"You got in trouble at school?"

"I was known to hold my own in a fight."

He chuckled. "You sound proud of that fact."

"I am. When I was young, I had a very good friend, June, a black girl. She went to the colored school, but we lived nearby and played together, always in secret. If Daddy had found out, he would have beaten me and locked me in my room for a good long while. I also helped June with her homework. She was the best and most loyal friend I had.

"Anyway, people in our town made fun of her and her little sister." Nellie's chest tightened at the mere mention of June and Velma. "I made sure that no one teased them or threw rocks at them or anything. After a few fights on their behalf, I was an outcast, but I didn't care."

Though her efforts weren't enough to prevent the awful things the adults did to June's father and the rest of her family.

"We could have used you in the Maquis."

"You can. I'll give forging those documents a try if you can secure the blank papers."

"First thing in the morning, then, we'll get to work. Tonight we'll pray that the Germans will leave you and the sisters in peace. I'd better get back. I've been gone long enough."

She touched his cheek. "Be safe."

He clasped her hand for the briefest of moments before he felt too much. "You too."

And then he slipped into the dark night.

ᴤ CHAPTER FOURTEEN ᴤ

Wednesday, July 5, 1944

There were too few of them. Too few of his fellow countrymen who were willing to help the Jews and others in their society. There always had been.

For years, Jean-Paul had been all-too-well aware of this fact. A few printed pamphlets, some downed Allied pilots smuggled from enemy territory, a handful of clandestine radio messages, most of which the Allies ignored.

And several groups of children smuggled over the border.

Jean-Paul mused on this as he drove Weber through L'asile's cobbled streets, the late-afternoon sun warming the stones of the centuries-old buildings until they glowed golden. This quaint town was much like all the others. When the Germans invaded, they had been welcomed by the French people afraid of communism. And they, along with the Vichy government, had collaborated with their occupiers.

That was what made Jean-Paul's work now so difficult. He couldn't contact an underground network, because one didn't exist. *Oui*, there was the *Oeuvre de Secours aux Enfants* and other groups like it. Some resistance cells. Other than the relatively small band of Maquis though, nothing organized.

Nellie would try her hand at the forging. At least she had her camera to take pictures of the nuns for the identity papers.

The difficult part was getting blank booklets for her to work on, just in case they were stopped by the authorities. Eight booklets, at least, but preferably a few more.

"You're deep in thought today." Weber's rumbling voice interrupted Jean-Paul's musings.

He gripped the wheel all the tighter. "Just a small problem I have to deal with."

"Ah, say no more. Women problems. That must be where you disappear to each night."

There was that problem. He'd tried to avoid the convent, but the visit last night had been necessary. Critical. He'd been careful, but could he be careful enough? "*Oui,* I do have a special friend I visit." His face warmed despite the rush of air across his cheeks as he maneuvered the Kübelwagen through the narrow streets.

"If I can be of any help, let me know. I'll see what I can do."

Weber could be of great help if Jean-Paul could manage to come up with a reason why he needed the blank identity books. But nothing sprang to mind. He'd have to find another way.

A short while later, they pulled up to the town hall. Instead of leaving him in the vehicle as usual, Weber invited Jean-Paul into the brown stone building, a laurel wreath carved above the door, bright pink petunias blooming in boxes in front of the eight-paned windows.

Perhaps he could snoop around. They must keep their identity cards in this building.

He moseyed to the clerk's window. A young blond with curls that framed her small, oval face sat behind the desk. As soon as he spotted her, Jean-Paul knew what he needed to do.

"*Bonjour, mademoiselle.* I couldn't help but notice how beautiful you are." Oh what a terrible opening line.

She peeked at him through her long, dark lashes, a dimple flirting with her right cheek. "All the men say that."

"Only because it's true."

Her face pinked. "*Merci.* Is there something I can help you with?"

"There is. You see, Major Weber is hosting a little get-together at his headquarters tonight. Honestly, with the Allies closing in, it's more like a going-away party. And I don't have a lovely lady to escort. I'll be the only one alone."

"And what a pity that would be." She affected a pout.

"A great one, I assure you. So won't you have some compassion on me and allow me to escort you to this party? I happen to know there will be plenty of food and wine." That was a fact. Who knew where Weber managed to get his hands on such riches? The rest of France lived on meager rations.

"And what is your name? You speak French very well for a German."

"That is thanks to a French mother. I'm Herman Bauer. And yours is?"

She pursed her lips, as if giving away her identity was a matter of national security. "Hélène."

"So is your answer *oui*?" He used his most charming smile, the one he took out for special occasions.

"You are very persuasive. You may have grown up German, but your mother taught you a thing or two about how to play the part of the charming Frenchman. Fine, I will accompany you tonight." She gave him her address.

This time his smile was a little more genuine. Though he had come inside on a whim, he now had a solid plan in place. The nuns might have their papers as early as tomorrow morning.

A thumping of boots on the tile floors brought Jean-Paul's attention to Weber striding down the hall. He shifted his focus from Jean-Paul to Hélène. When he came even with Jean-Paul, he slapped him on the back. "Ah, now I know where you sneak off to in the evenings. Very good choice."

Allow Weber to believe what he would, but Jean-Paul couldn't let Hélène hear and contradict him. He leaned closer. "She will be coming to your party tonight."

"Wonderful."

Jean-Paul glanced over his shoulder at Hélène. "I'll pick you up at six o'clock."

They made their way to the Kübelwagen. Weber chuckled. "Here I had you pegged as rather a stiff, formal, and uncomfortable young man. Yet you have managed to sweet talk Hélène. Did you cast a spell on her?"

"What do you mean?"

"Only that half of my staff have been trying to get a date with her for years now. She always turns them down. And firmly, I may add. You've barely landed in town, and you already have her agreeing to be seen in public with you. Well done."

Though Jean-Paul tried to wave it away as nothing, he could only credit it as God's providence.

The trouble was that he was only using her, making her comfortable so that tonight he could lure her from her desk and get the identity cards they needed.

What would Nellie think about this?

Why did he care what Nellie thought?

He shook his head and kept his gaze on the road in front of him as they returned to Weber's headquarters. From what he could tell, Hélène was the opposite of Nellie—prim, graceful, demure.

So why did the idea of spending an evening in the company of Hélène do nothing for him, while seeing Nellie always sent a tingle sparking to his fingers?

———— ≈ ————

Like a heavy black mantle, the weight of what was happening settled over Nellie. She was a photojournalist from the United States, for crying out loud. How did she get caught up in the middle of a war in a foreign country?

Oh right, this had been her choice. She had asked for this. Pleaded for it. Stowed away on a hospital ship for such a chance. But this wasn't what she'd bargained for.

Then again, she had been warned.

She stood against the rough stone exterior of the town hall, looking over the alley, her fingers gripping the wall as if that would keep her from being seen. At least she had the black dress the nuns had given her. In it, she would be another shadow among the shadows.

Much like that humid summer night almost twenty years ago, when she had hidden among the trees, the darkness blanketing her but not blocking out the evil hovering like the smoke from the burning crosses.

The white-hooded men, Daddy among them, dragged June's father to the clearing in the woods just because his doctor brother from up north had bought June's family a car. Uppity, Daddy had called Mr. Joe.

In their grip, he squirmed worse than a cat that didn't want to be held. "String him up!"

Daddy, no! Nellie swallowed the cry stuck in her throat.

"Daddy, no!" June shrieked. She and Miss Franny raced close enough to touch Mr. Joe, but the men beat them, raining blows on them, until they had no choice but to fall back.

One of the men—his hood hid who he was—tied a rope around Mr. Joe's neck.

Nellie crouched behind June and her mama, who both sobbed like the world was ending. She didn't let them know she was there. Just sat real still and watched.

She didn't want Daddy to beat her too. She knew what that felt like.

The men led Mr. Joe to the edge of the woods and made him stand on a chair. They swung that rope over the thick branch of an old oak tree, so big it would take two men to circle it with their arms.

Moisture trickled down Nellie's back. She couldn't draw a deep breath. Even the crickets had silenced. So had June and her mama.

Once they secured the rope on the branch, they kicked the chair from underneath Mr. Joe.

The screeches of a man and a woman arguing jolted her back to France. This may be a different place and a different time, but the way men treated others who were not the same as them hadn't changed. Nellie's chest tightened as if a belt were being cinched around it.

Clutching the side of the building, her fingernails breaking under the pressure, she worked to steady her breathing and erase the images seared into her brain. She would never forget, but for a time, she could put them away, to a place where she didn't have to see them for a while.

Right now, she had a job to concentrate on. She was a little girl when June's daddy died, unable to stop the gang of ruthless, heartless men. On that day she vowed she would never be that helpless or powerless again.

Lives hung in the balance now, as precarious as an elephant on the tip of a pin.

She was not Daddy. She was not those white-hooded men. She was not even their wives who watched in horror but kept their mouths shut.

Jean-Paul had wanted to be the one to do this, but she'd overruled him. He'd begged her, not wanting her to be caught like Simone. Again, she wouldn't hear of it. He couldn't both distract Hélène and swipe the blank identity cards. He needed help. Her help.

As the arguing down the street quieted, she slunk around the corner of the building to the back door. She pulled two pins from her hair, strands of it falling into her eyes. She tucked them behind her ear.

For an hour this afternoon, all that Jean-Paul could spare, the two of them had practiced picking locks. All the locks in the convent. But how much different would this one be?

She inhaled long and slow, even though she got a lungful of air tainted by cooking oil and cat dung. She bent one of the pins into a little lever and slipped it into the lock. The other, she opened up, bent it to a ninety-degree angle, and also pushed in. Then she jimmied it. Nothing happened.

Once more, she jiggled the pins in the lock.

Still nothing.

Jeepers, this wasn't working. She closed her eyes and sucked in another round of air. All of Jean-Paul's instructions rushed back at her. As she worked with the hairpins, she identified the lock pins that were seized. As she kept pressure on the lever, she forced those pins up.

With a series of clicks, the lock released, and she opened the door.

Her breath whooshed out in a single rush.

She resisted the urge to whoop and holler. Instead, she slipped inside and locked the door behind her.

The palest slivers of moonlight brightened her way as she tiptoed to Hélène's office. This door wasn't secured. She hurried inside and riffled through the filing cabinet and desk drawers. Most of the papers were in French, but what she was searching for didn't require her to read the language.

They weren't here though. Not near Hélène's desk anyway. She spun around. Where might they be? Behind her was another door that led to another office.

Perhaps in there. She swallowed hard.

Time was ticking away if she wanted to get this done tonight.

Just as she entered the inner office, heels clicked on the floor. The tapping of high heels.

Her throbbing heart pressed hard against her ribs. No one should be here. Jean-Paul had assured her they would all be at the party.

The footsteps approached.

What if they came in here? Where could she hide?

The dim light from the window illuminated a large potted plant in the corner.

Just as the door to the office opened, she dove behind it.

≣ CHAPTER FIFTEEN ≣

Tremors passed through Maria-Theresa as she sat in the hard pew staring at the crucifix she had gazed on thousands and thousands of times over the decades.

Always before this, it had brought her peace. Peace when she had been abused in the most horrible way. Peace when word reached her that her beloved father had died. Peace when cannons and ammunition from another worldwide war rent the air around them.

But tonight, the tremors didn't leave her body, and the peace she sought never flooded her.

"Why, Lord? Are you still here?" Never before had she doubted His presence. Like the most faithful companion, the Spirit had been beside her and within her. Now only emptiness filled her.

What was this strange foreboding? Was it anything at all other than her imagination? With each passing day, sleep came harder and harder. More often, as now, she spent the deepest hours of the night wandering the convent, as if she were a specter haunting it.

At times, her brain was muddled. Too many thoughts crowded inside to untangle them all. Sometimes they got lost in the endless web of memories. Was that what was happening now? Was that why a cold wind blew through the crevices of her heart?

The soft creaking of the chapel door turned her from the cross. A flash of light lit the space for a moment before the door shut again and Sister Angelica made her way to where Maria-Theresa sat.

"May I?"

Maria-Theresa motioned for her to sit. "I was meditating on many things."

"We are all doing a great deal of that these days. Have you come to any conclusions?"

"I fear difficult days are in store for each of us."

"You are likely correct. The journey we will embark on in the coming days, Lord willing, is going to be fraught with tension. Not an easy trek to make, to cross enemy-held territory while battle rages."

"And what of the children?" Maria-Theresa turned her full gaze on Sister Angelica whose blue eyes shimmered with tears in the flickering candlelight.

"I can only pray that we all make it to safety." Her voice was husky. "But we have to be prepared to do whatever God requires of us so the children are kept safe. They are the most important ones in all of this. Will they make it across the border?"

"Only God knows the answer to that."

"But the thought of never seeing them again is breaking my heart." A few tears leaked from Sister Angelica's eyes. She might have a tough exterior and come across as somewhat gruff, but inside her chest beat a tender heart softened by the Holy Spirit.

It was all Maria-Theresa could do not to weep herself. But what good was there in that? It would change nothing the Lord had planned for them. "If it is His will, you will stay together. If not, you must be accepting of that." Oh but that they would be able to stay with these sweet children and kiss their dimpled cheeks. *Lord, may it be Your will.*

Sister Angelica stared at her. "*I* stay with the children? What about you?"

"Do you expect an old woman such as I to take this journey? *Oui,* Jean-Paul will be driving us, and then we will be on a train, but what if events take a turn for the worse? What if we need to abandon the plan and walk any distance? I would not be able to keep up, and my pace may well end up being the death of all of us. I cannot have that on my conscience."

"You are planning on staying here?" Sister Angelica blinked fast several times.

"I am."

"We would rather die together than be separated from you."

Maria-Theresa patted Sister Angelica's hand, a gesture she had learned from her own mother seventy years ago. At last she had identified the unease settling like an ache in her bones. "You have much work left to accomplish for the kingdom. Mine is almost completed. *Non*, I will stay here. If I were twenty years younger, I wouldn't hesitate to leave. But as it is, I cannot."

"You must reconsider."

"It's not best for the rest of you." She wouldn't be the reason for the death of seven others.

"We all go or none of us goes." Sister Angelica scurried away, the usual dignity of her carriage replaced by the urgency of her footsteps.

Oh, and Sister Angelica was a stubborn one. Maria-Theresa had little fight left in her. The group must flee as soon as possible. It would be better without her. The Nazis would not leave a corner of the abbey unsearched. They would examine every stone, every crevice, every crack in the floor or walls. They would move every piece of furniture and pick up every rug.

There would be no hiding from them, even in this vast space. Even if she hid in the secret passageway, they would eventually find her.

They must leave. Should she go?

The cold emptiness in the pit of her stomach was now replaced by a warm, glowing fire. A fullness enveloped her. She had been mistaken earlier.

She was not alone. She had never been alone. All along, the Spirit had been beside her and within her, and there He would remain for the rest of her days, how many or how few of them there may be.

Jean-Paul and Nellie would return soon. *S'il vous plaît, Père, may they have met with success.* So many obstacles to overcome before they would be free. Would they surmount them?

She rose, her arthritic knees popping and cracking as she came to her feet. Once again, she studied the gold-covered crucifix, a reminder of the suffering her Lord had borne for her.

If He could endure what the Father had in store for Him, surely she could endure what He had waiting for her.

———— ≈ ————

Only he could sprain his ankle—his right one at that—by missing a step at the Nazi's headquarters. Jean-Paul huffed out a breath as a searing pain shot through his foot and up his leg. Putting any weight on it at all was agony.

And here they were, in front of the village hall. Hélène had driven him here in the Kübelwagen. Before he had a chance to set his good foot on the ground, she was at his side.

"I'm not an invalid." His growl brought a scowl to her face. "*Je suis désolé.* It's just that I'm not very good at being injured."

"I don't think any of us are." She offered to help him up, an offer he refused.

On the rare occasions he had spent time with Vater, all the man had ever done was drill into Jean-Paul how weakness was not to be tolerated. Every time he had skinned his knee or bumped his head, Vater had scolded him for the tears that had gathered in his eyes.

After a while, he learned how to control them. How to grit his teeth and keep on. Like a good little German boy should.

Jean-Paul managed to get himself out of the vehicle. "Why are we here?" It was the last place they should be. Right this very moment, Nellie was supposed to be inside pilfering those blank identity cards. The ones in Hélène's office.

She jogged ahead, her curls bouncing against her shoulders, to unlock the door for him. "This is where I have a first-aid kit with a splint and a bandage."

"You don't have one at home?"

"*Non.* And even if I did, it wouldn't be proper for me to take you there. My neighbors would talk. Don't worry. We'll get you fixed up as good as new in no time."

"I'm fine." He stood in the building's threshold. "It hardly hurts anymore."

"It is swollen to almost twice its usual size. You are not fine." She stuck out her lower lip in a small pout. One most men would find attractive. "With me, you don't have to play at how strong and invincible you are. *S'il vous plaît,* let me help you."

"Really, I don't want you to go to the trouble." He leaned against the stone exterior to take some of the weight from his throbbing ankle. It had been as large as an elephant's when Hélène had examined it earlier. "Can we go back to the party? I promise I'll sit all evening. You can wait on me hand and foot." He threw in a wink, as if he was flirting with her.

"I will not take no for an answer."

And that was why they found themselves here, in front of the village hall now lit by a slice of moonlight and the glow of a thousand stars. He dared a glance at the window that fronted the street. The one where Hélène's office was.

All sat dark and silent. He could only pray that Nellie had already come and gone.

They hadn't been at the party long. Really not enough time for her to pick the lock, find what she needed, and get out again.

In all likelihood, she was still inside.

If they stumbled on her, how would he explain her presence to Hélène?

"Well, whether you come with me or not, I'm going to get the first-aid kit. Suit yourself." She stepped inside and allowed the heavy oak door to shut behind her.

Like the prison door slamming behind him. For an instant, the dank odors of mold and urine, the whines of suffering men, the core-deep chill of the place washed over him again.

At best, a German prison was Dante's seventh circle of hell. At worst. . .

He couldn't allow his mind to go there. And he couldn't allow Hélène to stumble upon Nellie. Because he would do all in his power to ensure that no one else he knew ended up captured by the Nazis.

As fast as possible, he half ran, half limped inside and down the corridor. "Hélène, please wait." Perhaps Nellie would their hear footsteps or him hollering for Hélène and have a chance to escape.

Hélène halted and turned to him. "*Bien.* I see that you came to your senses."

He bit his lip as he hobbled toward her. "You win, just this once. I'll allow you to play field nurse, even though it's not necessary."

"If I don't wrap it, you won't be able to get your foot into your boot come morning."

She had a point. As they passed down the hall, their footsteps echoing in the corridor, he glanced at a picture of Hitler hanging on the wall, tilted a good bit to the left. It was this madman that had Nellie creeping around in the dark in order to save six innocent lives.

He refrained from spitting on the photograph. Perhaps the despot would topple like the picture looked like it might.

Using the wall for support, Jean-Paul headed toward the office, the plaster smooth underneath his hands. To give Nellie time, he fell behind Hélène.

She paused and waited for him to catch up. His ploy was working. "Why do you keep a first-aid kit in your office? I can't believe you see that many injured people here every day."

"Plenty of paper cuts. The French are not as strong as you Germans."

"I'm really more French than German."

She tilted her head to one side. "Is there a difference these days?"

Not much.

They came to the office, the door swung wide open. Hélène scrunched her forehead. "That's strange. I'm pretty sure I closed it before I left." She leaned over the knob.

If only he was fast enough to get between her and the door. But he wasn't.

"What's this?" She pointed to an open file cabinet drawer. "I know I didn't leave it like that."

"Perhaps your boss did."

"He has no reason to be going through these papers." Her small, delicate hand quivered as she straightened her desk.

"Oh." He did his best to sound surprised. And then an idea flashed across his brain, a bolt of lightning on an impossibly dark night. He grabbed Hélène by the arm and pulled her from the room. "Get to the car. Now."

"But—"

"Now." He leaned close enough to catch a whiff of her lilac-scented perfume. "You're right. Someone broke in. Whoever is here might be armed."

"What about you?" She kept her voice as low as his.

"Just go. Now."

She nodded, her eyes wide under the artificial glow of the light bulbs.

Only when the click of her high-heeled shoes faded into the distance did he dare call to Nellie in a loud whisper. "Where are you?"

A potted plant in the inner office rustled, and she appeared. "That was close. Why are you here?" She also whispered.

"It's a long story. One I don't have time to tell. Let me get the first-aid kit and get out of here. As soon as you hear us pull away, you need to leave too."

"But I haven't found the cards yet."

"You had better make quick work of it."

Clacking of heels on the floor stopped them in their tracks.

"Who is she?"

At the sound of the feminine voice, Jean-Paul's entire body froze.

Hard ice filled Hélène's words. "Who is she?"

⧅ CHAPTER SIXTEEN ⧅

"*Bonsoir.*" Nellie stared at Jean-Paul and the curvy blond standing beside him. She tipped her head and grinned as if it was perfectly normal to be in someone's office in the middle of the evening after having broken in. She even managed to keep the quaver from her voice, though her knees knocked like crazy.

Jean-Paul glowered at her before turning to the other woman. He spoke so fast and so low, she didn't catch what he was saying. But his tone was tense and terse, his words tight. After a rather lengthy explanation, he returned his attention to Nellie. "*N'est-ce pas vrai?*"

How was she supposed to answer if that was the truth when she hadn't caught a word he'd uttered. "*Oui?*"

"This is my girlfriend, Margot."

"Your girlfriend?" The Frenchwoman lifted her lip in a sneer. "What do you see in her? She is plain and dull. Nothing compared to what you might have had in me."

"But now you can understand why she was jealous and came here. She wanted to find something that would make you look bad so I would pay more attention to her than to you. But you have to understand. She is nothing to me." He pushed Nellie to the side.

She stumbled against the desk, leaning against it for support. Nothing to him?

"*Non.*" The blond batted her long lashes. Was that a tear clinging to one of them? "This is why I have never gotten involved with any Germans before. You have women wherever you go. I thought because you were part French, you would be different. You aren't." By this time, her voice had reached a fevered pitch.

Then she pointed a well-manicured finger at Jean-Paul and Nellie and motioned out the door.

She wanted them gone. Now.

Nellie didn't have a problem with that. She started for the door until Jean-Paul grasped her around the waist and prevented her from leaving.

He held her fast while continuing the conversation with the other woman. "You have to understand. I'm not like the rest of them. The moment I saw you, my heart stopped beating. I've never beheld such a beautiful creature as you."

Nellie gazed at the ceiling and gave a slight shake of her head. Could anything be sappier than that?

"I pleased myself with her, never knowing there was someone like you waiting for me. You're everything I've ever dreamed of."

"We hardly know each other. And the little I know of you has proven to be false."

"Just give me a few minutes to talk to her, and then we can speak more. I'm not willing to give up on you. Besides, I need a ride back." He glanced at his foot.

"Fine." The blond huffed. "Five minutes. And what you say to me had better be good. I have half a mind to leave you stranded. It would serve you right." With a mad clicking of her heels, the blond exited the office, leaving Jean-Paul and Nellie alone.

"Where do you have left to search?"

Nellie pointed to the two filing cabinets. Faster than a car at the Grand Prix, he picked the locks and set to searching one of them. She got busy with the other.

Not a minute later, he held up several booklets. "I got them."

She opened her pocketbook and slipped them inside.

"Now listen. This is what we're going to do. We have to make this look convincing to Hélène. We'll come out of the building together. I'll push you away. You stumble down the street and turn the corner out of sight. You're going to have to walk back to St. Roch."

"That's how I got here."

"I'll go back to the party with her. At least, I hope she'll forgive me enough to drive me back. I twisted my ankle."

"Is that why you're here?"

"*Oui.* Hélène has a first-aid kit here. She was going to play nurse."

He didn't need any light to know that Nellie was smirking.

"I'll be at the convent toward the end of the day tomorrow, and we'll leave then. So you have a long night of forging in front of you."

"You don't think she's suspicious?"

They exited the room and Nellie locked the door behind them before they made their way down the hall. Jean-Paul labored to limp as little as possible. No use in worrying Nellie. "If she is, I'll try to talk her down."

"So you're dumping me for her?" Her voice was light, teasing.

Bien. At least she wasn't panicking. "*Je suis désolé.* You have to understand. She has so much more to offer."

"Blank identity cards?"

"*Oui.*"

"I can't fault you for that."

They reached the door. "I'll see you tomorrow afternoon. Get those done. And do a good job. Ready?"

She nodded.

He opened the door. Hélène leaned against the Kübelwagen, the glow of her cigarette lighting the blackout conditions. He turned to Nellie. "Get out of here. Leave me alone. It's over. Over, I tell you."

"You are a despicable excuse for a human being." Nellie turned and fled around the corner and out of sight.

Jean-Paul drew in a deep breath and prayed that Nellie would make it back to St. Roch without any trouble. Then he approached Hélène. "My apologies for that. I knew she was a desperate woman, jealous that I was taking you to the party tonight instead of her. It never occurred to me that she would break into your office in order to try to find something unflattering about you."

"Are you sure you aren't using me?"

"Using you? Of course not. I would never do such a thing. She's nothing to me. You, well, you are the kind of woman that every man dreams about. She was a dalliance. You are not a woman a man would ever toy with." He brought every bit of French charm to the fore, stroking her silk-smooth cheek. "You take my breath away."

She lifted herself on her tiptoes and kissed the tip of his chin. "You have a way with words."

"*Merci, mademoiselle.*" He leaned over to kiss her.

She pushed against his chest. "*Non, non.* I want to go back to the party."

"Are you sure?"

"Positive. Let me bandage your foot and then we can go."

He winced as she pulled off his shoe and sock and wrapped his ankle. This would hinder him in their escape tomorrow.

Because of the pain and swelling in his foot, he couldn't drive, so she slid behind the wheel, just as she had on the way here. When they arrived at the party, he hopped up the steps and into the house, which was lit like a city street behind the blackout curtains. Though the crowd wasn't large—maybe two dozen people or so—the conversation, laughter, and music swirled.

They paused on the threshold for a moment before Hélène turned to him. "I'm going to powder my nose." She walked a few steps, turned back, gave a tiny wave, and blew him a kiss.

Perhaps he had played his part too well.

He stepped to the table in the living room laden with food, but he couldn't eat anything. Not when the sisters and the children barely had enough to keep body and soul together. Zimmer joined him and slapped him on the shoulder. "How lucky can one man be? You're here with the most beautiful woman in L'asile, the one every other man wants."

Jean-Paul nodded. But he didn't take his gaze from Hélène as she chatted with Weber.

They both turned and stared at him.

Tremors ran through him.

———— ≈ ————

Thursday, July 6, 1944

Off in the distance, the gonging bell, rich and deep and echoing off the abbey's stone walls, called the sisters to morning prayers and pulled Jean-Paul from his deep sleep, curled in a ball on the narrow bed in the house the Germans had requisitioned. He rolled over and stretched.

Ah. His ankle. As he came more fully awake, the throbbing

increased. He swung to the side of the bed and attempted to put weight on his right leg.

Sharp pain shot through the ankle and up his shin. He bit his lip and tried again. To no avail.

He stood with all his weight on his left leg. Now he managed to hobble the short distance to the door. More like hopping, to be honest.

How on earth was he going to drive Weber around today? And tonight, when they were to begin their journey, how was he supposed to drive them to the train station about twenty kilometers away?

Nellie had said she had a back-up plan. He huffed at the idea. She couldn't drive them. Could she?

Non, she had probably been up all night working on those identity papers. She would be in no shape to drive.

The best scenario would be for him to be behind the wheel. That way, Nellie wouldn't have to speak if they encountered any German checkpoints.

Using the wall for support, he limped down the hall and to the stairs. Then he hopped down those, clinging to the banister. By the time he made it to the kitchen, he was panting. He plopped into a chair at the wobbly table.

From his vantage point at the stove, pouring a cup of coffee, Weber raised an eyebrow. "I see your ankle is still a problem."

"No, sir. It's fine."

"I insist that you rest up. Besides, we have a visitor coming today. I need you to make sure he's taken care of."

"Who?" Jean-Paul would wait until his ankle stopped throbbing so much before getting up and pouring himself a cup of coffee.

"I can't remember his name off the top of my head. Don't worry. It will be fine. I'll have someone else take me where I need to go today. Too bad that you don't get to drive and maybe have another chance to flirt with Hélène."

"That is a shame." It was amazing enough that she bought his story about Nellie being his very jealous girlfriend. And who knew what she had told Weber. Nellie had been caught breaking into an office. That merited serious charges.

Thirty minutes later, his almost-cold coffee now down to the dregs, the house fell silent with the last click of the door as those officers billeted here left for their duties, which now included destroying incriminating documents before they left for parts east.

When Weber had outlined his plans for the day, they hadn't included anything about raiding the convent. They had to leave as soon as possible, perhaps even later this morning since he was now relieved of his driving duties, but the tension did ease from his shoulders, and his headache lessened. His bum ankle might be a blessing in disguise. He would be able to get away sooner.

But before he could get himself together and away, a knock came at the door. More like an insistent pounding. "I'm coming."

The banging continued the entire time it took him to limp to the front door.

When he threw it open, he stumbled backward.

Because there on the threshold, stood a broad-shouldered man with Jean-Paul's height, eyes, and chin.

Almost a mirror reflection of him, only thirty years older.

His father.

Her eyes burning and gritty from lack of sleep, Nellie sat at the abbey's kitchen table and added the final flourish to Claire's identity card. The last one. She had started with her own to practice forging the handwriting, how and where the stamps were placed, each and every detail. All their lives were important, and it was critical that each booklet was as perfect as she could make it.

If the authorities questioned one of them, they would question them all.

She'd saved Claire's for last. Because by now, her hands were steadier, her eye more practiced, her fingers defter at their job.

Claire's was almost perfect.

She sat back and studied the information on the cards, going through all of them to ensure they were each as good as she could make them.

Her acts of forgery in school had finally paid off.

Pastor Martin back home said God worked all things together for good. Guess he was right.

She pushed herself away from the table and moved to the stove to pour herself a cup of coffee. Not that what flowed from the spout resembled her favorite drink in any fashion, but it was warm, and she could pretend that it would keep her awake.

Just as Nellie turned to resume her seat, Sister Angelica swept into the room. "Are they finished?" Her blue eyes were rimmed red and punctuated by dark half-moons.

Nellie nodded. "Just now."

"You've been up all night?" she asked as she poured herself a cup of coffee. "You look it."

"I'm sure I do." Nellie brushed several stray hairs off her cheek.

Sister Angelica slurped her coffee, her still-youthful hands wrinkled from years of washing stacks of dishes. "*Je suis désolé.*" She smiled. "Sister Maria-Theresa often scolds me for my dour attitude and forthrightness."

"I'm not offended. In America, a genteel Southern woman would never speak her mind, no matter what her thoughts might be. I'm finding the opposite to be quite refreshing. And if I can be as blunt with you, you appear not to have gotten much rest last night either."

"Albert didn't want to take his bottle. Sometimes, with all of their limitations, the children have a difficult time feeding. Last night was such a night."

"Why don't you go get some rest. We have to be prepared to leave as soon as possible. We have no idea when the raid on St. Roch is going to take place, but we do know it's going to happen. I'm going to take Claire and Leo to the garden for a little fresh air and more practice on our hide-and-seek game while you get some sleep."

"You've been up all night too."

"I'm one of those people who doesn't need much sleep. Besides, it will energize me to romp with them. I missed putting Claire to bed last night." And her heart ached for Velma. "Go. I'll be fine."

"Let Sister Raphael watch them for a while."

"I'll think about it."

With a heavy sigh, Sister Angelica pushed away from the table and shuffled from the room, her shoulders bent much like an old lady's, except that she couldn't be more than forty.

The weight of what was happening, the price on their heads, and what they were about to do weighed on all of them. They each bore a heavy load.

"I don't pray much, Lord, but I need You now." Outside, she whispered the prayer. Inside, she screamed it, pleading with the Almighty. Would He hear? Had He ever heard?

Perhaps so. They had managed to get out of the scrape with Hélène last night. Perhaps God wasn't as far away as Nellie imagined.

With a little bit lighter step, she bounced down the stairs to the nursery. Claire and Leo were busy with some pencils and a few well-used sheets of paper.

Claire looked up when Nellie entered and her entire face transformed into a shining light bulb. "Nelwee, Nelwee!" She squealed and all but jumped into Nellie's arms. The way she slurred Nellie's name only endeared her more.

Nellie nodded at Albert, at last sleeping in his crib. "Shh. You'll wake the baby."

Claire imitated her actions, chubby finger pressed to her lips. "Shh, shh."

"That's right." Nellie kept her own voice low. "Who wants to play hide-and-seek with me?"

Now it was Leo's turn to squeal. He ran to Nellie and hugged her leg to the point of cutting off her circulation.

With a scowl, Claire shushed him. "Shh. Baby sweeping."

Sister Raphael rose from her rocking chair and smoothed Leo's curls from his forehead. "Why don't you snooze in the chair and allow me to take the children out?"

The lure of a few hours of shut-eye was strong and pulled her in the direction of the chair. But then Claire patted her face. "Pway."

Pway. Velma had always begged to play, even when June and Miss Franny were deep in mourning for Mr. Joe. Even when June was heavy with child and alone and overwhelmed with life. And so Nellie had played with her for hours on end. Together they had formed mud pies, walked in the woods, and sung to their baby dolls.

When the heat was unbearable, the relentless Mississippi sun beating on their heads and sending perspiration sliding down their faces, they had splashed in the stream, the water cool against their skin. They always came home soaking wet but happier than two dogs romping free.

Velma couldn't say Nellie's name, but she'd held her hand and hugged her tight. That was better than gold. Nothing Nellie got at home from her always-disapproving father and her distant mother was better than that.

The way a vine slowly curls a path up the side of a house until it covers the entire structure was the way her love for Velma grew.

The weight of her on Nellie's lap, the scent of cocoa butter on her skin, the fuzz of her hair tickling Nellie's chin—all those memories rushed back with a force that almost knocked Nellie to the ground.

She shook the remembrances from her brain like you might shake crumbs from a tablecloth. "Let's go play. Remember our special game."

The two children raced up the stairs but stopped at the door. They knew better than to go outside without an adult. Nellie peeked out, glancing both ways. Shadows hid people. Evil monsters who wanted to harm these precious ones.

But the sun shone warm and bright, reflecting off the puddles left by a rain shower during the night. In the birch tree in the corner of the garden, a bird sat on a branch and chirped his happy song, a bit of normalcy in a world gone mad.

She led the children outside, diverting them when they headed straight for the puddle. They practiced their hide-and-seek. Claire was getting especially good at the game, able to squat into a tight ball to keep from being seen. Leo was still a little too giggly. He might need a dose of cold medicine to keep him groggy.

Several hours from now, when darkness fell, they would begin their trip.

The most dangerous trip of her life.

⅀ CHAPTER SEVENTEEN ⅀

"Are you going to stand there with your mouth hanging wide open, or are you going to let me in?" Vater's thick, dark eyebrows lowered as he frowned.

With few other options, Jean-Paul opened the door wider and stepped back so Vater could enter. "What are you doing here?"

"That's an inane question."

Jean-Paul couldn't argue with him.

"Did you truly believe you could come here without any orders, use my name, and not be discovered? The moment I was called into my superior's office and told that I was in this village in France, I hopped on a train and made my way here."

Jean-Paul hobbled to the couch. "I would offer you coffee, but as you see, I'm supposed to be resting my sprained ankle."

"Bah." Vater waved away Jean-Paul's complaint. "You were always a crybaby. I thought I had beaten that from you."

Jean-Paul clenched his jaw. Those unpleasant summers he spent with Vater, despite his pleading objections to Mère, were far behind him. Though Vater continued to hold plenty of power to harm him.

"The question remains as to what I'm going to do about you. There's a reason you used an assumed name. There's a reason you didn't want to be discovered. What is it?" He sat in the armchair across the coffee table from Jean-Paul and folded his arms across his still-solid chest.

He'd done that hundreds, maybe even thousands, of times throughout Jean-Paul's life. There was little point in waiting him out. Jean-Paul had tried that before. It never worked.

But he couldn't share the truth with Vater. He wouldn't hesitate to turn Jean-Paul in. Probably would haul him back to Berlin and throw him into the deepest hole. That French prison where he was would look like Versailles compared to where Vater would take him.

"Your brother is serving honorably not too far from here. He does our family proud."

The implication was not to be missed. Vater wasn't pleased with Jean-Paul's decision all those years ago to forsake the glorious Fatherland and all it had to offer him, the sweet temptations of power and glory, to follow his French roots. When he was called up for service in the German military, he'd fled to the forests and joined the Maquis. For many long years he'd managed to avoid detection.

It was not a matter of whether he would regret slipping up and blurting out Vater's name when Weber had asked. It was only a matter of when. When had now arrived.

"You know my stance. I refuse to fight against my own people."

"Your people are the Germans." Vater's voice, so deep and authoritative, rumbled in Jean-Paul's chest.

"I have no desire to be associated with them or their barbaric acts."

Red gushed into Vater's face, and the vein in his neck, the one that always indicated his anger, stood out to a degree Jean-Paul had never witnessed. "You are a coward. A disgrace."

"I am proud of my decision. Nothing you can say or do to me will change that." He allowed his tongue free rein. He should corral it for the sake of Nellie and the children, but he could no longer control the words that streamed from his lips. "Germany is on the brink of falling. You don't have to look far to see that. The Allies are advancing daily, and they are bombing German cities to rubble. Wake up! Look at what is happening to your beloved Fatherland."

Vater stood over Jean-Paul, his hands fisted so hard his fingers were white, his long, pointy nose almost touching Jean-Paul's. "We will yet prevail."

"Get your head out of the sand and begin preparing yourself for what will happen to you when the Third Reich topples."

Vater struck him across the cheek. Jean-Paul had so practiced to school his emotions that even the sting of it didn't bring a single tear to his eyes.

"How dare you speak to me in such a manner." It was surprising that Vater's roar didn't shake the windows.

"I only speak the truth."

This earned him another slap. He'd been hit so many times, it didn't faze him in the least anymore.

"You are the most selfish, insolent child. This is why I divorced your mother and returned to the Vaterland. My mistake was in allowing you to stay with her, little simpering brat that you were. I should have kept you as I did Josef. Instead, I can barely stand to look at your face." He turned away.

In reality, he had turned away from Jean-Paul the moment he divorced Mère and destroyed their family. Mère blamed herself for what happened, calling herself a foolish woman. But it was Vater who was the fool.

"Why did you come here?"

"You have two choices. You can either return with me to Berlin and join the military like your brother. Make me proud. Show yourself to be a true German."

"That's nothing more than a desperate move on your part. Germany is running out of men. You need bodies, and you'll get them from wherever you can. Old men. Children. Mercenaries."

Vater backed up a step, his face red just a minute ago but now as white as his always-pressed handkerchiefs. "Your other choice is to return to Berlin as my prisoner."

"I would rather suffer in chains for the sake of freedom than be free for the sake of tyranny."

"Then you have made your choice."

Though his blood chilled at the images running through his brain—darkness, confinement, torture—he swallowed the rising lump in his throat and nodded.

Nellie and the sisters knew what to do. At least how to get to Annemasse. They could make the trip without him. It would be a long journey on foot to the station in the neighboring town, but once on the train, the excursion would be easy. Once at the border, they would have no trouble locating a smuggler to get them across. Perhaps they would even run into Georges Loinger or Marcel Mangel.

Vater returned to his seat, the hard lines of his face reverting to a mask of haughtiness and vanity.

Love your enemies.

Why would the Lord bring that verse to mind now?

Pray for those who persecute you.

Vater would need all the prayers he could muster once the Allies got ahold of him. There was no doubt that he had committed heinous war crimes. Jean-Paul would pray for his eternal soul.

Love your enemies.

"Vater, would you like a cup of coffee?"

Vater narrowed his eyes and tilted his head, studying Jean-Paul. At last he cleared his throat. "Fine."

Focusing all his attention on getting to the kitchen without limping, Jean-Paul made his way across the room.

If thine enemy be hungry, give him bread to eat; and if he be thirsty, give him water to drink: For thou shalt heap coals of fire upon his head, and the Lord shall reward thee.

Was that the answer? Could he lull Vater with kindness and either find a way to make him relent or find a way to escape?

———≋———

The day wore on, the children long since tired of their games and playing in the nursery, and yet no sign of Jean-Paul. He had hoped to get away early, to help them prepare. Something must have come up that detained him. A general hush fell over the convent.

With Sister Maria-Theresa downstairs keeping watch over the children, Nellie and the other two sisters went to the kitchen to prepare supper. Although they had already packed most of the food for their trip, they were forced to dip into their precious supplies to at least give Claire and Leo something to eat.

As Nellie sliced and buttered some bread, she kept her musings to herself. She gripped the knife with all her might to keep her hands from trembling.

Sister Raphael passed behind her and touched her shoulder as she went. "Don't fret. He will be here in time."

"I hope so. But this weight presses on my stomach. After last night, I can't help but worry that something might go wrong."

"Worry is natural for someone you care about."

"I don't care about him, not more than I do about anyone. I hardly know him."

"But he's kind and compassionate. Good with the children. From what I've heard, he's done much for our cause." Sister Raphael's words were tender and motherly in a way Nellie hadn't experienced since June's mama passed more than ten years ago.

"I know it doesn't change anything—"

Sister Raphael murmured in agreement.

"—but I can't help but be concerned. And I can't help but wonder what we're going to do if something awful happens to him. We can't stay here. We know that much."

"If the worst occurs, we go on with our plans." Sister Angelica spoke as if she were talking about alternate arrangements for a rained-out picnic.

Sister Raphael sliced several strawberries, their juice staining the cutting board red. "We know how we are going to get to Annemasse."

"How do we even get to the train though? Jean-Paul said we need to leave from another town because of the chance of someone here recognizing us. It's too far for us to walk, especially with three small children and all of our luggage." And there was no way she was going to leave her camera behind.

"God will provide." Sister Angelica's voice was steady and even. Like it always was.

"Don't you ever get tired and sick at heart over the evil in this world? Don't you wish there would be an end to it all? Don't you wonder why God has allowed such sin?" Nellie set her knife down and peered out the small, rippled window at the darkening sky, the herald of a storm to come.

"That's what all of this is meant for." Sister Raphael stood so close that the sweet fragrance of incense wafted from her clothes.

"All of what?"

"This suffering is meant to make our souls long for heaven. This world wearies us and weighs us down. Oh, but there is another world where we will never weary and where we will never long for anything better."

Nellie clamped her lips tight. If God truly loved His people, He wouldn't make them suffer at all. Not the way Mr. Joe had. Not the way the French were. Sister Raphael had to say the things she did because of her profession.

That didn't mean Nellie had to buy into it.

Men were cruel. God was little better.

From the corner of her eye, she spotted Sister Angelica nodding. "I know that's a difficult concept to believe, but that doesn't make it any less true. Think about it for a while. Read and pray. You'll see we're right."

Nellie turned to the food packed in boxes and retrieved the jar of schmutz to smear on the children's bread. June's mama always talked about the glory land and light and momentary troubles, but it made as little sense now as it did then.

A short time later, Sister Maria-Theresa climbed the stairs with Claire and Leo in tow. Their chatter broke the tension in the room just as the storm outside burst. Lightning zigzagged across the sky, and thunder rumbled like an earthquake under their feet.

Leo scurried to Nellie and pressed against her side. She rubbed his sleek dark hair and held him close. With the next crack of thunder, Claire was also clutching her leg. Strange how a child who had endured what Claire had was still frightened of a storm. Perhaps the cracking of thunder reminded her of the retort of the guns that brought down her father.

Nellie sighed. "There really is no going now."

"The storm will buy us more time." Sister Raphael placed two plates on the table and beckoned the children to come eat.

"We need a plan. A way to get to the train station if"—she glanced at the children—"if he doesn't arrive soon. Is there anyone you can trust? A farmer with a cart would be better than having to walk."

"We'll wait for him." Sister Maria-Theresa lowered herself into a chair and bit off a corner of her bread.

"What if he doesn't come?"

"He'll be here." The old woman chewed and smacked her lips.

"You don't know that. You can't know for sure. We could wait and wait only to have the Nazis at our door instead. He would want us to go and not risk our lives in the hope that he might show up."

"You must trust and be calm, child."

Though the temptation to pull at her hair and stomp her foot was strong, Nellie resisted. "Tomorrow morning. That's all the longer I'll stay. If Jean-Paul doesn't arrive by first light, I'm taking the children and leaving."

"That won't be necessary." Sister Maria-Theresa settled back in her chair and sipped her very weak tea.

She might believe Jean-Paul would show up, but Nellie had no guarantee. She would do what she had to do.

Another flash of lightning brightened the dim room.

Even if it meant going alone.

☰ CHAPTER EIGHTEEN ☰

As always happened when she entered the chapel, the spicy fragrance of incense enveloped Maria-Theresa and embraced her, holding her close and soothing her soul.

A place of refuge from the storm outside. A distant rumble of thunder curved her lips upward. Not that kind of storm. The storm of the soul. The storm of evil that brewed right outside the door.

It hadn't always been the Germans who had driven her here, not during either war. Though France was a Catholic country, she had been brought up in a Protestant home. Her parents raised her in that faith. They loved her, cherished her, and did all they could to protect her.

But it wasn't enough. They couldn't stop her uncle from doing what he did. Sullying her body and her reputation.

And so her parents had brought her here. To heal emotionally. And to get back what was most precious to her.

This place, this chapel, was where she met with God. True, she could meet with Him anywhere, but here was where she was most at peace with Him and with life. It was here in these rough-hewn, time-smoothed pews that she'd found the Healer. And the healing.

She inhaled vanilla and cinnamon, then made her way to her pew. The second one on the right. As always, she sat on the aisle and bowed her head.

And as always, she whispered her prayer. Somehow, if she spoke aloud, her connection to God was stronger. Like they were having a conversation.

"Oh, Lord. We don't know where Jean-Paul is, if something awful has befallen him, or what might be detaining him. I know that You sent him and Nellie here for a reason. You always have a plan and a purpose for everything that happens to us.

"We have this dangerous journey that we must make. Jean-Paul knows what to do. I'm afraid that we're inadequately prepared. He has the most experience at this sort of thing. He has the knowledge that we need.

"*Père*, I'm frightened. I will not admit it to the others, but I am scared. Afraid that we will not make it to the train. Afraid that one of the children will give us away. Afraid that the journey will be too much for some of us.

"I could go on and on and list each one of my fears, but that would mean I would be here all night and long into the morning. Not that I would mind the time spent with You, but preparations must be made. And You know that this old body can't function without rest.

"I'm afraid."

For several minutes the only noise that invaded the space was that of her own breathing, rattled by age. The solid pew underneath her didn't even squeak in protest as she shifted positions. For the first time in many years, the future frightened her. The way ahead was dark, twisting and turning so she couldn't see beyond the next curve.

"*Père*, what are we to do? I beg for Your guidance, for Your wisdom in this matter. Do we leave without Jean-Paul? Do I go with them as they have begged of me? Will that only endanger us further or will that save us?

"Whatever happens, I know it is Your will. Not a hair falls from our heads without You seeing it. What great comfort that has brought me throughout the long life You have enabled me to live.

"It's not so much for myself that I am afraid."

Was that even the truth?

"Maybe a little bit. That is why I don't want to leave. I know that I will be united in heaven with You sooner rather than later, but I always believed that would happen in my own bed here in these walls that have sheltered me all these years. I never imagined that I would pass beyond these gates again. I haven't since the day I arrived, and that was fine with me."

Sister Angelica's and Sister Raphael's pleas rang in her ears, urging her to go.

She chuckled. "You're upsetting my plans, Lord."

What were her plans compared to His? Nothing but a rushing wind in a tunnel. A puff of air visible on a cold winter's morning.

"I am trying, *Père*, to submit to Your perfect will. But it is difficult. This is difficult. These children You brought here have inspired so much joy in my heart. They are a substitution for the ones I never knew. I would do anything for them."

Anything? She bit the inside of her cheek, testing the veracity of her words. *Oui,* she was not lying. She would walk from here to Switzerland on hot stones if that meant saving even one of the precious lives hidden in the dark cellar.

She had her answer.

"I believe I know what is to be done. I thank You, Lord, for this time in Your presence. For the precious blood of Your Son that enables me to come before You.

"And now I beseech You to be ever near us as we strike out and make our way to the border. Close the eyes of the Germans. Hide us under Your wings. Hold us in the palm of Your hand.

"Deliver us."

The day wore on, stretching to endless seconds, minutes, hours to Jean-Paul. There was a reason Vater was the best at his job, a fine Nazi elite. Because he never failed in his duty.

Even though Jean-Paul showered him with kindness and attentiveness throughout the day, Vater never took his eyes from him. Just sat as straight as an arrow on the utilitarian brown sofa that had seen better days.

Usually the house was abuzz from early morning until late at night. Today of all days, it sat as quiet and empty as a tomb.

And that sent shivers up Jean-Paul's arms just as much as when he'd had to walk through the cemetery to his grandfather's grave in a chilly drizzle.

For the most part, he and Vater sat across from each other, staring each other in eyes so alike there was no doubt they were cast from the same genes.

What was there in the house that could make Vater drowsy? A bit of beer, but the taste was impossible to hide in coffee. Perhaps a little vodka left from last night's party? He had no idea. And if he could rummage it up, how would he slip it to Vater when he never let Jean-Paul out of his sight?

This was proving to be an impossible task. Vater was too keen and observant, too diligent at his post.

At last, Jean-Paul hitched up his pants legs, and sat, leaning toward Vater. "Can we talk?"

"Ah, so you are ready to do your duty to the Vaterland of your own free will?"

"Not quite. I'm your own flesh and blood. We may resemble each other only in our physical features, but I am your child. Your son. Does that mean nothing to you?"

"It meant nothing to you when you chose your mother over me."

"Josef and I were little boys. What an impossible choice we were given. And then for you to steal away in the night with my brother, not a backward glance at me or Mére, what was I to think? You loved him more than you loved me." Heat rose in Jean-Paul's chest. After all this time, didn't Vater understand?

He drew in a long breath. It would serve no purpose right now to attack Vater for the way he left Mère alone, how Jean-Paul had had to become the man of the house overnight and take care of her. Vater may have given them money out of a guilty conscience, but she still needed someone to love her.

Jean-Paul was that someone.

That was why he was loyal to France. That was why he had compassion on the less fortunate. On those society shunned.

Because Vater had shunned him.

He rose from his seat and paced the room even though his ankle throbbed, fingers combing his hair several times over.

"You thought that by appealing to my father's heart, I would let you go. As you said, I made that mistake once before, leaving you behind. I intend not to repeat my earlier foible."

It was true. Vater didn't understand. He never had, and he never would. But the only emotion Jean-Paul could identify in those swirling about in his chest was pity. He pitied Vater for missing out on the love of one of his sons. And his wife.

He had traded his family for the Vaterland.

And a sorry trade it was.

Finally, as the fading daylight streaked the sky a dusty pink, came the hum of the Kübelwagen from the yard.

And Jean-Paul's chance. Ignoring the burning pain in his ankle, he shot from the house and toward the vehicle. "Hurry, hurry, it's an emergency."

The two in the Kübelwagen eyed him, but his panic must have truly shown on his face, because they hopped out of the vehicle within seconds. As Vater emerged from the house, shouting obscenities at him, Jean-Paul was climbing behind the wheel.

Zimmer, one of the soldiers who had just arrived, must have heard Vater, because he leapt in front of the vehicle.

Jean-Paul laid on the horn. "Get out of my way, or I'll run you over!"

Zimmer didn't budge.

Jean-Paul inched forward and nudged him with the front of the vehicle. Meanwhile, Vater approached and reached out for Jean-Paul. He nudged Zimmer again and again and again, holding the steering wheel with one hand while fighting off Vater with the other.

Vater grabbed hold of Jean-Paul's shirt. "You will not get away from me."

One more tap of the bumper to Zimmer's shin, this one harder but not hard enough to knock him down, and Zimmer scurried out of the way. Jean-Paul spun the wheel and hit the gas, tires spinning and shooting gravel like a machine gun.

He sped down the street as fast as the Kübelwagen would go. An American Jeep would be quicker, but he had to take what he could get. Thankfully, it would take some time for Vater and Zimmer to secure other transportation.

By then Jean-Paul and Nellie and the others would be well on their way out of town to catch the train.

He raced away from the village toward St. Roch. Once he arrived, even though his ankle shot pain through his leg, he hobble-ran to the rusty iron gate and shook it. "Open up! Open up!"

Not two flashes later, Nellie was there, unlatching it and catching him as he stumbled through the entrance.

"Lock it! Lock it!"

She did as he bid. "What happened?"

"No time. We leave now. Get the children and the sisters. I'll gather our supplies. We only have minutes."

Thankfully, she didn't protest but scurried away to do his bidding. He limped as fast as possible to the kitchen where the food stores sat stacked in boxes.

Nellie and the others met him there, Nellie holding Claire by the hand, a suitcase in the other. Sister Angelica and Sister Raphael each held a child and a suitcase. Even Sister Maria-Theresa clutched a battered carpetbag in her hand.

Bien. They were all prepared to leave.

"Let's go. My Kübelwagen is outside. We don't have a moment to lose. Remember, children, the game I taught you? We're going to play it now."

Before they had a chance to step into the courtyard, he heard voices at the gate.

Vater's was among them, crying out for Jean-Paul's blood.

☰ CHAPTER NINETEEN ☰

At the rattle at the front gate, Nellie broke into a cold sweat. "Why now?"

Jean-Paul's face crumpled. "It was me. It's my fault. They followed me from the house."

"No time for that now. We have to get out of here."

"*Non*, we must hide."

"They know you're here. They'll search until they find you."

Claire whimpered, and Nellie turned to her. "*Shh*. Very quiet. You mustn't make a single noise." Thank goodness Sister Raphael had already administered the cough medicine to Albert. He slumbered in her arms, his lips pursing from time to time.

Jean-Paul gathered the group together. "Nellie is right. We must leave."

"But are you going to be able to make it?"

More rattling at the gate. More shouts in German and French. More threats. Time was running out. They'd soon climb the fence or sever the lock.

"I'll be fine." Jean-Paul gathered the food supplies.

He had to be okay. At least he was here. At least he would be able to help them. She could have done it alone, would have done it alone, but it was nice to have him here.

"Let's go." Sister Angelica whispered the words and motioned for the rest to follow her.

The voices came closer. They must have gotten inside. With her hands sweating, Nellie gripped Claire and the suitcase, and on soft feet, scurried down the corridor to the basement stairs.

Time was of the essence, but Sister Angelica tempered her steps so Jean-Paul and Sister Maria-Theresa could keep up.

The shouts approached. One voice in particular called for Jean-Paul.

Nellie picked up her pace, almost dragging Claire along with her. They scampered down the stairs and through the nursery. At the far end of the room stood a large dresser. Sister Angelica shoved it to the side and revealed a door, presumably to the hidden passageway she'd told them about.

The sisters scurried forward first with Jean-Paul bringing up the rear, still limping.

Nellie reached out to him when he drew even with her. "How are you doing?"

"Fine, fine. Don't worry about me. You go ahead."

"Will you be able to slide the dresser back?"

"If Sister Angelica could do it, so can I."

Nellie slipped into the passageway, flicking on her flashlight to banish the complete darkness that enveloped her. A blast of cold air struck her as she scampered farther inside. The dresser scraped the old stone floors and then Jean-Paul shut the door.

His footsteps closed in on her. Good. He was keeping up. She wouldn't ask him about his ankle again.

As soon as he shut the door, the hollers coming from upstairs ceased. The walls and ceiling were thick and lined with aged, moss-covered stone.

In front of her, Sister Maria-Theresa slowed.

"Keep going. We can't stop."

"I'm slowing you down." She shook her head, her gray curls bouncing with the motion. No more wimple.

"We need you to take care of the children. It's not far now."

"I know, child, I know."

Her words held a wishful, longing quality, like she was speaking about something else entirely.

Jean-Paul came alongside them. "No stopping now. Not for anything."

Claire took Sister Maria-Theresa by the hand, and together the three of them resumed their trek.

Was that a sound at the door behind them? Had the Nazis discovered the secret passage? Nellie's heart flapped around in her chest, thumping into her ribs, its rhythm unsteady and uneven.

As they hurried, she glanced at Claire. Her eyes were big and round in her face. Poor kid. She didn't understand what was happening but knew enough that it frightened her.

It frightened all of them. Nellie gave Claire's hand a good squeeze. Claire gazed at her and smiled the tiniest of bits. Enough to reassure Nellie that she would be all right.

"Are we almost there?" Jean-Paul's voice in her ear startled Nellie.

"I think so. Pray that they didn't leave a sentry outside."

"I have been doing that every step of the way."

The passage narrowed, and Nellie had a difficult time drawing a deep breath. The old stone walls, crumbling in places, closed in on her.

And then finally, there was the door, a simple but sturdy one, the rest of the group waiting for them there. Nellie released her grip on Claire and hurried forward. "We can't burst out of here. They might have a guard waiting for us. I'll scout it out."

Jean-Paul nudged her out of the way. "I'll do it."

"You're the one they're searching for. If they find me, I can come up with a good story. Or pretend I don't understand them."

"*Non*, it's my job."

"Will someone look out there?" Sister Angelica harrumphed.

Before Jean-Paul could protest further, Nellie cracked open the door. "Everyone stay back."

Night was fast approaching, and making out anything was difficult. She couldn't shine her flashlight, so she gave her eyes a moment to adjust to the dim light.

To her right, a tree stretched out its branches, the leaves clinging to it as a gusty wind swept across it. There was no other movement. No other shadows.

Holding her breath, she peered to the right. There was nothing in this direction but open fields. A hedgerow marked the far boundary of the property. Again, all was still and quiet.

But that didn't mean they were in the clear. Just because she didn't see anything right now didn't mean someone wasn't lurking around the corner, ready to nab them. It didn't mean that a guard might not be posted near the front entrance where the Jeep was.

She breathed out and relaxed her shoulders, infusing her voice with a confidence that didn't fill her chest. "I don't see anyone. We can go."

Jean-Paul pushed by her. "Let me double-check."

"Don't you think I have two good eyes in my head?"

Sister Raphael touched Nellie's arm. "Let him look. What good is an argument going to do us right now?"

With a huff, Nellie stepped aside and allowed Jean-Paul access to the door. He glanced both ways, then turned to the group. "There's no one out there."

Nellie huffed again. Why couldn't he trust her?

He led them out of the hidden door on his gimpy ankle, limping around the corner, turning every now and again to shush them when someone stepped on a dried leaf or a twig.

The air was so fraught with tension that even Claire picked up on it and clung to Nellie's leg. Though she attempted to loosen the child's grip on her thigh, it was to no avail. Now she was almost as hobbled as Jean-Paul.

He approached the convent's final corner. Once they turned this one, they would be by the Jeep. They were a hair's breadth away from escaping undetected.

He flattened himself against the building, and everyone fell into line behind him. The ancient stones were still warm from the day's sunshine, even though the rain had come and gone, and only lightning flashed in the distance.

Nellie stood on her tiptoes to whisper in his ear. "Anyone there?"

"I don't see—"

The old-age squeak of the gate interrupted him, and German voices poured from the convent's entrance. Though Nellie couldn't understand the language, there was no mistaking the tone. They weren't happy. Words flew from their lips like spittle.

Jean-Paul sucked in a breath. Whatever they were saying wasn't good.

She whispered again, the scent of soap and fresh air clinging to him. "Tell me."

"They aren't giving up."

As if to verify what he said, flashlight beams swept over the gravel drive and sifted among the bushes and vines hugging the convent's exterior.

Jean-Paul pushed them farther back into the darkness.

Her breath came in short, rapid spurts. Any minute, the Nazis were sure to round the corner and discover them hiding here. Should they head back inside? Was it safe in there now?

Leo whimpered, and Angelica covered his mouth to silence him. That was all they needed, for the children to make noise and give them away.

Jean-Paul turned to her, this time whispering to her, the tip of his nose tickling the top of her ear, sending a shiver skittering down her spine. "They're sure we're in there somewhere. They're going back in to check but leaving one outside to watch."

He leaned forward a little bit and listened. "When there's just one, we take turns running to the hedgerow."

"We have to get to the Jeep."

"We will. One step at a time."

Still holding on to Claire, she pulled even with Jean-Paul and peeked around the corner. There was a Jeep, with another one behind it. The soldier left outside to stand guard lit a cigarette, the red glow of it a bright spot in the night. His heavy boots crunched on the gravel as he paced the length of the convent. The only other sound was that of the crickets chirping their love songs.

Nellie stood statue still as the sentry paced several more times.

Jean-Paul turned to her. "As soon as the guard has his back to us again, you pick up Claire and race for the bushes. Lie flat under them, and don't make noise."

She nodded, though it was doubtful he saw that in the dark. For several long minutes, she waited, every muscle tense and ready to spring into action. A few moments before the guard turned, she hoisted the heavy girl into her arms.

As soon as the soldier turned on his heel, Jean-Paul gave the signal, and she raced across the rain-soaked grass, her feet slipping as she went, her stride awkward because of the child's weight. Her chest heaved as she lugged Claire with her. Never had a few feet been such a long distance.

Just as the soldier reached the end of his route and was about to turn, she dove under the row of bushes, sliding on the mud, her face in the dirt.

She had made it. But how would the others? How would a lame Jean-Paul and a frail Sister Maria-Theresa manage to cover that much ground in such a short time?

Sister Angelica was next, with Leo in her arms. Within moments, she was in the mud at Nellie's feet. Claire squirmed, but Nellie refused to let her go. She whispered as softly as possible, and Claire relaxed at last.

Sister Raphael, cradling Albert, now scrambled across the grass, almost losing her footing but managing to make it across, settling in front of Nellie.

Could the other two accomplish the same before the Nazis gave up their search of the interior and made their way outside again?

If only she could create a diversion. Something that would buy the two of them more time to cross the no-man's land.

That was it. That was the answer. She leaned close to Claire. "Stay here. Don't move. Don't make a sound."

Sister Angelica raised her head, and Nellie shook hers. When the guard turned and Sister Maria-Theresa and Jean-Paul set off across the lawn, Nellie bent over and waddled toward the end of the hedges. Then she reached out and picked up a large rock from the drive, stood for a split second, and hurled it over the soldier's head.

He stopped short, raising the weapon in his hand, shouting into the darkness.

For a moment, Jean-Paul and Sister Maria-Theresa paused. Then they picked up their pace and scurried under the hedgerow just as the soldier turned.

The soldier called in French, "Who is there? Weber, Jung, Braun, come here. They're out here."

Nellie duck-walked toward Jean-Paul, who yanked her down, not releasing his grip on her wrist even when she attempted to pull away.

"What did you do? Now we're in more danger than ever."

⋚ CHAPTER TWENTY ⋚

Though Jean-Paul kept a tight grip on Nellie's wrist, she managed to yank free of him. "This is what we're doing." She pointed toward Sister Angelica, then the convent and the door they had exited not so long ago and then whispered loud enough for him to hear. "Go!"

Without hesitating, without so much as looking both ways as you would when crossing a street, Sister Angelica picked up Leo and sprinted across the lawn.

Before Sister Angelica had even returned to the shadows, Nellie pointed to Sister Raphael and gave the same command. Again the nun obeyed without question. This was insanity.

Nellie turned toward him. "Follow with Sister Maria-Theresa." In the space of a heartbeat, she too was dashing toward the convent, Claire bouncing against her chest, her footfalls soft but rapid.

What choice did he have? Beams from the Germans' torches swept across the lawn, miniature searchlights hunting for any sign of them. He was crazy to trust Nellie, but he picked up Sister Maria-Theresa, who gave a slight squeak, and hustled toward the dark side of the building where the others had disappeared.

Once there, he stood the nun on her feet. Already, Sister Angelica and Sister Raphael had slipped through the doorway and out of sight. A moment later, Nellie was also inside.

Sweating and muddy, he led Sister Maria-Theresa into the building. The rest of the group stood against the thick walls, chests heaving from the flight. He wasted no time in shutting the door and then pulling Nellie to the side.

The front of her shirt and pants were covered in mud, and some of it streaked her face. A few clumps even clung to her hair. She didn't simper or whimper or even attempt to wipe it away.

He cleared his thoughts, not giving the heat in his chest time to cool. "What in the world were you thinking? You could have gotten us killed. You still might. A stealthy resistance worker, one who stays alive, thinks through various scenarios before committing to a plan."

She had the gall to toss out a throaty scoff. "I would believe the opposite to be true. I'm sure you've had to make split-second decisions, even ones of life and death. Too much time deliberating could mean your demise or that of others."

He swallowed hard. He would never admit it to her, but she was correct. Sometimes there wasn't the chance to run through all the possibilities and their implications. Sometimes you had to act and pray for the best. "Have you had a chance to figure out how we're going to escape?"

She opened her hand, and the glow of his torchlight fell on the rock she held. "You all go to the front gate. Or at least as close to it as you can get without being seen. I'll heave this stone into the bushes, which will send them over there."

"And we'll jump in the Kübelwagen. Right under their noses. But you'll never make it through the passageway, up the stairs, and outside before they stop searching the hedgerow."

"Then you'll need to come up with a distraction for them. I know you can think of something."

How cheeky could one woman be? Before he could formulate an appropriate reply, she had marched away and was speaking with the sisters, heads bent together.

Like American football players breaking their huddle, they stepped apart, Nellie hanging back while the nuns headed down the passageway. He scurried in front of them, then glanced backward at Nellie.

She nodded. "Get going before they stop searching outside. I was the fastest runner on my school's track team. I'll be fine."

Was she displaying false bravado, or was she truly as confident as she sounded?

Like she said, he didn't have the luxury of time to dissect it and mull it over. They had to hurry before Vater and the others returned to the front.

He led the nuns through the passageway. Between the two younger sisters and himself, they made quick work of pushing the door hard enough to move the dresser. Then he led them up the stairs, and outside to the front gate. The clouds overhead parted, and a soft beam of moonlight illuminated the scene.

Careful to stay low and as invisible as he could make himself, he opened the gate little by little so it wouldn't squeak. The area in front of them was clear. No one, not even the guard from earlier, was in sight. No motion. No noise.

Nellie's diversion must have worked, though there was no telling how much time it had bought them. His pulse thrummed in his neck. He flushed hot and cold.

He strained to hear Nellie's footsteps behind them but was met with only quiet. Even the children were still and silent.

But they couldn't wait. It would take a minute to get everyone settled in the Kübelwagen, especially the children and Sister Maria-Theresa.

Their footsteps would make noise on the gravel and perhaps draw the attention of Vater and his comrades. That made speed of the essence. If only Nellie were here.

"Let's go. Fast." He pushed Sister Angelica, Sister Raphael, and Claire ahead of him, then grabbed Sister Maria-Theresa by the hand and hurried along with her.

His breaths came as fast as water rushing over a precipice and hurt his chest as much as water slamming against it.

Sister Angelica and Sister Raphael dumped the children inside before opening the door and climbing in themselves. He and Sister Maria-Theresa arrived at the vehicle moments later and within a few seconds, they were both inside.

Still no Nellie.

Where could she be?

He fumbled near the ignition. Cool metal slipped past his fingers. Good. The key was still here. As soon as he started the engine, the Nazis would come after them. They had no time.

German voices and hurried footsteps broke the stillness of the night.

He gulped and turned the key. The machine roared to life.

He shifted into first gear. Pressed his foot to the gas, just a little bit, just enough to roll forward.

He glanced over his shoulder. There came Vater, leading the pack, like a hunting dog sniffing out blood.

If they had any chance of getting out of here, they had to leave now. Vater wouldn't hesitate to shoot.

But how could he leave Nellie? He'd failed Simone. He wouldn't fail another woman.

———≈———

Nellie pounded down the passageway, drawing on every reserve of strength she had. While she'd boasted to Jean-Paul that she had been on the track team, that was years ago. She'd done more than her share of walking in London, but this was different.

This wasn't a stroll down the street. It was a flight for her life.

She dashed up the stairs and through the kitchen. If only she could see or hear what was going on outside. But the thick walls that had cocooned them blocked out all sight and sound.

So she kept on. She would either run into the Jeep or straight into a Nazi's arms.

She gulped in lungfuls of oxygen, her leg muscles screaming in protest. But she couldn't give up. She wouldn't.

A stitch in her side almost doubled her over. But she refused to give into it. Instead, she willed one foot in front of the other. She would make it. She would. She had to.

At last she burst into the warm summer night. The moon lit the path in front of her, the one toward the front gate.

The Jeep's motor chugged to life.

No! No! Was she too late? Had they been spotted?

Maybe she should turn around and hide. Or maybe it was best to go forward.

She continued through the wide-open gate and onto the drive.

It wasn't too late to turn back.

From her right came the Germans, shouting, waving their weapons, shooting into the air. The first crack of gunshot sent her heart into cut time.

The Jeep swung around in a wide arc, now approaching her.

This was her chance. Even as it picked up speed, she ran alongside it. Sister Angelica held out her hand to Nellie, but that would do her no good. She should have tried pole vaulting in school.

Lungs burning, chest about to burst open, she sprinted for all she was worth. With one giant leap, she landed in Sister Raphael's lap in the front passenger seat. "Go!"

The shout took the last of her breath. The sudden forward jolt of the vehicle pressed her against Sister Raphael.

Behind them, a motor roared to life. More shots volleyed around them.

Nellie ducked. More shouts.

She concentrated on pulling herself all the way into the Jeep. She jerked as Jean-Paul shifted gears. Which was a feat in itself since she lay halfway against the stick.

The Jeep picked up speed. Once they turned off the convent property and onto the road, Jean-Paul shifted again. By this time, she had managed to right herself, though she sat on the emergency brake and straddled the gearshift, one hip pressed against Sister Raphael's leg, the other pressed against Jean-Paul's.

Funny how a tingle ran up only the left side of her body. She scooted over, closer to Sister Raphael, pressing her against the door, and Leo crawled onto her lap.

The anemic light gave her a chance to study Jean-Paul's profile. His high cheekbones, his prominent chin, his angular nose, the scar across his cheek.

What was she doing, thinking about him like this? They had just escaped with their lives. And only barely.

"That was close." She managed a half-hearted laugh. The other half of her heart, she'd left behind in St. Roch.

"Too close. I thought you were a good runner."

"It's a long way."

Sister Raphael shifted positions. "We're just happy you made it."

Jean-Paul sped through the deepening night, bumping over potholes and flying around curves. Nellie had nothing to hang on to other than Leo. She managed to brace herself against the dashboard. Her palms were sweaty. She peered over her shoulder. The Nazis were behind them but weren't gaining any ground. Holding steady. "How are we ever going to get away?"

Jean-Paul shrugged. "That's Weber's vehicle. I'm betting that they didn't have any time to fill it with petrol. Soon they'll run out. Weber had plans to visit with some of his fellow officers in a town a good distance from here. We just have to keep ahead of them a little while longer. Because as soon as they return to the house, Weber and my father will alert every German between here and the border."

"Your father?" She must have misunderstood him. His father was in Germany, wasn't he?

"He was the man leading the charge. It's a long story, one I'll tell you later."

In Sister Angelica's arms, Albert stirred, then let loose a mighty wail, one that was noticeable even over the roar of the engine. She shushed the baby, but he continued to cry.

"The medicine must have worn off. Can someone find it in one of the bags?" Sister Angelica's voice held a note of weariness.

And their journey had only begun.

Nellie couldn't move, but Sister Raphael bent over and within a minute or so had located the medication. Before long, Albert returned to his slumber.

Nellie glanced over her shoulder every couple of minutes. Then the hum of the engine behind them quieted. When she looked this time, the major and Jean-Paul's father were falling behind. More and more every second.

They sputtered.

Stopped.

Jean-Paul rounded a corner, and all fell quiet.

"We did it." She grabbed his upper arm. "You did it. I believe they're stranded."

Jean-Paul nodded but kept his focus on the road and his foot on the gas. As they continued, a heaviness settled on Nellie's lids, and she gave in to the temptation to close her eyes. Just for a minute or two. Just to rest.

The next thing she knew, a bump jostled her awake as she leaned against Jean-Paul. She bolted upright and gazed around. Everyone else slept. "Are we almost there?"

"My brother always used to say that when we took the train to Germany every summer before my father left us."

"Why was your father here?"

"Summoned to cart me to the Fatherland. By whatever means necessary."

Nellie sucked in a breath. "Your father was here for you? Is that what took you so long to get back to the convent?"

"*Oui*. It took me a little bit of time to escape from his clutches. This isn't the first time today I've stolen this Kübelwagen."

Imagine being hunted down by your own father. She was all too familiar with people stalking others like predator and prey. She'd witnessed the consequences of it. And she understood the depravity of the men behind such witch hunts.

But it was truly evil when it was your own father who would arrest you and hand down an almost-sure death sentence.

She stared into the darkness. They both had a past they were running from. And who knew what lay ahead of them.

⦚ CHAPTER TWENTY-ONE ⦚

In the middle of the night, with blackout restrictions in place, the train yard in this good-sized French town, so much like all the others Nellie had seen since arriving on Omaha Beach, sat as quiet as the countryside. Jean-Paul had explained that coming to a city this large was a calculated risk. It was far enough away from the convent that Weber and his father might not think to look here. Then again, with so many more people, someone might spot them and report them.

They ditched the Jeep—Kübelwagen as Jean-Paul insisted it was called—a couple of blocks away from the station. To his credit, he carried their supplies and limped along without complaint. Claire, now fast asleep on Nellie's shoulder, snored through her open mouth. At least Nellie was able to throw a blanket over her head to keep her safe. The same with the other two children. If only they would sleep the entire way to the border.

Her arms ached with Claire's weight, and she shifted the child to the other side.

"Do you want me to take her?" Jean-Paul kept his voice low and quiet. No need in alerting the authorities that there was a group of undesirables out in the middle of the night trying to board a train illegally and cross the Swiss border without permission from either government.

Nellie shook her head. Even with Claire pressed against her, her camera bounced against her chest, a comforting friend in this strange and hostile world. While her fingers itched to press the shutter, if they were caught and she had pictures of anything, they could incriminate her or others.

She kept the envelope of photographs she'd already developed stuffed in her brassiere. She shuddered. What would they do to her if they discovered those pictures, especially the one of Claire? The only option was to keep from getting caught.

Her boss would be pleased with the images. Hopefully pleased enough that she wouldn't get in trouble for the escapade that brought her to France in the first place.

Overhead, too high to be any threat to them, came the rumble of engines. Planes, British Spitfires, on their way to bomb German interests in Europe.

The nail in the coffin.

Months from now, a year from now, this would be free land. This continent would once again teem with life.

But they couldn't wait that long. By then, the Nazis would have discovered the children.

And would have exterminated them.

Like the way Mama had scrunched cockroaches beneath her shoes.

A shiver coursed through Nellie.

Jean-Paul turned toward her and raised an eyebrow. She shook her head, then peered over her shoulder at Sister Maria-Theresa, who dragged behind the group.

Nellie fell back and nudged the older woman with her elbow. Sister Maria-Theresa offered her a small smile.

"We're almost there. Then you can rest. The remainder of the trip will be easy."

"Don't worry about me. I'll be fine. I won't slow you down. The Lord is my strength. Nothing is more powerful than that. You would do well to remember that. He overcomes everything."

Jean-Paul turned back and hushed them. "No noise." His whisper was harsh.

And he was right. In this slumbering town crawling with ruthless Nazis, they had to watch their every step. Already, she'd had too many run-ins with them. Not to mention that Jean-Paul was a hunted man. Each of them had a price on their heads.

At last they arrived at the train depot, a rather plain brick building. The station's windows were shuttered and, like all of France, like all of Europe, it was unlit. In the distance, a dog barked. A web of train tracks crisscrossed the yard. Where were the spiders? Lying in wait to wrap up their prey?

Silence reigned. No hissing engines. No clanging bells. No humming throngs.

Too quiet. Too still.

Nellie hardly dared to breathe.

Jean-Paul came to a halt and studied the trains in the yard. Nellie stopped beside him, shifted Claire once more, and leaned toward him. "How do you know which one is going east?"

"We guess."

"Guess?" Her voice was loud enough to stir Claire. "Just like we guessed with the vegetable truck?" Had that been less than a month ago?

"Only troop trains are going west right now. A passenger one is most likely going east. Follow me."

"Are you sure you know what you're doing?"

"Trust me."

Could she? Should she? Did she have a choice?

Though she had longed to be part of the Allied forces and follow them as they liberated France, finding themselves in this part of the country because of their choice of the farmer's truck hadn't been all bad. She had a story to tell. Just a far different one than she'd planned.

Deep in the tangle of engines and boxcars and flatbeds, away from any potential spying eyes, Jean-Paul set down his supplies and instructed the women to wait there. But Nellie was never one to sit around.

How many times had Daddy told her to wait for him? Did she ever? Until Mr. Joe's death, she hadn't. After that, she'd stayed put, pulling her covers over her head, praying for the people who might be Daddy's victims that night.

She settled Sister Maria-Theresa on her suitcase and handed Claire to the older woman. The light of the setting moon was just enough for her to make out Jean-Paul's retreating form. She hurried after him.

When he jumped into an open boxcar, she hopped up after him. He spun around. "Nellie?"

"This would be a good one to take."

"Do you ever obey directions?"

"Not usually, *non*."

He sighed and rubbed his stubbly chin.

"Explain to me about your father."

"You get right to the heart of the matter, don't you?"

"Forthrightness. That's what it's called. It's why I never made a good Southern belle."

"As I told you before, my father is German. When I was ten years old, he took my brother and returned to Germany, leaving me and my mother behind. It was my choice to stay in France. Right afterward, he took my brother and left in the middle of the night. But how could I leave my mother to go live with a man who beat me whenever I made the slightest infraction? I'm his greatest disappointment. And he is willing to sacrifice me on the altar of Germany's downward spiraling ideals. That's all there is to it."

She understood the beatings. And fathers who were monsters. "*Je suis désolé.*"

"There's nothing to be sorry about. You did nothing wrong. I did nothing wrong. Vater is. . .is. . . That's all I can say about him. And you're right. With the hay in here, it gives us the perfect place to hide if the authorities stop and search the train. It will be comfortable for the sisters and the children."

Even though Jean-Paul stood in front of her, all she could see in her mind's eye was Velma's dark, trusting face. "Just get us to Switzerland."

Friday, July 7, 1944

Albert's cries jerked Jean-Paul awake. Weak morning light filtered into the boxcar. Even though it was early in the day, the interior was warming. Summer was coming in full force, and even now, straw stuck to their sweaty bodies. Sister Raphael scratched at the red welts on her bare arms.

And the train had yet to move a smidge. On the other side of the boxcar, Sister Angelica searched about in their boxes for bread for Albert. The other two children slumbered, a light snore coming from Claire. The nun found the bread and fed some to Albert, who ceased his fussing.

Beside him, her disheveled hair tumbling about her shoulders, Nellie stirred. She yawned and stretched. "Where are we? Have we stopped for passengers?"

"We haven't moved yet." The truth cut him worse than any knife.

Her hazel eyes widened, enough that the gold flecks in them stood out even more. "Are you sure?"

He nodded, his lack of sleep a testament to that fact. He'd planned on dozing once they moved. That had never happened. He yawned.

From outside the boxcar, whose heavy door they had closed and barred soon after boarding last night, came voices. Though the thick metal kept out the exact words being spoken, the cacophony of sounds testified to a great number of people out there. Dogs gave deep, throaty barks. Most likely German shepherds with their teeth bared.

Then the crack of a rifle sent everyone in the car jumping and startled Albert from his infant slumber. Everyone except for Sister Maria-Theresa, who knelt in the far corner in deep, fervent prayer. Was she even aware of what was happening outside of their door?

Then again, perhaps it was best she wasn't. Or else she had such peace about the situation that fear was unknown to her. Oh, to experience even a small measure of that peace.

"And now we can't even get off and try a different train." Nellie's shoulders sagged.

Claire wandered to her, plopped in her lap, and patted her cheek. "Nelwie cwy?"

"*Non, ma petite amie,* I'm not going to cry." Nellie sat up straighter, but the smile she offered the child was as fake as Hitler's claims that the Jews were going on holiday when they were transported by the trainload.

Is that what was happening outside of these doors? If so, the Nazis would want this boxcar for their human cargo. And a barred door was not going to do anything to stop them.

Jean-Paul scooped Claire from Nellie's lap and swung her to the other side of the car. "I'll bet you are ready for some breakfast. How about some bread and water?"

She nodded, her braids bouncing with the motion. Nellie had styled her hair that way before they left to keep out the lice and tangles. Still some straw, the same color as her locks, stuck out from between the plaits.

The voices outside grew louder, until they were right outside the railcar where they hid. Everyone froze. Even the children understood they were now to play hide-and-seek.

The bar rattled. Jean-Paul held his breath. Making very little noise, Sister Raphael rocked Albert back and forth to keep him silent.

And then the voices moved on. The air whooshed from Jean-Paul's lungs.

"That was close."

He turned to Nellie, the deep V in her forehead softening. He chuckled. "That was nothing. We've come through closer scrapes already." He allowed the unspoken comment about there being many more narrow shaves ahead to hang in the air.

Just as he bent over to take the bread from Sister Angelica, the train jerked. Claire shrieked and clung to Nellie's neck. Leo simply laughed. How like a boy.

After several halting stops and starts, the train picked up speed and momentum. At last, they clacked over the rails. Sister Raphael poured water into a cup and passed it around to everyone. Jean-Paul only took a sip in an effort to preserve their precious rations for the women and children.

Throughout all of this, Sister Maria-Theresa had not broken off her prayers. He went to her as she knelt in the corner and tapped her on the shoulder. She sat back and turned toward him as he offered her the meager breakfast.

"*Merci.*"

"Do you trust God?" The question slipped from his lips before he had a chance to check it.

"Of course. Why would I not?"

"Even in the middle of this chaos? Not knowing who is on the right side and who is on the wrong? Even when people have failed you and betrayed you time and time again?"

"What people do doesn't affect my view of God." She took several healthy gulps of water. "Man is fickle. God is not."

Jean-Paul brought his bread to the boxcar's corner, on top of the heap of hay, and chewed on both the meal and the elderly nun's words. According to her, God wasn't like man. Why, then, did He change His mind so often? First the Jews were His chosen people, and now they were hated and hunted. He could make no more sense of it than a kitten could make sense of a tangled ball of yarn.

As the train sped eastward Nellie came and joined him on the hay-stack. "You are very deep in thought."

"Am I?"

"We haven't known each other long, but I recognize that look in your eyes, like you're watching a movie instead of living real life."

He quirked an eyebrow. "I've never heard an expression quite like that one before."

"In American English, we ask for a penny for your thoughts."

"But the penny is the smallest coin. Is that all they're worth?"

"I'm sorry about your father. It's difficult to come to terms with the man who gave you birth and yet spawns such evil." Now she had the same faraway gaze in her eyes she'd accused him of having.

"We aren't speaking about just my father, are we?"

"Of course we are." Her answer was too quick and too bright.

He leaned towards her, their hands just brushing each other. His heart rate sped up a little as he studied her, her delicate profile a stark contrast to the bleak settings. "Tell me about him."

⚡ CHAPTER TWENTY-TWO ⚡

Nellie couldn't stifle a bitter laugh when Jean-Paul asked about her father. Such a contrast to the sheer delightful giggles from Claire and Leo as they played with the sisters in the straw. Even Albert was in an unusually good mood, smiling at Sister Maria-Theresa who rocked him as if he were the Christ child Himself.

"I think our fathers might have been best friends if not separated by an ocean."

"Oh?" Jean-Paul chewed the end of a piece of hay. If they weren't fleeing for their lives in the middle of war-torn France, Nellie might have laughed at his impersonation of a Nebraska farmer.

"He hated the Negroes. Called them uppity and said they didn't know their place."

"I studied something about that at university."

"He especially hated when they were more prosperous than him or when they had nicer things than he did. That really grated on him. Made him madder than a hive full of angry bees. And meaner than them too." Even her French was laced with traces of her Southern roots. "Have you heard of the Ku Klux Klan?"

He nodded.

"I didn't realize you were such an admirer of Americana."

"To me it seems like a place flowing with milk and honey. At least it did when I was a boy, before I learned that it wasn't so different than anywhere else."

"That's too true. Anyway, Daddy was the leader of the KKK in our area. He killed my best friend's father, leaving her mother with two young girls. Velma was—is—Mongoloid."

Even in the bleak interior, his face shone with understanding. "Now I know why you were so good with the children from the very beginning."

"Claire is so much like Velma. Sometimes just looking at her makes me miss home."

"Did your father ever pay for his crime?"

More children's laughter echoed in the clacking train car. "He died of a heart attack when I was sixteen. Even before that, I had little to do with him. I couldn't stomach the sight of him, always remembering that night and what he did to Mr. Joe. I was glad he was gone and couldn't hurt anyone else."

All Jean-Paul did was nod.

And it was enough. He understood. All her life, no one other than June had known what it felt like. And she didn't even truly feel the full impact. Didn't know what it was like to be the spawn of such a perpetrator of evil. To lie awake in the dark, trembling, waiting to become as horrible as the man who had brought her into this world.

Did evil run in families? What about God punishing the children for the sins of the fathers to the third and fourth generations? But Jean-Paul understood all those fears. At last, she had discovered a kindred spirit. "How do you handle it?"

He didn't have to ask what she meant. "Most of the time, I try to close my mind to the thought. When I am confronted by a situation, I ask myself what my father would do. Then I do the opposite."

Now it was Nellie's turn to nod.

"What happened to Velma? And your friend?"

"Their mama died the year after Daddy. June doesn't have a husband and is struggling to provide for her two little ones. The minute I got a job in Chicago, I sent for Velma and found a good place for her to live. When I worked there, I visited her as often as I could." Again, the pain of missing the sweet young lady stabbed in the middle of Nellie's gut.

"Mère would say that God worked everything out for good."

Nellie snorted, then repented of the unladylike action. "All I see is evil, as thick and as common as the air we breathe. It doesn't matter where we are, whether France, the United States, or Germany, it's there. But when I peer into Velma's eyes or Claire's or Leo's or Albert's, then what I see is goodness and pureness. An innocence that must be protected at all costs."

She couldn't think or talk about this anymore. The flooding memories threatened to overwhelm her and send her into sobbing spasms. She'd cried enough tears over Mr. Joe and Velma. At least now she was able to take some action. This was far better than sitting in England, photographing mothers waiting in line for milk for their children. Here she could use her photographs to tell a story that would touch the world. Like the one of Claire in front of the church.

She dusted off her pants and lifted her camera from her chest. If they got caught by the Nazis she could always expose the film before they had a chance to snag her camera from around her neck.

Even though the light was low and the shutter speed slow, she managed to capture Claire's face bathed in the sunshine streaming in from the vent. The golden hues of the sun highlighted the gold in her hair. She laughed, wide-mouthed. If Nellie ever got a chance to develop it, it would be a beautiful picture.

The heat inside the boxcar built as the day wore on. The children's early energy waned, and Albert was fitful again. For now they didn't need to keep him quiet, so they saved the cough medicine for when they would have to. Nellie got a picture of Leo sleeping in Sister Raphael's lap.

Eventually, Nellie couldn't sit still a moment longer. This confinement was going to drive her crazy. She moved around the boxcar adjusting their food supplies, brushing the hay into neat little piles, and smoothing the children's damp hair from their sweaty brows. Moisture dotted her forehead and ran down her face.

And then something in their movement changed. They were slowing. The train's whistle sounded several times. She peered at Jean-Paul, who had come to his feet. He climbed on top of a suitcase and peeked out the grate. "Looks to be a good-sized town."

"Do you know which one?"

He turned to her and gazed at her, narrow-eyed.

"I guess that was a stupid question."

"It may be that we'll be here long enough for me to find out some information, like if we're on the right track, so to speak, and how much farther we have to go. If we have farther to go at all."

"You mean we could be in Annemasse?" What a blessed relief it would be to get out of this stifling boxcar and stretch her legs.

One more step toward freedom.

"I'm not sure. Probably not. I figured the trip to be longer. I'll go find out. You stay here with the sisters and the children." He pierced her with his glare.

But he was out of his mind if he thought she was going to stay put. Hadn't he learned that about her yet?

He slid the boxcar door open just a crack, then peeked out both ways. After a moment, he jumped down, and with one glance backward, disappeared, leaving the door ajar.

Nellie pretended to be busy entertaining Leo and Claire, but she was really waiting for Jean-Paul to be out of sight. After about five eternal minutes, she stood, brushed the straw from herself, finger-combed her hair, and turned to the sisters. "I'm going to go and see for myself what's happening."

Sister Maria-Theresa shook her head. "Jean-Paul has only been gone a few minutes. I don't think you should be rushing after him."

"I'd like to take a few photographs and see for myself where we are."

"Why can't you wait for him?"

"I'm chafing just sitting here and waiting for someone else to take action. I'm a doer, not a sitter."

"You must learn patience, my dear, in all aspects of your life. Sometimes we have to wait on the Lord and His perfect timing. And sometimes we must wait on others and trust them to do what they have said they will do."

How succinctly she put it. Waiting. Never Nellie's strong suit. And more than once, it had gotten her into trouble. Not just the night of Mr. Joe's murder, but many, many other times.

"I'll be very careful. Men aren't detail oriented. They don't notice the small things like women do. And with my trained photographer's eye, I see more than most people."

"And what is there to find out? All we need to know is where we are." Sister Maria-Theresa shook her head, her frown deepening. "It's best if you stay put and do as Jean-Paul has asked. Trust him."

But there was a world out there. She might suffocate if she stayed in here. "I'm going. I promise not to wander too far and not to say anything to anyone." She kissed Claire's cheek and jumped out.

As she leapt, she leaned too far forward, and her momentum drove her to her hands and knees, the sharp edges of the gravel biting into the soft flesh of her palms. But she wasn't about to be deterred. She brushed off her hands.

Careful to keep close to the train so she could dive under it if needed, she slunk along the cars snaking toward the station a short way in the distance. The dark two-story brick building overlooked a pair of tracks, a copse of trees opposite it.

Small and charming, just as she had always imagined France to be. She snapped a couple of pictures. Ahead, a few passengers stepped from the platform and onto the train. Not many. Just a handful. No tearful goodbyes from any of them.

The sign on the station read GARE DE PONT-DE-VEYLE. Not that it meant anything to her. She still had no idea if they were headed in the right direction or not.

If only she could walk up to the conductor standing on the platform in his navy-blue uniform, a cap on his head, calling out what she assumed must be a boarding call.

Not much of a chance to do any surveying. Without taking too long to frame the shot, she snapped a few pictures of the station. One of them included a Nazi in his brown uniform, a dog straining on a leash. Even here they kept tight control on the people, much as they had in every other French town she had been to.

She had turned to go back to the boxcar when a deep voice called out to her. "*Madame.*"

She ignored him.

"*Madame.*" Louder this time, so there could be no mistaking that he was calling to her.

If she ran to the boxcar, she would lead him to the sisters and the children. They may not have time to hide. But if she answered him, he would hear how poor her French was, laced with her American.

"*Madame.*" His footsteps crunched closer on the gravel.

She could no longer pretend he wasn't behind her. As slowly as she could manage, she turned around, as if she didn't have a care in the world. "*Monsieur.*"

He was the soldier she had spotted before, the one in the tan uniform, shiny black boots to his knees. At least he was German. He wouldn't recognize her terrible accent when she spoke in French. And she didn't have to pretend that she didn't speak German.

"Where are you going?" His French was even worse than hers.

What should she say? If she told him their true destination and they were on the wrong train, the German would put her on the correct one, and she may never find Jean-Paul and the others again. Already she had been ripped away from Velma. To lose Claire would be almost too much to bear.

But how would she explain herself walking away from the station and passenger cars? "I was stretching my legs."

He raised a blond brow at her. Was he questioning her, or didn't he understand what she said?

"Where are you going?"

"I needed a break from sitting so much. My calves were cramped."

Again with the raising of the eyebrow.

"*Madame.*" He motioned for her to make her way toward the platform.

She could come up with no reason why she shouldn't follow him. She trudged toward the front of the train. "Annemasse?"

"*Oui, oui.*" He eyed her from the top of her disheveled hair to the tips of her muddy boots. If he recognized them as American, he didn't give any indication.

He led her to the passenger car and helped her aboard.

"*Merci.*" She sank into the plush though a little worn seat. How wonderful it was to relax in the depths of such comfort. The beds and chairs at the convent had all been hard. She hadn't sat in a cushioned chair since London.

It was a bit of heaven on earth.

But she didn't dare get too comfortable. Before the train left, she would have to disembark and run to the boxcar. The sisters must be worried about her. Perhaps even Jean-Paul was.

If she wasn't there when the train started to move, would they get off?

She pressed against the window. The weather was too warm for her to steam it up. Straight and tall and clutching his rifle, the German solider never left his post on the platform. His gaze roamed up and down, but he didn't turn his back, not even for a second.

And then with a toot of the whistle, the train chugged to life.

⚊ CHAPTER TWENTY-THREE ⚊

Jean-Paul squinted against the bright sun as he limped to the boxcar, making sure to stay on the far side of the train, away from the platform. The heat grew more intense by the moment. If the others smelled half as bad as he did, it was going to be a long trip to Annemasse.

At least they were on the correct train. He had verified that with the German soldier who had stopped him and asked for his identification. Nellie's forgery was so good that the Nazi didn't even take two glances at it. He would have to compliment her on her handiwork.

Each of the chocolate-brown cars resembled the others, making it impossible to distinguish one from the other. Good thing he had counted the number of cars from theirs to the front of the train.

He hadn't needed to, though, because Albert's wails pierced through the heavy steel car and carried outside. Anyone walking by would be able to hear them.

As fast as possible on his injured ankle, he slid over the coupling and around to the car, hoisting himself inside the stuffy carriage.

Sister Raphael gazed at him as he entered, her eyes glazed with unshed tears as she jiggled Albert in an attempt to still his cries. Claire, sucking her thumb, snuggled against Sister Maria-Theresa while Leo jumped up and down, rocking the car.

"We have to get Albert quiet. Where's the medicine?"

"We're running very low on it." Sister Raphael shifted Albert over her shoulder so she could pat his back. "I thought it would be best to save it for Annemasse."

"We can get more when we arrive. Right now, he might be drawing attention to us. He certainly doesn't sound like a cow or another animal that might be in here."

Sister Angelica shuffled through their stores until she came up with the medicine.

While he'd been out, he had refilled their water. Sister Maria-Theresa was as wilted as a philodendron that hadn't been cared for in a month. He handed her the canteen first.

Wait a minute. Not everyone was here. "Where is Nellie?"

Sister Raphael's mouth dropped open. "She wasn't with you?"

"She left here?" Of course she did. The heat flushing his face had nothing to do with the ambient temperature.

"She is a headstrong one. I've never known such an independent woman in my life." Sister Angelica handed the medication to Sister Raphael.

"That's Americans for you. Though I wouldn't call Nellie independent. Foolish might be a better word."

Sister Maria-Theresa clucked at him. "Don't be so hard on the girl. She is young and a little naive."

That was one thing she wasn't. She'd seen much in her life and been through a great deal.

"She wants to make a difference in the world and right the injustices that have been done." Sister Maria-Theresa withdrew a snow-white handkerchief from her skirt pocket and dabbed at her upper lip.

"And how did she propose to do that in a train station in Pont-de-Veyle?" He plopped on a pile of hay, and Leo climbed on his lap. Right away, his shoulders relaxed. The child trusted him. He had to do everything in his power not to break that trust.

"I don't know, but she longs to be part of the action. That's a quality she needs if she's to change the world."

Changing the world. That was what had led him to join the resistance in the first place. Such an unrealistic ideal. How many had he actually made a difference for? Perhaps a small handful. Not enough to change the tide of the war, that was for sure. Certainly not enough to change the world.

"Even if you only help one person, that is enough. By aiding a single individual, you have changed one world."

Albert's wails quieted. Even Leo was content to nestle in Jean-Paul's lap.

A single individual. Was it truly enough? Could helping just one person make a difference? To that person, to their loved ones, to the people they would touch one day, it did.

But there were so many in need right now. Six of them just in this boxcar. Without a great number in the resistance ranks, it was a Herculean effort to assist all those who required assisting.

"What are we going to do about Nellie?" Sister Angelica sat and rubbed the back of her neck. "What if she doesn't come back before the train leaves the station? What if she's been detained? If they torture her, she might give us all up. She's a fool."

Sister Maria-Theresa chuckled. "They will not torture her. And she's feisty enough that I don't think she'll betray us."

"But we do have to get her back here. She'll be out of luck if she gets left behind, especially with her atrocious French." Jean-Paul sighed. "I'll have to go find her." Even though his ankle protested the thought.

But before he could set Leo aside and rise to his feet, the train's whistle blew, and the boxcar rolled down the track.

As she settled into the seat, Nellie slipped on an air of confidence she was sorely lacking. Too many questions swirled in her brain.

In the seat across from her, an infant cried, loud and full-throated. Not like Albert. While he could wail, he sometimes had a difficult time getting enough air into his lungs. The mother rocked this infant and shushed him, and he nestled into her arms, his eyelids fluttering closed.

Would Albert ever know his mother's singular love like that? Cherished by the woman who had given him birth? Though their papers were false, the sisters had sewn their true identities into their clothes. Once they were in Switzerland and France was liberated, their families could be notified.

Albert and Leo's families, at least.

What would happen to Claire? No one wanted children like her. They ended up in institutions, like Velma. While Nellie had made sure to find the best place possible for her, it wasn't home. It never would be.

In front of her, a man in a black bowler hat snapped open his paper. Thank goodness no one had come to sit beside her. The last thing she would be able to do now was make small talk in a language that wasn't her native one.

They clicked and clacked along for a while. The seat was comfortable, and her eyelids shut of their own volition. How good it was to be able to get some rest where her back didn't ache and straw didn't poke at her skin.

She couldn't have slept for long before the rotund conductor made his way down the aisle. "Tickets, *s'il vous plaît*. Have your tickets ready."

Nellie sucked in a breath. A ticket. The thought of needing one had never crossed her mind. What was she supposed to do? She flicked her gaze around the carriage, scanning the floor, the seat beside her and around her. No tickets. Nothing she could try to pass off. Certainly nothing that the conductor would accept.

As she scanned the interior, the man in front of her got up and went to the lavatory.

The lavatory. That was it. The answer to her problem. Not in this car, but if she could scoot into another and maybe hide out in that one until they arrived or at least stopped again, she'd be safe.

When the paunchy older man bent over to punch the young mother's ticket, Nellie made a dash down the aisle, a brief hop over the coupling, and into the next car. She slowed her pace but moved through this one, almost empty, to the last one.

Only an old woman, her fingers gnarled with age, occupied this carriage. She bent over her knitting. Somehow, despite the arthritis which afflicted her, she managed to turn that yarn into a scarf. Something recognizable. Beautiful, almost.

Right now, Nellie didn't have time to ponder what she saw. With so few passengers, the conductor wouldn't be far behind. She slipped inside the minuscule room and slid the lock shut. As she stood with her back against the door, she allowed herself only shallow breaths. Perhaps he wouldn't even notice the lavatory was occupied.

Each beat of her heart was an eternity. She swallowed, the sound of it much too loud in the confined space. Perhaps the conductor was even now standing outside the door waiting for her. Ready to nab her and send her off to those horrible places Jean-Paul had told her about.

Voices floated underneath the door. One warbled. The old lady. The other was deep and strong. The conductor.

The train swayed, and Nellie steadied herself against the tiny sink, so close she couldn't even stretch her arms out all the way.

Would he turn around and leave the car? Perhaps he had forgotten about her. Maybe he hadn't even seen her before. She wasn't that memorable. It was possible.

The knock at the door sent her jumping. She bumped her knee on the sink and gave an involuntary cry of pain.

"*Mademoiselle,* are you hurt? Can I help you?"

She couldn't answer him. She worked in vain to steady her breathing.

"*Mademoiselle?*"

What to do? What to do? Hold on. She wasn't the master at getting excused from school for nothing. It had been a while, but she would never forget how to do it.

She retched. Not really, but hopefully the sound would be enough to convince the conductor that she was sick and it was best not to disturb her.

"*Mademoiselle.*"

She retched again.

He didn't call out for her anymore. Even if floors on board trains creaked, she wouldn't be able to hear them over the *tickety-tackety* of the wheels on the tracks. That meant she had no way of knowing if he remained outside the door or not.

She would slump to the floor and wait out the rest of the trip, but there wasn't room.

All she could do was lean against the door and focus on the fact that each turn of the wheels carried them closer and closer to the Swiss border.

She couldn't allow her mind to wander to the others. The walls closed in even more when she brought them to mind. Claire's laughter rang in her ears, even still. The most beautiful, most melodic sound in the world.

At least Velma was safe, away from the bombs and the gunfire and the human-sniffing dogs.

Or as safe as she could be. Her father had lived in the United States, in an America that was supposed to be at peace.

But its citizens weren't all at peace with one another. And for much the same reason as America now fought against the Germans. At the very least, maybe what was happening in Europe would bring a new awareness to her people that everyone had the right to life, no matter what blood flowed in their veins.

Nellie sighed. This string of thoughts wasn't leading anywhere productive either.

Without the little light on, it would be dark enough in here to develop her photographs. Ones of smiling, laughing, happy children.

Ones of a world the way it should be. Of a world she prayed she would live to see.

⫸ CHAPTER TWENTY-FOUR ⫷

Though the straw pricked at her crepe-like skin, Maria-Theresa sat on the pile of hay without flinching. Heat from the sun beating on the car warmed her from the outside in. The pain that she endured now and the discomfort she had endured since coming to St. Roch was nothing to the pain she had been subjected to as a child.

Because she had survived that, she could survive anything. God had given her peace and bestowed it on her in abundance.

Too many of these young people today didn't have that peace. Not just freedom from conflict but peace in their hearts. After the Great War, many of the soldiers suffered so because of what they had experienced. It was likely to be the same once this war ended.

Jean-Paul might be among them. Even as the train crawled ever eastward toward freedom, he paced the boxcar. When the train rounded a bend, he stumbled but never ceased moving. His face was redder than the reddest rose, and beads of sweat lined his brow. Even his slicked-back hair wilted.

He moved toward her, and when he approached, she reached out and grabbed him by the elbow. He tried to shake her off, but she didn't release her grip. The human will could overcome even arthritic fingers. "Come sit with me for a while."

"I can't."

She didn't narrow her eyes or glare at him but kept her gaze steady. "Sit."

He plopped beside her.

"Tell me what is the matter."

He leaned away and stared at her. "You have to ask?"

"Ah, it is what I suspected. You are worried about Nellie because you care a great deal for her."

"Shouldn't I be concerned? We don't know where she is or what happened to her."

"I know." She patted his sweaty hand, her blue veins bulging. "I know. But she is safe in God's hands. That's safer than you could keep her."

"I feel so helpless."

Ah, there was the crux of the matter. "You like to be in control."

"*Non.*" He fiddled with a piece of straw, twirling it between his fingers. "*Oui,* I suppose I do. But these days, I have so little of it."

"That is where trust and hope come in. Trust that God knows what He's doing. He's much smarter than you."

That earned her a snort of laughter.

"He is. Why wouldn't you trust the One who created and sustains the universe?" She allowed the question to hang in the thick, close air.

"He hasn't been very kind to me."

"If you sat down and thought about it, you would see that He has been. In every little detail of your life."

He sighed. "And what about the hope?"

Hope. What every human longed for but so few possessed. "Hope that He has life in control. He holds Nellie in the palm of His hand. All of us. Not a single hair falls from our heads without His knowledge or apart from His will. Because of that, we can trust in the hope we have for the future. A life eternal in His kingdom. And that is far better than any hope. Even the hope of getting across that border."

Jean-Paul clasped his hands and leaned forward. Even though he didn't close his eyes, perhaps he was praying. That was what he needed to do. The best medicine she could prescribe for him.

For it was in prayer that she had discovered her solace. In a crazy, mixed-up, evil world, it was the only place of peace and hope.

So, as Leo and Claire played at her feet and Sister Angelica and Sister Raphael snoozed, she went before her faithful Father. Out loud, so they could all hear her. Perhaps her words would bring them the peace they so needed.

"Almighty Father, this is a frightening time for each and every one of us. We have embarked on this mission to save the lives of these three precious children. You go before us. You go behind us. You surround us with legions of angels.

"But *Père*, we are scared. We don't know where Nellie is or what has happened to her. Wherever she may be, please protect her and provide for her every need. Grant her serenity and wisdom. Help her to know that she is not alone, that You are with her, watching over her.

"Be with us as well. Ease our alarm, and provide us a rich measure of Your peace. May the children not miss her or fret over her. Hold them in the palm of Your hand and keep them close to Your heart. You created them. You love them with an everlasting love. They have a purpose in this world. May they live to fulfill that purpose.

"Blind the eyes of those who hunt us. May the rest of this trip proceed without complication. May we be reunited with Nellie very soon. Above all, may we each be drawn closer to You throughout this experience.

"May the grace and peace of God the Father, Son, and Spirit be upon us all. Amen."

Everyone chimed in their amens, even Sister Angelica and Sister Raphael, who had awakened.

The train moved along at a snail's pace, or so it seemed from where Maria-Theresa sat. They stopped at every little town and station along the way. Though it was daytime, there was still the threat of Allied planes in the air. The Allies bombed German positions and cities day and night.

They pulled some bread from the supplies and gave the children a little bit to eat. Angelica moistened some of it with water and fed that to Albert. They each took a turn drinking from the metal canteen, the taste of the water matching that of its container. But it was wet, and she would not complain against it.

Sister Raphael sang songs to the little ones and occupied them the best she could.

Slowly, the little light that filtered through the grate dimmed. The air inside cooled. Night must be approaching.

Though he had paced on and off all afternoon long, limping on his ankle which must throb, once darkness descended, Jean-Paul came and sat next to her again. "I understand what you are saying about trust and hope and peace. That's all fine. But where is Nellie? I need to know."

———— ≋ ————

How much longer Nellie's trembling legs would be able to hold her up was anyone's guess. There was no toilet—just a hole in the floor—so she couldn't sit. As the train lurched to stop and start, so did her stomach. The small lavatory stank, the foul odor churning her stomach even more. Pretty soon, the pretend retching wouldn't be so fake.

After the first two stops, the conductor didn't pester her anymore. Either a new conductor boarded the train or the old one figured she was too sick to bother with. Thank goodness he never brought anyone to force open the door.

After their last stop, there was no doubt it was a different conductor. This one's voice was deeper and richer. His French was stained with a German accent. He didn't knock on the lavatory's door. Perhaps the other conductor had warned him about the sick woman. Whatever the reason, she managed to let out a breath and relax the slightest of bits.

A few times, her heavy eyelids demanded to close. What could it hurt? Annemasse was the end of the line. The train wouldn't continue into Switzerland. But the cramped space didn't allow for more than a few minutes of shut-eye.

And each time she gave in to the pull of slumber, the train rocking her like a mother to her baby, horrible images filled her brain. Children wrenched from their parents' grasp. Men's broken bodies. Mr. Joe, Clarence. The stench of burning flesh as the church went up in flames and the retort of gunfire as the Nazis mowed down the village's men.

She shot up straight, banging her knee hard against the sink, so hard she couldn't stifle the yelp. Her pulse ticked in her wrist. Had that gunfire been a dream or was it real?

Several minutes went by as she held her breath, waiting for more.

There wasn't anything other than the toot of the train's horn as it continued on its journey.

If it had been real, it was over.

And it couldn't have been Jean-Paul and the sisters. If they were on this train, they were tucked into the boxcar in the back. Someplace the Vichy or the Germans couldn't reach while the black snake sped across the countryside.

Please, God, let them be on this train. I don't want to face crossing the border alone. Because with or without them, there was no turning back. She had to make it out of German-held territory and find her way to the Allies.

She clutched her camera strap, the film inside holding the precious, valuable pictures. Every now and again, she patted her chest where the envelope with the photographs of Claire and her village rested.

Another reason she had to escape as soon as possible. The world needed to see these prints to understand what the Europeans had been suffering through for over four years. The Allies had to finish the job with the utmost urgency.

When her calves cramped so that she had to bite her lip against the pain and she couldn't stand for another minute, the train slowed. The conductor called, "Annemasse. Annemasse. End of the line."

By half bending and half lifting her leg, she managed to massage away the cramp by the time the train belched to a stop at the station. She couldn't draw attention to herself, so she waited for a couple of minutes before turning herself around and unlatching the door.

The old woman who had been in the carriage when she'd entered so many miles ago was now gone. Darkness had descended. Good. She wrapped herself in its cloak as she made her way down the metal stairs and onto the platform.

A few other people milled about the station, but most of the place was quiet. Perfect for her to slip away.

In the distance, the moonlight reflected off a mountain. How different this part of the country was to anything she had ever seen. Mountains. They must be majestic during the day.

After checking all around, she left the platform and scrambled over the coupling between two cars to the far side of the train. She plastered herself against the car and crept down the line, making as little noise as possible.

How was she going to find which boxcar they were in? If they were even still there at all. If they had stayed on the train after Pont-de-Veyle perhaps they jumped off as soon as it halted. They might be well away from here already.

A weight fell on her shoulders, and she fought to draw in a deep, steady breath. They weren't in the first few cars, that much was sure, so she moved down the line several carriages and knocked on the metal side. "Jean-Paul." She kept her voice as low as possible, while still speaking loud enough for anyone inside to hear her.

No sounds. Nothing but the stillness of the night filled the air.

She kept on for a while, banging on several more cars. Each time she did, she sucked in a breath. All the commotion she was making was only drawing attention to herself.

She had to come up with a different plan. This wasn't working. By now, Jean-Paul and the sisters had to be far away. Her throat burned.

No. She shook herself. She wouldn't give up. She wouldn't give in. Crying had never gotten her anywhere. Only by being strong had she overcome so much in her life.

That wouldn't change. Especially not now.

She moved toward the next boxcar.

The gravel behind her crunched.

She spun around. No one was there.

She strode forward.

The footsteps picked up. Closer now. Ever closer.

Now she really couldn't breathe. Whoever it was must hear the blood whooshing in her ears.

"*Arrêtez.*" Stop.

But she had no intention of obeying that command. Instead, she took off on a sprint.

Not fast enough.

He called something to her, but the blood pounded in her ears so hard it drowned out his words.

Whoever was chasing her grabbed her by the arm and pulled her close.

ⵥ CHAPTER TWENTY-FIVE ⵥ

"Nellie, *arrêtez, arrêtez*." Jean-Paul held fast to her. "Hold still. It's me. Jean-Paul."

She relaxed the tiniest of bits.

"I'm here. We're here. And we're so glad we found you in one piece." At his words, she melted into him. "Jean-Paul?"

"*Oui, oui*, it's me."

"Oh, you're here." Her voice shook. "And the others? Are they okay? Are they with you?"

"We're all here."

"Even the children?"

This maddening, headstrong, bull-nosed woman had a soft spot for those little ones. "Even the children. They've been missing you."

He released his hold on her, brushing her hair from her eyes. Those golden-green eyes brimming with unshed tears.

Though he had half a mind to shake some sense into her and scold her for running off the way she did, he couldn't do it. In this moment, even though her hair had come loose from its pins, she had never been more beautiful or vulnerable.

Underneath that gruff exterior, a true heart beat. One that got as frightened as every other human being. One who hurt and loved as much as anyone else.

"What happened?" He kept all traces of accusation from his tone.

"I should have listened to you, but I was mad that you took off and didn't include me. I wanted to see for myself where we were."

"You hate to be left behind."

She nodded, the tears pooling in the corners of her eyes.

"Were you in a different boxcar?"

This time, she shook her head. "I spent the entire trip in the lavatory." The story poured from her, along with those shimmering tears.

He drew her into his arms, his anger and worry melting like snow in summer. Like puzzle pieces coming together, they fit each other, and she sobbed into his dirty, straw-covered shirt.

He hadn't held a woman this way since Simone.

She was so soft. Before this, he would have guessed her to be hard on the outside just like she was on the inside. Actually, neither was true. Her silken hair cascaded through his fingers, and her cheek was smooth as he brushed away her tears. The moonlight fell on her pale face, accentuating the redness of her lips.

Very kissable lips.

He trembled from head to toe, longing to draw her even closer. To touch those amazing lips with his.

With more strength than Hercules, he held her at arm's length. "I'm just glad nothing happened to you. That I found you."

"Me too." She giggled, and he couldn't help but join in her laughter.

Wait. Was that pool of brightness coming from a flashlight? He covered her mouth to stifle her laughter. Again, another difficult task but so necessary.

They stood stock still, moonlight spilling over them. If the guard or whoever was out there moved to this side of the train, there would be no hiding. No way out.

But the circle of light bobbed away from them. After several more long minutes of holding his breath, Jean-Paul finally released it in a rush. He grasped Nellie's delicate hand. "Let's go. The others are waiting for us in the woods a little ways from here. We have to get to Mayor Deffaught's house as soon as possible. Albert is sure to wake up any minute and start to fuss."

"We do need to get the children to a safe place. Wash them up, feed them well, and tuck them into bed. Maybe we all can sleep tonight."

He hustled her along the backside of the train and then into a stand of trees keeping guard over the station. Not too far in, the trees thinned into an opening. There sat the three sisters, each with a child on her lap. As soon as Claire spied her, she jumped from Sister Angelica's hold and raced to Nellie, clasping her around the leg. "Nelwie! Nelwie!"

Nellie knelt on the leaf-carpeted ground and embraced the little girl, who hugged her neck like she might never let go. Nellie did the same.

While it would be wonderful to stay and drink in this scene, they couldn't remain here. They had to get safely inside as soon as possible. Their exposure out here was too great. "Come on. It's not far to the mayor's house. We'll all be glad to get there."

He lent a hand to Sister Raphael and Sister Maria-Theresa to help them stand, and once he had scooped up Claire, he whispered in her ear. "Remember that we are playing hide-and-seek. We don't want anyone to know where we are going, because we don't want them to find us, so you have to be very quiet. Right?"

She touched her lips. "*Shh.*"

"That's it. You're so good at this game. Let's play for a while." He limped off, leading the way to Mayor Deffaught's house. After chasing down Nellie, his ankle was sore. But like he'd told the others, it wasn't far.

As long as they kept their heads down and didn't get noticed by any authorities, they would be fine.

They had to be.

He'd been to Annemasse a few times before, enough to know the back way to Mayor Deffaught's house. They kept blankets over the children's heads. Leo and Claire were quiet enough, but the baby whimpered. The sooner they got there, the better.

They crept through the city, skirting the beautiful town square bordered by three- and four-story eighteenth-century buildings. No need in alerting the authorities that, because it took a while to reconnect with Nellie, they were out beyond curfew.

Just around the corner was the mayor's house. But the hairs on the back of Jean-Paul's neck stood straight, and a chill ran down his spine. He handed Claire, heavy in his arms, to Nellie. "Turn right, and his home is the small white stucco cottage with a red-tiled roof. Tell him I sent you. I'll be along in a few minutes." He limped more.

"We'll wait for you."

"*Non.* If I separate myself from the group I can draw the attention to myself. We need to get the children inside as soon as possible."

"And you, because of your father."

"Just go. Now, before you're spied."

"Hurry." Her voice was husky. "I don't want to leave you."

"Just a matter of minutes."

A moment or two later, they turned the corner and disappeared from his sight. He had almost made it to the bend himself when a shout came from the street.

"You there. What are you doing out this late at night?"

<hr />

Someone strong and beefy pulled Nellie and the others into the house, almost shoving them inside. Then he shut the door and latched it.

"*Bienvenue.* Welcome, welcome." The rotund man with a double chin and a receding hairline flashed Nellie a warm smile that relaxed some of the tight muscles in her shoulders.

"*Merci.* I'm Nellie Wilkerson." She made the rest of the introductions. "Jean-Paul Breslau will be along soon. He was right behind us."

He nodded. "*Oui,* I know him. It will be good to see him again. You can tuck the children into bed. The room is all the way down the hall."

Lord, just keep them quiet.

Nellie led the sisters down the passage to the far bedroom. A window was open to catch the evening breeze, and the lace curtains floated on the soft air.

The bed was large, and the sheet had been pulled back, almost as if the mayor had been expecting them. Or expecting someone, at least.

The four of them got busy nestling the children on the soft mattress, including Albert, Sister Maria-Theresa pulling off their shoes, Sister Angelica tucking the covers around their ears.

Nellie bent over Claire and Leo. "You must go to sleep now."

"Eat. Eat." Claire pouted and attempted to crawl from underneath the sheet.

Nellie pressed her down. "*Non,* you must stay there and sleep. For a little while."

She sat on the edge of the bed and unbraided Claire's hair, running the kinky locks through her fingers to soothe the child. And herself. Jean-Paul would be here any minute. They hadn't come this far only to be caught. She had to remind herself to breathe. To keep calm for the children's sake, even though she strained to hear the opening of the door for Jean-Paul's arrival.

Over and over again, Nellie smoothed Claire's hair, more for her own peace of mind now. Still no Jean-Paul. Claire's breathing had turned soft and steady and even. She slept. Oh, to be young and unaware of the danger surrounding you.

Nellie had lost such innocence on a sweltering Mississippi night so long ago. She could never again see the world through rose-tinted glasses after she'd witnessed the evil men could perpetrate against each other.

Because no matter the passage of the years or the change in location, the evil remained the same.

An evil that pressed on her chest and sent her temples throbbing.

The mayor peeked in. "Jean-Paul isn't here yet. I'll go search for him." Nellie's throat swelled shut. All she could do was nod.

Sister Maria-Theresa came and sat beside her and held her hand. The old woman's dry, knobby fingers touching hers were somehow a comfort. Sister Maria-Theresa's lips moved though no sound came from her mouth. Whatever prayer she prayed, Nellie prayed God would answer it.

After an interminable period of time, the mayor entered the room. Nellie jumped to her feet. Jean-Paul should be right behind him. But he wasn't. She twisted so she could see around him. Perhaps the mayor's girth hid Jean-Paul. But he wasn't there.

"Where is he?"

The welcoming smile that had greeted them had disappeared, replaced by a deep scowl. "I'm afraid the Gestapo has taken your friend to the Hôtel Pax, part of which they have converted to a prison."

Prison. The word alone froze Nellie's heart.

Just when she and Jean-Paul had made a connection, she had lost him. The way he held her at the train station and allowed her to cry, the way he cradled her close, the way he dried her tears and stared at her as if he wanted to kiss her told her more than any words ever could.

He felt something for her. Something she felt for him as well.

Now that she had opened her heart to him, he was ripped from her, a fresh wound gaping in her chest. One among many.

But this one was different. It cut deeper and hurt more than any other. Worse even than the sword that had pierced her the night she discovered that her father was a murderer.

This was as if a wild animal were tearing her arms and legs from her body.

She couldn't lose him now. She wouldn't.

"It seems that a German man was searching for his son and had alerted the authorities here that he might show up in an attempt to cross the border. Seems they were right."

Nellie clamped her lips tight. They knew nothing of this man standing before them. It could be that he himself had tipped off the Nazis and had been lying in wait for Jean-Paul.

The grin returned to his chubby face, though not quite as large as at first. "Don't worry, *ma petite*. Your friend would not be the first one I have rescued from that prison." A cloud passed over his face before it brightened again. "We will get him released."

Sister Raphael approached the mayor. "You have to be quick about it. Once his father arrives, there will be no getting Jean-Paul out."

Why was she sharing this information with a stranger? She could be signing Jean-Paul's death sentence. All of theirs.

Monsieur Deffaught nodded. "I understand. I have a plan in place that I was going to use just last week, but we had to abandon it. My one regret in all of this awfulness." His eyes shimmered, and he bowed his head. "Marianne Cohn gave her life for thirty-two children. If only I could have saved hers."

Marianne Cohn? The woman from the station in L'asile? It couldn't be. No. Jean-Paul would be crushed to learn of her death.

The mayor straightened. "But now is a good time to pull out the plan and use it. I believe it to be a solid one. With Monsieur Breslau's connections and history, the Gestapo won't release him to his father so fast. The Germans will have him on a work detail. They will march him there each day. When they do, we will nab him and hustle all of you over the border."

Nellie's blood flowed through her body again. "You can get him out? You're sure this is going to work?"

"We'll try our very best."

Would it be enough? Would she see Jean-Paul again and get the chance to tell him what he meant to her?

⣿ CHAPTER TWENTY-SIX ⣿

Even though blackout conditions existed, enough moonlight shone that Jean-Paul could make out the Hôtel Pax where the Gestapo was taking him. The brick three-story building wasn't large, just three windows wide on each level, but it sat squat and square overlooking the street. Shutters flanked each window, giving the place an almost homey appearance.

Almost.

Because Jean-Paul had already experienced what happened behind those walls. This was no comfortable residence on the outskirts of Geneva.

It was a place of horror.

He would be lying to say he wasn't shaking from head to toe.

The two Gestapos who arrested him, each dressed in a gray-green uniform, led him into the building, one of them holding a gun that dug into his lower back.

A grand staircase sat in the middle of the open room, sweeping to the second story with a railed balcony ringed with doors. The cells, most likely. The paneled first-floor space featured several doors as well. The third-story dormer ran the length of the room, the skylight illuminating the entire scene.

Nothing like the prison he had been in before. Nothing like it at all. Almost hospitable. Was this due to Deffaught's influence? Perhaps so.

But Jean-Paul wasn't about to allow himself to be swayed by the pleasant interior. He may have been cloistered in an abbey, but even he'd heard about what happened to Marianne Cohn just weeks ago, how she had been arrested with a group of children she was escorting to Switzerland. The Nazis were crowing over it, as if they'd had something to do with her capture. Deffaught had managed to secure the release of some of the children.

Marianne had been executed not far from here.

A chill ran up his spine to the base of his neck, and he shivered.

"Let's go." The beefier guard shoved Jean-Paul forward, toward the stairs, and he stumbled up them.

The smaller soldier grabbed his already bruised arm and led him to one of the doors opposite the second-floor railing. The guard unlocked the door, pushed him inside, and locked the door again.

The fading moonlight filtered in through the barred window in the corner of the room. The size of it wasn't bad at all. He'd been in smaller apartments in Paris. There was enough room for two beds. The mattress was thin, but a blanket sat folded at the end of each bed.

He had no roommate.

Just as well.

He sat on the edge of the bed against the far wall, leaned over, and rubbed his throbbing head.

Would Nellie and the others be safe at Monsieur Deffaught's house? Or had the Gestapo taken them all away?

They must not have been harmed or else they would be here with him. When Marianne was arrested, the children in her care, the very children he had spied at the train station in L'asile, had been taken with her and brought here as well. He glanced around the room once more.

How awful for those kids, to have to try to survive here without a parent to comfort them. The guards said that Marianne did everything in her power to keep them calm and happy. She had been a good woman that way.

He rose and paced the five steps or so that it took to cross the room. *Non.* Not a room. A cell. He turned and did it again. Then again. *Lord, please keep them safe. Watch over them. What happens to me doesn't matter. My earthly father may despise me, but You will never forsake me. Just don't allow him to harm the women and children.*

Vater. How long would it be before he arrived in Annemasse? What sort of punishment—or more likely torture—did he have in mind for his wayward son?

No matter what, Jean-Paul would never give up the women and children. He would never do anything to jeopardize them.

Or had he already done it? Vater must have known he was making a break for the border. That was why the Gestapo was ready and waiting for him. *Non*, he wouldn't even care about the others, wouldn't give them a second thought at this point.

Non. Jean-Paul himself was the prize Vater was after. The only one. He would be the feather in Vater's cap. Capturing him meant bringing down part of the French resistance. With each kilometer the Allies pushed inland, the German's paranoia increased tenfold.

Their little band had almost made it. He had almost been free of Vater forever.

If only. But if onlys didn't change their circumstances.

At some point he lay down and must have dozed off, for the clinking of the key in the lock woke him. He bolted upright and smoothed back his hair. Crazy, really, since it had been days since he'd pulled a comb through it.

The guard, the big one from earlier, stood on the threshold, his frame filling the entryway. Even if Jean-Paul wanted to attempt an escape, there was no room to slip by him.

The soldier glared at Jean-Paul. "Come with me."

No use in pretending he didn't understand German. He came to his feet and followed the Gestapo agent around the balcony to the stairs, then to a door on the first floor. The guard knocked and, without waiting for an answer, opened the door and flung Jean-Paul inside, shutting it behind him.

It was an office. Nothing more than that. A desk. A bookcase. A typewriter. Papers in neat piles on the desk and a gray steel filing cabinet in the corner. One upholstered chair sat behind the desk, two metal ones in front of it.

And sitting behind the desk was an officer, his uniform decorated with iron crosses and an eagle on both the sleeve and his billed cap, his face grim, his mouth downturned. He motioned for Jean-Paul to sit in one of the metal chairs.

He followed the order.

"You know why you are here, Johan Braun?"

"My name is Antoine Duval." The name on his forged identity card.

The Nazi inhaled several very deep breaths and fisted his hands. "Your name is Johan Braun. That is the one you were born with." Each word was measured.

"Antoine Duval."

The German came around the desk and stood in front of Jean-Paul. "I will only ask you one more time. What is your name?"

"Antoine Duval."

Quick as a cat after a mouse, the Nazi struck Jean-Paul on the side of his head.

"What is your name?"

"Antoine Duval."

Another strike to the other side of his head.

"What is your name?"

"Antoine Duval."

This time, the punch was to his nose, snapping his head backward, the sound of bone breaking all he heard. Stars shot in front of his eyes, fireworks of blue and red and green. Blood ran down his face, the metallic taste of it on his tongue. He didn't wipe it away.

"What is your name?" The German's roar filled the small room.

"Antoine Duval."

The beating continued. Each time, the same question. Each time the same answer. Each time the same consequence.

If only the agony would end. Every square centimeter of his head throbbed. But he wouldn't give in. Never, never would he claim his birth name.

The thought of it alone churned his stomach.

He vomited.

And blackness overtook him.

———— ≈ ————

Saturday, July 8, 1944

A soft summer's morning sun teased Nellie's eyelids open. She squinted against the light, one little body pressed against hers on one side and another on the other. Leo and Claire still slumbered, the peaceful sleep of the innocent.

She checked her watch, the black band encircling her wrist, the hands moving along as if all were right in the world. Nellie must have been more tired than she had realized to even get the few hours of sleep that she had. Already, half the morning was gone.

Careful not to wake the children, she slid from between them and padded to the kitchen. No one else was about, but the coffeepot sat percolating on the back burner. After rummaging through several cabinets, she came across a couple of chipped mugs and chose one for the hot ersatz coffee.

Would Switzerland have real coffee? Would they ever make it there?

She shook away the thoughts and sat on the davenport in the living room with her mug. The curtains remained drawn, likely to keep anyone from seeing them in here. Curious eyes could lead to flapping lips.

How had Jean-Paul fared last night? What were they doing to him?

Again, she forced herself to push away the thoughts that sent her leg to bouncing. But even as she stared at the off-white curtains sprigged with red roses, her mind wandered to the Hôtel Pax, where Monsieur Deffaught had said they would likely hold Jean-Paul. How long before his father showed up? Monsieur Deffaught said they had to put their plan in motion before Jean-Paul's father arrived in Annemasse. But was that a matter of hours or of days?

It was sure to be a short amount of time, no matter what. Nellie set aside her hot drink and, after freshening up, checked on the children. They had both awakened but had gotten so good at playing hide-and-seek that they had snuggled under the covers.

The two little lumps wriggled. But Nellie would play along with them. "Where are Claire and Leo? I can't imagine where they've gone to. I'm sure they were here when I left the room."

The blanket muffled their soft giggles.

"Where are you, Claire and Leo? I miss you."

Leo's dark red hair peeked from under the covers, but Claire pulled him back. While it had taken some time and effort to teach her the game, once she knew how to play it, she played it well.

"Maybe I'll sit on the bed and think about this."

As she settled herself beside one of the mounds, more giggling ensued. This time, Claire joined in. The corners of Nellie's mouth turned up, despite her best efforts to contain her mirth.

"If only Leo and Claire were here."

The covers flung back, and Leo and Claire emerged. "*Ici! Ici!*" Claire exclaimed. "Here! Here!"

Now full-scale laughter erupted, both of the children tackling Nellie, the three of them rolling around, howling with laughter, tangling themselves in the sheets.

Nellie glanced up to discover Sister Angelica standing in the doorway, arms crossed, her mouth turned down. Their merriment died away.

"I'm sure you're aware that it's imperative to keep the children quiet." Sister Angelica's words were firm but not scolding.

"They just needed some time to be children. To play and laugh. Although they may not understand exactly what is going on, they know that all is not right with the world. They sense our fear, and it invades their hearts too."

Sister Angelica uncrossed her arms and came to sit beside Nellie on the bed. Leo climbed into her lap, and she snuggled with him. She wasn't heartless. She understood and loved these children as much as Nellie. "It's been hard on everyone. But what else are we to do if we are to save them? If we don't teach them to be quiet, it may cost them their lives."

And ours. The unspoken words hung in the air. "I understand, and I'll try to be more careful from now on." Nellie turned to Claire, only to find a tear tracking down her cheek. She pulled the girl to her. "Hush, hush. No need to cry. You're fine. No one is angry with you. I just forgot how to play hide-and-seek."

Sister Angelica stood, Leo on her hip. "Monsieur Deffaught has returned from getting some bread for us. And he'd like to go over the plan he has for rescuing Jean-Paul when he goes on work detail."

Nellie set Claire on her feet, and hand in hand, they made their way to the kitchen. The dark-haired mayor stood at the counter slicing a fresh loaf. This was one of the best parts about being in France. No one matched them for bread. Even with rationing, they continued to manage to turn out the softest, most yeasty-flavored baguettes and rolls.

Nellie's stomach rumbled. Claire patted it and then her own. She was hungry too.

In short order, Monsieur Deffaught had them all seated at the table with their breakfasts. Somewhere he had even managed to come up with milk for the children. With a great deal of vigor, Albert sucked on his bottle.

Their host stood at the kitchen counter and faced them, his lips drawn into a thin, grim line. "I encountered some disturbing news while I was out. In fact, a number of people confronted me, inquiring about the party that arrived at my house last night."

Nellie dropped the piece of bread she was holding.

"They know we're here?"

"So it seems."

"Then why haven't they come to arrest us as well?"

"I don't have an answer for that. All is know is that we have to act, and we have to act as soon as possible to get Jean-Paul out of prison and all of you across the border. We don't have a moment to lose."

"What if he doesn't start the work detail right away?" Their plan may never get off the ground. And because Jean-Paul and the sisters hadn't given up on her, she refused to give up on him.

"We'll have to pray that he does. Otherwise, you'll be forced to cross without him."

"That's out of the question."

"It's very much a possibility." Monsieur Deffaught turned to the sink to wash the serrated knife.

But it was one option Nellie wouldn't consider. She wasn't going anywhere without Jean-Paul. She hadn't been able to help Mr. Joe. She hadn't been able to save Clarence. But she would do everything to ensure that Jean-Paul crossed that border in one piece.

⧉ CHAPTER TWENTY-SEVEN ⧉

The afternoon wore on, and Nellie's nerves frayed. She chafed at having to stay indoors on this glorious summer day. The sun was bright, and the mountains she spied through the back window beckoned to her.

But here she sat. Monsieur Deffaught was about his business. Hopefully, that included finding a way to get Jean-Paul released. Or putting into motion the escape plan he had outlined.

She circled the small kitchen several times. At least at the convent, they'd had the walled yard where they could enjoy the pleasant days and allow the children to run and be children for a little while. She turned and circled the small room in the other direction.

This wasn't getting her anywhere, so she went to the bedroom where the children all napped. Albert was on the floor, curled in a drawer they had lined with blankets, sucking on his fist, his long eyelashes brushing his cheeks. They weren't as round as they should be, but he did retain some baby fat. The sisters slept in the other room.

As she turned to leave, she spied her camera sitting on top of her suitcase. She had three frames remaining. This might be her last chance to capture shots in Nazi-occupied territory. It was her obligation as a member of the press to record what she could.

To let the world know what was going on here. What Hitler was doing to those he deemed undesirable.

For too long, too many had been silent. She had a chance to give voice to those who were helpless. She couldn't allow it to pass.

She grabbed the camera and slipped from the house. On the streets, people went about their business. A woman with a canvas bag over her arm hustled away from the bakery. An older man in a business suit emerged from the bank. And a group of young girls giggled together on the street corner.

As if the world hadn't gone mad.

As if there weren't people down the street who were being held in prison, their very lives at stake.

Nellie would never be the same. The evil she had experienced at a young age and the evil she was experiencing now permeated even deeper into her soul.

She worked hard to appear to be strolling down the lane without a care in the world, enjoying the sights, drinking in the beautiful buildings from the last centuries in every shade from white to brown. Several of them sported balconies, and on one of the balconies sat an older woman, drinking in the sunshine.

A crisp red-and-peach striped awning covered tables set in front of a café. Farther down the street, a blue awning proclaimed the shop to be PALAIS DU VÊTEMENT. The Clothing Palace. With rationing, there couldn't be much clothing at all in that particular shop. Clutching the camera strap for all it was worth, Nellie drew in a steadying breath and blew it out. Last night, when they had been speaking to Monsieur Deffaught about the plan to get Jean-Paul out of the prison, he had mentioned where the Hôtel Pax was located.

Even with one wrong turn, she arrived at the prison within minutes. She stood in front of the innocuous building, blinking against the sun. This was the place? This was the place of horror? It could have been the home of a well-to-do cotton farmer in Mississippi.

Then she glanced up. Bars crisscrossed the windows on the second floor. No, this was a place of incarceration. A place where, according to Monsieur Deffaught, Marianne Cohn had died just a few short days ago. And where children were being held against their wills.

She lifted the camera to her eyes and peered through the viewfinder. Once she was satisfied with the scene, she depressed the shutter, and the camera clicked.

A brown-shirted officer stepped from the building and stared in her direction. She lowered the camera. He moved in her direction.

She mustered her nonchalance and strode in the opposite direction. She didn't dare turn around to find out if he followed her or not.

Instead, she ducked into the bakery and, with the few coins she possessed, bought a small roll. Not brioche, thanks to the lack of eggs and butter, but still soft. Though her pulse pounded in her neck faster than a drummer in a swing band, she strolled toward a park she had passed on the way here.

As she turned the corner, she glanced behind her. The soldier was still there. She resisted the urge to break into a run, keeping her pace steady. She entered the park and found a bench where she sat and bit into the roll. Very nearby was Switzerland. From this vantage point, if she squinted, she could pretend she could glimpse it. So close and yet so far. Someday, perhaps, people would stroll over the border. Live in one country and work in the other.

But that day wasn't today.

She swung her attention between her bread and a group of girls playing jump rope. Just as she and June had played, skipping and singing little songs, the lilt of them the rhythm of childhood.

And then a figure in brown stepped in front of her, obscuring her view. Blotting out the happy image. She peered at him through her lashes. He was younger than he had appeared, the scars from his acne still deep. "*Bonjour.*" She kept the word as sweet as Southern tea.

"*Bonjour, madame.*"

They stared at each other for a moment. Nellie took another bite and chewed, the bread dry in her mouth. She forced herself to swallow. Best to get this over with as soon as possible. "Can I help you?"

"You took a picture of the Hôtel Pax."

"I was only admiring it and thinking what a nice picture it would be. It's such a charming building and reminds me of home. I have a job in the bank here, but I'm from near Paris originally."

He raised one blond eyebrow. "You don't sound like it."

She bit the inside of her cheek. Her French teacher had always told her she still had an accent. And Jean-Paul had told her the same. She'd said too much. "We moved quite a bit."

"Give me your camera."

"*Pourquoi?*"

"Because I told you to."

"I don't understand."

"You were taking pictures of a prison."

"I wasn't taking any pictures."

"Identification." The soldier's face hardened and aged him ten years.

She pursed her lips as she dug her ID card from her pants pocket and handed it to him.

"You aren't dressed for working in a bank."

Drat. Her clothes. Mama always told her she should wear dresses more, that it would get her in trouble one day. Mama meant that she wouldn't be able to find herself a man to marry. She never would have imagined that it might land her daughter in prison. She must be frantic with worry by now. "I'm sorry. I'm new here and didn't know what that building was. I promise you, I didn't take any photographs."

He handed her booklet, the one she had forged, back to her. "The camera."

She couldn't allow him to take it. The pictures it contained were meant to show the world what was happening over here. "*S'il vous plaît, monsieur,* I beg you not to take my camera." She drew on her Christmas pageant acting experience. "My mother died not long ago. The last pictures of her are on this film. They mean everything to me." She dug her fingernails into her palms so hard that the tears she produced were real. "*Je suis désolé.*"

"Surely you have a mother. What if this were the only thing you had left of her? Show me some kindness. I would be bereft if I couldn't have these photographs."

The young man's face softened. He stared at something behind her, then redirected his attention to her. "Very well. But I had better not see you with this camera again. Is that understood? Next time, there will not be leniency."

"*Merci.* You are very kind." She wrapped her roll in the waxed paper, stood, turned her back to him, and strode away has if her heart weren't threatening to vacate her chest.

As soon as she turned the corner and was out of the man's sight, she broke into a run. Sweat ran down her face, plastering her hair to her cheeks. She couldn't breathe. Her lungs and her throat burned.

Despite the stitch in her side, as soon as Monsieur Deffaught's little house came into view, she picked up her pace and flew through the front door, slamming it and locking it behind her.

Sister Maria-Theresa came in from the kitchen, drying her hands on a dish towel. "What is the matter, child?"

Nellie raced into her arms, holding her as if that would make the world right. "I can't do this anymore."

"*Ma chère*, what can't you do?"

"This. I was almost arrested today. Again. Jean-Paul has been captured. If they killed that woman, what might they do to him? This is too much. The evil in the world is too great to overcome."

Sister Maria-Theresa allowed Nellie to sob for a while longer. When her cries softened to little hiccups, she handed her a handkerchief and led her to the davenport. "I know sometimes it can be so difficult to see the light for all the darkness. But if you peer hard enough, you will discover it. It's there."

"You're wrong. It's been snuffed out."

"Jesus said, 'These things I have spoken unto you, that in me ye might have peace. In the world ye shall have tribulation: but be of good cheer; I have overcome the world.' That's what we need to trust in right now. He promised us tribulation. That's to be expected. But He also promised that it will not last. He will defeat evil once and for all."

Nellie wiped her face with the handkerchief, a whiff of roses coming from it. "I wish He would hurry up about it."

Sister Maria-Theresa chuckled. "Me too. Ah, the heaviness of this world presses so on my shoulders and my chest. But the peace that God has promised keeps that weight from crushing me."

"How can that be?"

How was Maria-Theresa to answer Nellie's question? It was one that had plagued mankind since sin had entered the world. How can one have peace in the midst of great trial and sorrow?

She smoothed Nellie's hair from her sweaty brow. "Let me tell you a story.

"Growing up, we were very poor. Life was so difficult. Both of my parents had to work in order to keep food on the table and a roof over our heads. I was too small to be left alone, so they entrusted me to my aunt and uncle.

"My aunt was a harsh woman." The recollection brought a shudder. "But her abuse of me was nothing compared to what my uncle did." She barely whispered the words. Trembling overtook her, and she drew in a ragged breath. "No one should do that to a seven-year-old child. He had no right to steal my innocence."

"Oh, *je suis désolé.*"

"I told my parents. He said not to say anything, but I told anyway. They never sent me back to that house, but every time I slept, I had nightmares. Awful, horrible dreams. I couldn't eat. I couldn't laugh or play. He stole my childhood.

"Even though my parents were Protestant, they sent me to live at St. Roch. It was their last hope for me. And within the walls there, I found peace."

Nellie nodded. "It is a beautiful, quiet setting, away from the world and its troubles."

"That is not what brought me my peace. That was the work of Jesus alone. He healed my broken, wounded heart. Oh, I will bear the scars of what happened for the rest of my life. But I am no longer terrified. I no longer hurt as much as I once did. Because He has overcome the world.

"One day soon, my tribulations will end, and I will enter into eternal life and peace. In the meantime, I remember what Jesus said through Paul. 'Be not overcome of evil, but overcome evil with good.' And that's what you're doing. It's the right thing. Because Jesus defeated sin and evil at the cross, even if things don't work out in this life, we have the next. Hold on to that."

She patted Nellie's hand and went to stand, but Nellie pulled her down again. "So what we're doing, the danger we are in, is worth it?"

Maria-Theresa opened her mouth to answer, but just then, Claire rushed into the room and flung herself onto Nellie's lap, a squeal of glee filling the room.

Maria-Theresa smiled. The Lord had provided the answer in a much more concrete way than just words. "Look into Claire's eyes. The answer lies there."

A solitary tear trickled down Nellie's fair cheek. "You are so right. What we are doing is good, no matter the cost. With God's help, we will overcome the evil of this world."

"He will overcome it, child. It won't be long, and this will be over. He will not allow Hitler to rule forever." Now Maria-Theresa did come to her feet and went to the kitchen.

She leaned against the stove for support. All of these years, only her parents had known the truth behind the reason for her coming to live at the convent at such a tender age. And now Nellie.

Thank You, Père, that she didn't condemn me. Perhaps she didn't even fully understand what I was saying, but it was enough. Grant her the same peace You have granted me these many years.

Her strength waned. A sharp pain shot through her chest and down her arm.

The call came.

And she answered it, surrounded by unspeakable peace.

⫶ CHAPTER TWENTY-EIGHT ⫶

The day's dying rays filtered through the bars of Jean-Paul's prison cell. Throughout the long hours, he had stared through the window, watching the city pass in front of him, as if the people didn't have a care in the world.

And perhaps they didn't. Likely very few of them were fighting to get three very special children across the border before his father discovered them and eliminated them.

Non, eliminated was too clinical, too sterile of a word.

He wanted to kill them. Destroy them.

And everyone associated with them.

That included Nellie.

How had she managed to worm her way into his heart in such a short amount of time? Especially since she was one of the most exasperating women on the planet.

He grinned, then winced, his face still sore from the beating. In fact, a headache had plagued him all day. And his nose throbbed.

He sighed.

Earlier this afternoon, he had been sure he had spotted Nellie outside of the building with her camera. But that would have been crazy. They would be in hiding. Tucked away and safe from Vater. She would never risk her life and the lives of so many others by being out.

Would she?

And the photographs she carried were too precious. Especially the one. It had to make it across the border along with the children.

Then again, she was too stubborn and headstrong for her own good.

She would do her own thing. Once more he grinned, smaller this time so it didn't hurt so much.

That was what attracted him to her. If she weren't so brave and fearless, she wouldn't be Nellie. And these feelings that had implanted themselves in him wouldn't be sprouting and leafing out.

His stomach rumbled. How long had it been since he'd had a good meal? A very, very long time. He spun around, the room swirling. With a plunk, he sat on his bed and prayed for the pain to go away.

A short time later, as the shadows lengthened on the stained, urine-soaked floor in front of him, the door opened, and a tray with a thin bowl of soup and a cup of what was probably supposed to pass as coffee was slid to him. A moment later, the door slammed shut, the keys grating in the lock.

At least there had been no more interrogations since this morning, no more beatings. Surely Vater was already in the city. If not now, very soon. Though Jean-Paul carried the false identity card that Nellie had crafted with such expert care, they already knew who he was. Who his father was. And would not have hesitated in sending him the location of his son.

Jean-Paul slurped as much of the soup and coffee as he could before weariness descended on him. Just as he lay down and allowed his eyelids to flutter shut, the door opened again.

A bonus meal?

He could only be so blessed.

"Come with me."

This was a different guard from yesterday. He was tall and lean, his muscles bulging beneath his immaculate gray shirt. Not a hair was out of place, and his sideburns were perfectly even.

He led Jean-Paul down the wide staircase to the same room he'd been in yesterday. The officer pushed him into the metal chair and seated himself across the desk. He tented his fingers and stared narrow-eyed at him. "I hope that a day of reflection has changed your mind about the question we asked you."

"What question would that be?"

"Your identity." The man was the embodiment of patience.

"You know what my papers say. Why do you continue to ask me?"

"Because we know the truth."

He did. Which was what made this line of questioning even more ridiculous. "Again, why do you ask me if you already know?"

"Because we want to hear it confirmed with our own ears."

"I cannot confirm anything that isn't the truth. My name is the one on my card. I can tell you nothing else."

The man waved his hand. "It is of little consequence to us. We know who you are, Johan Braun. Tomorrow, you will go out on work detail with the other prisoners. When you return, your father will be here waiting for you. I don't envy you having to face his wrath."

Jean-Paul's throat closed, and he fought for breath. Vater wouldn't allow him to slip through his fingers a second time. His punishment would be swift and sure. The same men who had claimed Marianne Cohn's life a few days ago would claim his tomorrow.

The soldier sneered. "I don't think there's any need for a beating today. The pain in your heart should be quite enough, I believe." He scraped back his chair and returned Jean-Paul to his cell.

The officer wasn't wrong. A parent's betrayal had to sting more than anything in the world. If he couldn't trust the man who had fathered him, whom could he trust?

What had he been thinking when he had allowed his mind to explore the possibility of a future with Nellie? He didn't know her at all. They had barely met.

His heart screamed at him that she was different.

His head told him to tread with caution.

What did it matter though? By this time tomorrow, Vater would be here. His life would be over.

In God I will praise His word, in God I have put my trust; I will not fear what flesh can do unto me.

The verse Mère had drilled into him as a child surfaced. Her voice was as clear as if she sat beside him in this tiny room.

Could he do it? Could he trust God, even with his very life?

He didn't have a choice. He was backed into a corner. There was no one else to trust. No one else who could help him out of this situation. No one else who could bring him to heaven tomorrow.

And so, through the very long hours of the night, he bowed his head and spent his final night on this earth communing with his faithful Heavenly Father.

———— ≈ ————

The thump from the kitchen startled Nellie from her moment with Claire. She jumped from the davenport and raced to the kitchen. Sister Maria-Theresa lay in a heap on the floor.

"Sister! Sister!" Nellie's screams grated over her vocal chords. She knelt beside the elderly woman whose face was as gray as a Mississippi winter sky. She felt for a pulse, but there was nothing.

"Help! Help!"

Sister Angelica and Sister Raphael bolted into the room. "Oh. Oh." Sister Raphael knelt beside Nellie. Sister Angelica crossed herself, and her lips moved in prayer.

Tears burned Nellie's eyes, then fell freely down her face. "I think she's. . ."

Sister Raphael pulled Nellie into an awkward side hug. "She is at peace."

Strange that Sister Raphael would use that word mere moments after Sister Maria-Theresa had spoken to Nellie about that very subject.

Peace. The freedom from all that is evil. Now Sister Maria-Theresa had it in abundance. For the rest of them, it remained elusive.

"Go on." Sister Angelica nodded at Nellie. "Claire is wondering what is happening. Take her to the bedroom and keep her occupied. We'll tend to Sister Maria-Theresa until Monsieur Deffaught returns home. We can't go out and call for the undertaker ourselves. We can only pray that he knows someone he can trust."

Nellie rose and went to Claire, who swiped at Nellie's tears. "*Non, non.*"

Oh, if Claire only understood. How could Nellie explain to her what had happened and that she wouldn't be able to play with Sister Maria-Theresa anymore? "I'm sad, *ma chére.*"

Claire hugged her tight and then sang her very own version of "Frère Jacques." The song brought fresh tears to Nellie's cheeks. Very often, she and June had sung this very ditty to Velma. In English, of course, but the same melody.

They sang it to her after Mr. Joe died, to keep her calm and to distract her from everyone else's grief on that hot, miserable night. And now Claire sang it to Nellie on another miserable day.

Oh Lord, I need that peace right now. The hope that Sister Maria-Theresa is with You and that her suffering is over at last.

Nellie spent the rest of the afternoon in the back bedroom, keeping all three children occupied, happy, and quiet. As soon as Monsieur Deffaught returned home, she took Albert, instructed the other two to play with the dolls, and hurried to the front room.

He stood beside Sister Maria-Theresa's body, washed and laid out on the davenport. The wrinkles were gone from her face, and a slight smile graced her lips.

Darkness filled the little house, and they only lit a single lamp. No one ate much for dinner, including the children. Albert was fussy. They sensed that all was not right in the house.

Sister Angelica sat in a kitchen chair next to Sister Maria-Theresa, holding vigil, praying, and keeping Claire from trying to wake up the elderly nun.

Despite the great sorrow and heaviness in the room, Nellie pulled Monsieur Deffaught to the side. "Were you able to find out anything about Jean-Paul? Can we put the plan into place?"

He nodded, his jowls jiggling. "I visited the prison this afternoon. They didn't allow me to see Jean-Paul, but they did inform me that he would be heading out to a work detail in the morning."

"That's perfect." Maybe something would go their way.

"We'll have to see. My informant told me that his father is on his way here."

"His father? How did he discover he was here? He had the identity papers I forged for him." Maybe they hadn't been good enough. She refused to allow herself to contemplate any other reason he would reveal his true name.

"Never underestimate these Nazis. Especially a Nazi father with a wayward son."

"What will happen if his father arrives before Jean-Paul is taken out to work?"

"We'll have to pray that doesn't happen. If he does, there will likely be no getting him out."

"What time does the train arrive in the morning?"

"Early. Just about the time they march the work detail through the city's streets. It's going to be close."

"We will be successful." Though she imbued her voice with confidence, her insides still quivered. They had to make this work. There was no other way.

"But Sister Maria-Theresa's death is a good thing. It will provide us the perfect opportunity to get you and the children over the border." He outlined how he envisioned that would work.

Warmth filled Nellie's chilled heart. Even in death, Sister Maria-Theresa was helping them. She would be pleased. "That means we only have one chance to rescue Jean-Paul."

"Most likely. We'll hold the funeral late tomorrow afternoon. By this time tomorrow, Lord willing, you should be in Switzerland."

So many moving pieces had to fall into place to make that happen. How could it ever? Yet here was a good and honorable man willing to risk his life to help a group of strangers.

Jean-Paul was another man who did what was right even when it might cost him his life. He'd been imprisoned once before, but he hadn't let that stop him from jumping back into the work, even knowing firsthand what the consequences might be.

Perhaps there were those who were good in this world. Not good in and of themselves, but good because they reflected the light of Christ in the midst of this choking darkness.

Nellie settled Leo and Claire into bed and volunteered for the night shift of the wake. The house went quiet, and a stillness settled over it.

Once everyone else had retired, Nellie pulled up a chair and situated herself beside Sister Maria-Theresa's body. She held the nun's cold hand. "I don't know how to begin to thank you for everything you've done for us. For me in particular. You took in a bedraggled pair, showered us with love, and cared for our needs. You always put others before yourself. I can't imagine the pain you suffered as a young child, but you triumphed through it all.

"And today, with some of your very last words, you comforted me. Showed me a truth I have been blind to for most of my life. If you could overcome what your uncle did to you at such a tender age, I can too."

Nellie drew in a ragged breath in an effort to hold her tears at bay. Sister Maria-Theresa at last had everything she had ever wanted. That was a cause for rejoicing. "You showed me a better way to live. I can never repay that debt."

She leaned closer, as if sharing a secret with the sister. "You were right about everything you said. Evil no longer has a stranglehold on you. And it doesn't have to have one on me either. Light will always prevail. It chases away the darkness, banishing it, warming those around it.

"Tomorrow is going to be a difficult day. Everything is going to have to go just right for this to work. But you know what? I believe it will. This time, evil will not win."

At some point during the night, Nellie nodded off, her dreams taking her to a field full of wildflowers, their brilliant colors more vibrant than any technicolor movie, their fragrance sweeter than the finest French perfume. Overhead, a chorus of birds serenaded her.

And beside her, his hand in hers, was Jean-Paul. They stood together, side touching side, and lifted their faces to the cerulean sky and the streaming sunshine.

She turned to Jean-Paul. "Let's never leave."

He smiled at her, a look that took her breath away for the love it contained. "Never, never."

"Nellie. Nellie." Someone shook her shoulder.

She jolted from the vision to discover Monsieur Deffaught shaking her awake. She rubbed her eyes. "What time is it?"

"It's time to go."

⟨ CHAPTER TWENTY-NINE ⟩

Sunday, July 9, 1944

The thin gruel that Jean-Paul's captors fed him for breakfast did nothing to calm the rumbling in his stomach. Hopefully they fed the children arrested with Marianne better than they fed him. His gut told him that was not the case.

During the night, he'd heard several of the smaller ones crying, probably part of Marianne's group. They must have been frightened. If only he could have gone to them and held them to comfort them. He'd spoken to them through the thin walls, encouraged them, told them that their parents would want them to be brave; but he was a stranger, so his words mattered little to them.

The light at his window was still weak and dim when the guard opened his door. "Time for work. *Schnell, schnell.*"

Having no idea where he was going or what he was going to be doing, he left his cell and followed the lanky soldier down the hall. The guards had a group of men and women congregated at the bottom of the staircase. Some were ragged and thin while others were plumper and their clothes, though worn, were still tidy. They turned to him, eyes wide. He returned their stares.

The guards roamed the room, their gazes never leaving the group. But they didn't herd them anywhere. Jean-Paul turned to the man beside him, shifting his weight from one foot to the other. "What are we waiting for? Where are we going?"

One of the guards, a man old enough to be his father or grandfather, held his rifle higher. "Silence. Prisoners are not to speak."

The guard resumed his pacing. The man beside Jean-Paul leaned over and spoke in a whisper. "Sometimes to the hotel kitchen." He straightened as the guard peered in their direction. "Sometimes to dig ditches near the woods."

Word around the prison had been that Marianne was beaten to death in the forest with shovels. The pieces were fitting together. If he survived this, he would be able to tell what he knew. Like Nellie, he would share a story with the world.

And then little footsteps filled the space. Many of them. There had been thirty-two with Marianne. She and Monsieur Deffaught had secured the release of some of them. But not all. At least, that was what his fellow prisoners told him when they spoke through the walls late at night.

Those who remained marched across the balcony and down the stairs. Jean-Paul turned to his compatriot. "They work too?"

"They what?" The man's voice carried over even the noise of the children.

"I said quiet." The guard marched closer to Jean-Paul, his face a paper's width away, his breath stinking of coffee and last night's garlicky meal.

Before Jean-Paul could reply, the old man struck him on the side of the head with his rifle butt. Bright lights exploded in front of Jean-Paul's eyes. He staggered backward. Pain ripped through his already throbbing head.

Though his vision blurred and he swayed, he managed to stay upright. The poor children had been through enough. He pulled his handkerchief from his pants pocket and, barely touching his tender temple, wiped away the blood. He smiled just a little, just to the brink of agony.

"That is what happens when our orders aren't obeyed. Didn't you learn anything from what we did to that woman and the others last week?" At the guard's words, silence descended. No child even whimpered.

Why had he said anything? They might retaliate against the children or the man beside him.

He stared at his scuffed and mud-covered boots.

"Be careful. People need you." The words were barely audible.

How did this fellow prisoner know? They hadn't met until ten minutes ago.

People need you. People need you. The words reverberated in Jean-Paul's head. The four women and three children might need his help across the border. To carry things. To get them out of trouble if things went wrong. To help them once they were on the other side.

Did Nellie need him? She was a self-sufficient woman. One who would try to take on the world, given the chance. But she carried precious photographs. Pictures that had to make it into the hands of the Allied press.

She might need his help to do it, stubborn though she was.

People—seven of them in particular—needed him. They had come to trust him. What a position to be in. He couldn't let them down. How he would do it remained the big question. But he would find a way out of here. And he would help them.

Whether or not Nellie wanted or needed it.

"Let's go." A younger, more strapping officer barked this order. "Move out."

Three guards herded the children across the street. Jean-Paul had just exited the prison when the last of them disappeared into the hotel. A kitchen was a dangerous place for an eight- or ten-year-old. Perhaps the chef was kind to them and took pity on them.

The remaining guards, maybe a half dozen or so, marched the group of twenty men and women down the street. They must be headed to dig ditches today. If he was going to make an escape attempt, that would be better. It would be much easier to disappear from an outdoor work detail than from a kitchen.

Then up ahead, he spied her. The summer sun, now above the horizon, set her hair ablaze, streaking it red. She had tied a blue bandana around her neck.

What on earth was Nellie doing here? Most likely she had come up with some kind of crazy plan. Wait. A shadow lurked behind her, tucked between two buildings up ahead. Could that be Monsieur Deffaught?

Had God answered Jean-Paul's prayers so fast?

He wriggled his way from the middle of the pack to the edge, careful not to snag the sight of any of the guards. They were approaching the spot where he had spotted Monsieur Deffaught. Nellie strolled alongside the group, a basket swinging from her arm, as if she were on her way to the market.

Much as he wanted to stare at her, she kept her gaze straight ahead, and he followed suit. His mouth had gone dry, and all sound around him had muffled, drowned out by the pounding in his ears.

All of a sudden, on the other side of the street, there was Sister Raphael, her slight form unmistakable to him. She crumpled to the ground, screaming. Time slowed as he turned to go to her, fighting through the group.

But he couldn't move. Someone held him back. A large someone with a tight grip.

Jean-Paul glanced over his shoulder. Monsieur Deffaught. "Come."

"But—"

"*Rapide.*"

Jean-Paul stepped from the flowing crowd and toward the narrow alley where the mayor had been hiding.

Almost there. Almost free. An answered prayer.

Then a booming, commanding voice. "Where are you taking my son?"

Vater. He had arrived.

———— ≈ ————

Nellie pressed against the glass of the *boulangerie* window where she had ducked inside, awaiting the work detail. Her breath hitched when Jean-Paul's father's commanding voice echoed down the road. This had been a possibility. A very real one. They had prayed so long and hard that they would be able to get to him before the train arrived this morning.

But that wasn't the case.

From the other side of the road, Sister Raphael screamed louder. Her diversion wouldn't work now. Jean-Paul's father had spotted him. Knowing everything Jean-Paul had told her about the man, he wouldn't be dissuaded.

He approached Monsieur Deffaught and Jean-Paul, his strides long, the angles of his face hard. Now was Nellie's chance. The mayor would have to hold off Jean-Paul's father, if at all possible. The mayor had size on his side. From the way he filled out his officer's uniform, Jean-Paul's father had the advantage in strength.

Nellie burst out of the boulangerie, dropping her basket on the way out. She raced toward Jean-Paul, tugged his arm, and pulled him away from the scene.

"He's getting away." Jean-Paul's father had a voice even deeper than his son's.

"Now, now." Monsieur Deffaught's voice was calm and steady. He must be blocking the Nazi's progress. "What is this all about? Do you know that young man?"

"He's my son. And I've come here to arrest him."

By now, Nellie and Jean-Paul were far enough away that she couldn't make out Monsieur Deffaught's answer. A moment later, though, came his cry. "Hey, hey. Why are you after him?"

"Run, run." Nellie's breaths heaved in and out.

"I'm trying."

She glanced sideways at Jean-Paul. His face was bruised and battered. What had they done to him? "We can't stop."

"I know. But don't get yourself arrested."

"I'm not going to let you go." If she could slow her pace, she would. To do so would mean certain capture.

They approached the small woods they had seen from the train station. The heavy footfalls of jackboots continued behind them.

Jean-Paul was panting. More and more, she pulled him along, encouraging him to keep going by squeezing his hand.

"I can't."

"You can, and you will." She managed to keep the tremor from her voice. In fact, her own lungs cried out for air, but she couldn't stop. It would mean death for both of them.

Any moment, she expected a searing pain in her back when a bullet hit her. But none came. Wasn't Jean-Paul's father armed? Or was there some humanity in him, enough that he wouldn't kill his son?

They stepped into the thicket. Different from the kind of trees they had in the South, yet so much the same with branches and dead leaves and bushes that pricked arms and legs.

She zigged and she zagged, all in an effort to throw his father off their trail. After a while, the cracking of twigs behind them quieted, then stopped altogether. She kept going, circling around the small copse, slower and slower, though, because of Jean-Paul. Between his ankle and his face, he had been through an ordeal. At last, they halted. He collapsed against a tree, his breathing rapid, blood oozing from his temple.

"Sit here." She took off the bandana she had around her neck and dabbed at the jagged cut. "What happened?"

"Beating because I wouldn't tell them my name." He winced when she applied the cloth to his wound again. "Rifle butt today because I asked about the children working."

She sat back on her haunches. "The children?"

"Marianne's children, the ones who weren't released. They work in the hotel kitchen."

Her heart pinched. Another batch of young ones forced to grow up far too fast. "That's terrible. Maybe we can get them out and over the border with us."

"*Non.* There's no way we're going to get that many out. Perhaps with Georges or Marcel's help, Monsieur Deffaught can come up with a plan." He leaned against the tree and closed his eyes. "When do we cross?"

"This afternoon."

One eye popped open. "So fast?"

"You're a fugitive. And the timing works."

He quirked his eyebrow.

Nellie swallowed hard and pinched the bridge of her nose to hold the ever-threatening tears at bay. "Sister Maria-Theresa died yesterday."

"What?"

"A heart attack or a stroke or something. Fast." Nellie bit the inside of her lip. "Even in death, though, she's helping us. The funeral is the perfect opportunity to get over the border. The sooner, the better."

"*Oui,* I know what you're talking about. Georges has used that tactic a couple of times in the past. It's risky, but we can't send the kids over by themselves to fetch a ball."

"I was supposed to take you to a church, *L'église Protestante Unie,* to wait for the funeral. There are mourning clothes left for us, but we can't go there now. It's just down the street from the prison."

He furrowed his brow. "My mind is muddled, but that might not be the worst idea. Vater saw me disappear into these woods. That's where he'll search. He'll never think to look a few doors down from the Hôtel Pax."

"We're just going to march down one of the main streets in Annemasse in broad daylight?" This man had gone cuckoo. That head injury must really be affecting him.

"I'll keep my head down. We'll stay to back roads. Everyone is busy here. We have to go. Now." He struggled to his feet, steadying himself against the tree.

She reached out and stroked his cheek with the lightest of touches. "I'm worried about you. Can you do this?"

He mimicked her actions, his touch like a whisper of wind. "Together, we can. In a few hours, I can rest. Until then, I'll stay strong, but only if you're with me. I want you beside me."

The air was heavy with unspoken words. Things they couldn't say right now. Not when they were hunted. "Then let's go. You can lean on me."

"I plan on it."

⚡ CHAPTER THIRTY ⚡

The old, small church, alive with worshippers this morning, was now dark and rather musty, and as Nellie sat on a chair beside Jean-Paul, she shivered. Not really cold. Just...

"Don't think too much about it." He leaned against her.

"I'm trying. But it's hard. So much has happened in the past few days."

"I miss her too."

"When my father and the other Klan members killed Mr. Joe, I thought my world had come to an end. But it went on. More complicated than before, but it continued. I know it will now too, no matter what the outcome. Sister Maria-Theresa talked to me about overcoming. And we will. One way or another."

"You have some of her spirit in you."

The shiver ceased, replaced with a warmth that had nothing to do with the heat of the day. "I'm sorry about your father."

"Long ago, I had to come to terms with our relationship. Or the lack of it. He sees me as a pawn in his Third Reich game. That's all I am to him. He can be nothing in Hitler's eyes when he has a traitorous son."

"Even with Germany's end in sight?"

"They don't see it that way. Hitler is using propaganda to persuade his people to continue fighting, to never give up. Not until the Allies are on the Reichstag's doorstep will he admit defeat."

"What about your mother?"

"She is a fabulous woman. I have never felt neglected or that I had less than my brother. All I ever felt was loved and cherished. I hope you get to meet her someday."

"I would like that very much. She sounds incredible. She must be to have raised a son like you."

"She should have never married my father. How could she have been so blind to the monster he is?"

"He must have charmed her. Men can be very persuasive, especially when young women are involved. It's the only reason I can think of why my mother and father ended up together. And then she turned a blind eye to what he was doing all those years. She wasn't strong."

"Mama was young. And innocent. And even though he shattered that the day he walked out on her, somehow she continues to maintain this naivete about her. Something pure and beautiful. Something I see in you."

No one had ever said anything quite like that to her. No one had ever thought her beautiful. Her father talked about her wide forehead, telling her she had too many brains. Her mother told all her friends it was a shame that Nellie was short and stubby.

"Nellie?"

"I don't know what to say."

"I only tell the truth."

"Not to certain people you don't."

"To you, always."

"You are blind."

He leaned closer to her. "I see very clearly. And in front of me is a beautiful woman who has a heart to match. That is the truth. One I want you to know and believe in case. . ."

In case the worst happened. That was why he was being so nice to her. They were in a life and death situation. How sweet that he was trying to make her feel better.

"What time is it?" He winced as he shifted positions in one of the pastor's chairs.

She glanced at her watch, the one that continued ticking in spite of everything she had gone through. "Just a little while longer. Does your head hurt much?"

"I'm trying not to think about it. I'm more worried about the kids."

"I know you are. That makes you a beautiful person too." It didn't matter if he was talking about the ones in prison or their little group. He cared about them all.

Funny how she had to travel to war-torn France to find a man who did.

"I'm very tired." His yawn was cavernous. "Do you mind if I lean against you and try to sleep a little?"

"You can't sleep." She shouted the words, then covered her mouth. "I mean, you might have a concussion. No closing your eyes until we get you checked out by a doctor. As soon as we get to Geneva."

"Then you have to keep talking, or I will fall asleep."

"How about you do some of the jabbering? Tell me more about your mother."

"She's a hard worker, or she was until she started having back problems a couple of years before the war. She is an artist. Did I ever tell you that?"

"An artist? Like a painter?"

He nodded, then sucked in a breath. "She paints landscapes for a living, mostly ones around our home. Even though her colleagues told her she needed to be in Paris if she wanted to earn more money, she was happier in the countryside. She has always seen the world as beautiful and full of light."

"A picture of hope."

"Much like the one you carry with you."

"Claire's picture is a little different. That one is about the hope of survival in the darkest of times."

"Not so different. Her paintings give people hope in the worst of times. They can look at her work and, for a moment, they are lifted from their circumstances. And our hope is that people will look at your picture of Claire and it will give them hope that they will overcome despite the evil in this world."

Nellie couldn't help but smile. "You should be a poet."

"Maybe that is what I will do after the war. And you will go home." He didn't ask. Just stated a fact.

"I'm not convinced I will. I've never felt as alive as I have since I've been in France, even though I'm on the run for my life. The only thing that would make me return to America is Velma. And June. They need me."

"Then you must go to them."

That would mean leaving Jean-Paul. And Claire. How could she do that? Yet the *Tribune* would expect her to pick up her war correspondence work again. They could assign her anywhere.

She glanced at her watch once more, then nodded at Jean-Paul. "It's time to go."

———————≋———————

As they neared the *Cimetière d'Ambilly*, which hugged the border with Switzerland, Jean-Paul and Nellie were met by a funeral procession of thirty or more people. Monsieur Deffaught had come up with quite a number of mourners on such short notice.

In the crowd, he spotted Sister Angelica, dressed in black, wearing a hat with a black veil that covered her face. She carried Albert, wrapped in a black blanket, cradled against her chest. Sister Raphael, dressed similarly, led Claire and Leo by the hand. A veiled hat perched on Claire's head, sliding a little to the left.

A few women on the street, lines marring their still-young faces, babies clutched to their breasts, little ones clinging to their hands, watched the solemn procession. Jean-Paul and Nellie blended in with the mourners.

Like toys placed in strategic positions, German soldiers stood scattered about, each with a keen eye on the gathered group. Jean-Paul took note of them, scanning the area for any sight of Vater.

He was sure to be livid and wouldn't rest until he had his son, his own flesh and blood, in custody.

Lord, blind his eyes.

Jean-Paul pulled his borrowed black hat farther over his eyes and kept his head down but his gaze up. He slunk to the middle of the procession, Nellie moving with him.

"I don't see him. I'll stay right by your side to block sight of your bruises."

Always thinking ahead. Another of her admirable qualities.

The afternoon sun was strong as they approached the cemetery. Beneath his dark clothing, perspiration dampened his underarms. As soon as they were safe in Switzerland, he would need a bath.

Six elderly men lofted Sister Maria-Theresa's casket onto their shoulders, her slight weight nothing to them. Jean-Paul's throat burned. She had been a good woman. Wise and upright. Though she had never said anything to him about it, her demeanor bespoke a hard childhood. One, as Nellie had mentioned earlier, she had overcome.

Albert whimpered in Sister Angelica's arms, and she jiggled him to keep him quiet. Sister Raphael held fast to Leo, but Claire tugged free from her hold and clung to Nellie.

They came to the walled cemetery, the brown stone of it as somber as the group that approached. The iron gates stood open, ready and waiting for them, as heaven's gates had stood open, ready and waiting for Sister Maria-Theresa yesterday.

Claire begged to be lifted, and Nellie took her up in her arms. Like a school of fish huddled together, they moved as one body toward the back of the cemetery. A wall rose next to the spot dug for Sister Maria-Theresa's body.

And beyond that wall lay Switzerland.

He forced himself to keep breathing and to keep his attention away from the fact that freedom lay mere meters away. There, Leo, Claire, and Albert would soon be able to live in the open and be children. Perhaps one day they would be reunited with their parents.

Except for Claire. She was alone in this world. He flicked his gaze to Nellie. Well, maybe not quite alone. But what would become of her when Nellie returned to the newspaper and the assignments that were sure to be waiting for her?

The Protestant minister opened his little black Bible, the pages well worn with the years. He read a passage of scripture from the book of Psalms and then spoke to those gathered.

But no matter how hard Jean-Paul tried, he couldn't keep his concentration on what the minister said. A heavy weight pressed on his shoulders and on his chest. A presence that wasn't visible but that was as tangible as the ground beneath his feet. A dark foreboding. Despite the warmth of the late-afternoon sun, he shivered.

Beside him, Nellie wept. He drew her to his side, and she leaned against him, her shoulders shaking. His own eyes watered, but he steeled his spine. Right now, he couldn't let his guard down. He couldn't give in to his emotions.

The service continued. Claire wriggled, and Nellie straightened, swiped away her tears, and bent to whisper something in her ear. She nodded and stood still.

Then came one of the cemetery caretakers. That must be what he was, dressed in overalls, wearing leather gardening gloves and carrying a ladder. No one among the mourners paid any attention to him.

Jean-Paul peered around to make sure none of the Nazis had followed them here. None were visible, but he was unable to shake the heaviness.

A cloud passed over the sun.

The gardener positioned the ladder against the wall. First he climbed up it and swept his gaze around. By this time, their little band had squeezed their way close to the barricade. Jean-Paul went to him.

"It's clear."

Jean-Paul held his breath and willed his hands to cease their trembling. He was as bad as an old man. He motioned for the women to come. Sister Angelica, with Albert in her arms, was the first one up and over. Their contact on the other side would be waiting to escort her down another ladder, across a small creek, and into Switzerland.

Sister Raphael picked up Leo, and when he protested, she covered his mouth, muffling the sound. She spoke to him, just a couple of words, but enough to get him to stop wriggling. One agonizing rung at a time, she climbed the ladder.

A murmur rose among those around the grave. "Hurry up," he told Sister Raphael. Then he turned around to watch the area. To make sure no one stopped them from climbing to freedom.

When he turned around, Sister Raphael was just disappearing over the wall. He released a little bit of the breath he was holding.

Now it was Nellie's turn. If only he could kiss her. He had missed his chance in the church. Now it was too late. "Be safe. I'll see you on the other side."

She nodded and helped Claire onto the ladder. It was a challenge as the child didn't know quite what to do. Nellie kept her grip on her waist and helped her move one foot at a time to the next rung. The process was slow. Too slow.

As they neared the top, a man appeared on the other side. He gave Claire a small smile, then took her in his arms. A moment later, they were gone. Nellie completed her climb and also made it over the wall.

Just as she went out of sight, an uproar disturbed the funeral. Black cars flying the German flag raced toward the gravesite, screeching to a halt not far away.

As soon as they stopped, the doors opened, and Nazis with guns poured out.

Vater among them.

Jean-Paul went cold all over. He raced for the ladder, ascending it as fast as possible.

Several shots rang out, striking the wall next to him, plaster flying, chunks of concrete striking him.

His sweaty hands made it difficult to hang on. Another volley of bullets. Any second, one of them would pierce him. Because his legs were shaking so much and his ankle was throbbing, he almost missed a rung.

Just when he was about to swing his leg over the wall, someone grabbed his tender ankle and pulled him back.

Vater.

⫶CHAPTER THIRTY-ONE⫶

No sooner had Nellie's feet hit the ground on the other side of the cemetery wall than a commotion came from the opposite side. Voices. German voices.

And Jean-Paul's own, answering them in the same tongue.

The sheen of sweat on her arms turned to ice. His father had discovered him.

They couldn't have come this far without their entire band making it safely to Switzerland. Already, Sister Angelica was on the other side of the creek, running deeper into free territory. The German guards they had been told to expect weren't anywhere in sight.

Nellie raced to Sister Raphael's side, pulling Claire along with her. "I'm going back for Jean-Paul. Take her. And this." She slid the packet of pictures from inside her blouse and handed it to the nun, along with the camera from around her neck. "If I don't come back, see that it gets where it needs to go."

"But—"

Nellie forced her legs to go as fast as possible, the blood whooshing in her ears drowning out the rest of Sister Raphael's words. She scampered up the ladder and peered over the top of the wall at the scene below.

Jean-Paul's father had him backed against it, a gun pointed at the middle of his chest. A couple of other Gestapo stood behind him, each with their own weapons trained on Jean-Paul.

Her throat closed. What could she do that wouldn't get both of them killed? There had to be something. But she couldn't stand up to a bunch of armed Nazis when she had nothing to defend herself with.

Jean-Paul's father screamed at his son, the gun in his hands shaking with his wrath, his face raspberry red.

The sun, now lower in the western sky, teared Nellie's eyes and clouded her vision. She blinked away the moisture.

Wait. Was that something shiny in one of the mourner's hands? She squinted and focused. A gun. That was what it appeared to be. She scanned the crowd.

The pastor, standing at the head of Sister Maria-Theresa's grave, reached underneath his black robe. The way he held himself said he too was readying a weapon. A few others reached into their pockets or their waistbands.

They were going to fight back.

And so would Nellie. Unlike that sultry Mississippi night so many years ago, she wouldn't sit by and do nothing but watch an innocent man die. This time would be different.

The armed men glanced at each other. The sign to act. Time to move. With a great heave, Nellie flung herself over the wall and scrambled down a rung or two. Then she turned around and jumped with all her might.

As she hurtled toward the ground, she banged into Jean-Paul's father. For a second after she struck the grass, she was breathless. There beside her was his revolver. She'd knocked it loose. Shaking, she picked it up, the handle still warm from his grip, and pointed it at him.

From somewhere behind her, a shot rang out, the bang of it echoing in her ears.

Close. Too close.

She forced herself to stay still, her hands to quit trembling. Where was her backup? Had she misjudged? Weren't the men of the town coming to help?

The longest two seconds of her life passed in complete silence before the roar of voices rushed back, almost knocking her to the ground.

A dozen or so of the mourners streamed forward, thrust their gun muzzles into the backs of the Nazis, forcing them to the ground. Nellie's lungs tightened.

The pastor nodded in their direction. "Go, go!"

What consequences would he face for his actions?

Jean-Paul didn't give her much time to contemplate. He grabbed her by the arm and led her to the ladder. "Get up. Watch. The guards on the other side must have been alerted."

She shimmied up the ladder, much as she had climbed the drainpipe at home and back to her bed on that fateful night. When she reached the top, she didn't go all the way over but just snuck a peek at the other side.

"What?" Jean-Paul's breath was hot on her neck, his body almost covering hers as he stood no more than a rung or two below her.

"No guards."

"Perfect. Go."

And so she did. Once she dropped to the ground, she sprinted, splashing through the creek, Sister Angelica lifting the fence so she could crawl into Switzerland.

She moved out of the way so Jean-Paul could also get through, then collapsed to the ground, her shallow breaths coming hard and fast, her heart rate never higher.

And then he was through, and Sister Angelica lowered the fence.

They were free.

They had all made it.

By nothing other than God's grace was each of them sitting here.

Jean-Paul plopped to the ground beside Nellie, a half-grin, half-grimace on his face. "We did it. You're crazy, but thanks to you, we made it." His hand brushed hers.

Fire raced from her tingling fingertips straight to her heart. "The men in the crowd would have managed without me. I just don't like being left out."

"I would laugh if that didn't make my head hurt so much."

Sister Angelica and Sister Raphael, along with the children, joined them. Claire climbed onto Nellie's lap, and she held tight to the child. "You're free. You don't have to be afraid anymore. No one is going to hurt you. No more hide-and-seek." Tears streamed down Nellie's cheeks, dripping from her chin. Were there any sweeter words in any language?

At Nellie's declaration, Claire frowned. "*Non, non.* Pway."

Nellie kissed her forehead. "Such a good girl." One who hadn't understood the reason for the game. Perhaps now they could all enjoy it.

"Pway." She folded her hands.

She wanted to pray. "Oh sweet child, of course we can pray." And so, beside the fence, now on Swiss soil, they bowed their heads and thanked the Lord for their escape, each taking a turn to express their appreciation to the Father for His watchful care.

When they had all said amen, she turned toward Jean-Paul. The bruises on his face were deeper and darker than ever, standing out against his pale skin. "How are you?"

"Okay."

"You aren't."

Sister Raphael pointed to a group of men approaching them. "It appears that the Swiss authorities have discovered us. You'll get some medical attention."

Jean-Paul bit his lip. He must be feeling worse than he admitted.

Just as the Swiss border guards arrived, he slumped to the ground.

―――――≈―――――

Nellie stepped out of the official black car that had driven the women and children from the border and stared at the cold, sterile, dormitory-style building that loomed over them, the white lights emanating from it a stark contrast to the silken darkness. The housing on the campus of Mississippi State University was warmer and more welcoming than this.

"Why are we here?" She questioned the burly middle-aged man who had brought them to this place.

"This is the detention center where we process all those who have crossed the border illegally and determine what is to happen to them."

Her shoulders sagged. Had they come this far only to be imprisoned and possibly returned to where they had come from?

Sister Raphael spoke while she jiggled Albert, who was getting hungrier and whose pitiful wails were louder with each passing minute. "Sir, we had to flee for our lives. There were men shooting at us. They were coming for us and for the children."

He shrugged. "It's not me who makes the determination. I'm just to bring you here. I'm only doing my job. The women can come with me. You can bring the baby. The older children will need to go with the matron. They'll be placed in the ward with the others. We have a great many of them here just now."

Marianne Cohn's children. The ones she had given her life for. But Nellie refused to allow Claire and Leo to be taken from them. She shook her head. "These children can't be left alone."

"As I said, the matrons will take care of them."

"You don't understand. They'll be frightened without us."

Their escort blew out a breath. "Again, the matrons will be there. I assure you, they are very good with children."

Nellie took a step closer to him. "These children are Mongoloids. They will stay with us." She pulled Claire to herself.

He studied their little group. Jean-Paul wasn't with them, having been taken to the hospital to have his wounds tended to. Sister Angelica and Sister Raphael clung to the children. After a minute or so, the man crossed his arms. "I'm not supposed to do this, but I'll make an exception."

"*Merci beaucoup.*"

"My sister has a place here. Sometimes she takes in special cases. I think yours would qualify. You can go with the children. The other two women stay."

"*Non.*"

"Unacceptable." The nuns spoke in unison.

"That won't be possible." Nellie straightened to her full height and stared into the man's blue eyes. After all these years of blackout conditions, it was strange to have enough light this late in the day to tell the color of someone's eyes.

"That's my offer."

"I cannot look after these children by myself. Surely you understand that." She sweetened her voice with a generous amount of honey. "The little ones require a great deal of extra care that I cannot give them on my own. They're attached to us, and until they're returned to their parents, we must stay together."

"We all go, or none of us goes." Sister Angelica wasn't helping the situation. Nellie had just buttered up the man, and now she was making ultimatums.

Claire tugged on Nellie's arm. "Pway? Pway?"

She bent to Claire's level. Did she want to play or pray? "No, sweetheart, we don't have to play hide-and-seek anymore. We're safe here." She spoke the words more for the benefit of their escort than for the child. "This nice man is going to take very good care of us."

"Very well." The man huffed. "Sabine's place is not very big, but I'll allow all of you to go there. As I said, I'm not supposed to do this, but you're an extraordinary bunch."

"That is the nicest thing anyone has ever said to me." Nellie flashed him her highest megawatt grin. They returned to the car and climbed back inside, squeezed together.

Once settled, Sister Angelica nudged her with her elbow. "I think the extraordinary one among us is you."

She was nothing more than the daughter of poor Southern folks, one of whom was a murderer. "Most people would think I'm a tomboy at best and insane at worst."

Sister Angelica laughed. "Not true at all. *Merci* for keeping us together. I've been shaking ever since we left the convent. Even before that, if I'm honest. I've been afraid since Leo arrived on our doorstep two years ago."

"You hide it very well." Perhaps that was why she acted so gruff and grim. Perhaps she was only attempting to keep from breaking down.

"You should see me when I'm by myself."

"One of the last things Sister Maria-Theresa said has resonated with me. God will overcome evil eventually. At the cemetery, He did."

Soon they arrived at a pretty little cottage, roses growing up the home's brick exterior. Oh, how long it had been since Nellie had seen such a charming sight. London had been battered and scarred, a shell of its former self, and though the convent was comfortable and pleasant, it wasn't a home.

Their escort led the way to the house and spoke to his sister when she opened the door.

"*Bonsoir.* Look at all of you. And what sweet children." She smiled at Albert, who returned her grin with an even larger one of his own. "How long has it been since you've had a bath? And some warm food? Come in, come in, and I'll get you what you need."

The others followed Sabine, but Nellie hung back. "We're so grateful you relented and brought us here," she said to the man. "*Merci.* But when can we see our injured friend? I need to find out how he is and make sure nothing bad is happening to him."

"*Madame,* I assure you he's in good hands. But I cannot allow you to go out. You must be processed, and we have to make sure there is good reason for you to be in the country."

From underneath her shirt where she wore it on a chain around her neck, Nellie produced her press credentials. "I'm an American journalist. I've been helping these people for a little over a month, and we've just barely escaped with our lives.

"The man who was with us, his father was hunting him like an animal. If the Germans had discovered the children, they would have slaughtered them without hesitation. *S'il vous plaît*, you cannot detain me. I must go to him."

⚎ CHAPTER THIRTY-TWO ⚎

"*Monsieur, s'il vous plaît,* lie still. We cannot help you if you don't allow us to." The nurse leaned over Jean-Paul, the white-tiled walls and floors of the Swiss hospital bleak and sterile.

How could he remain here when he didn't know what was happening to the rest of their little group? From what he remembered Georges Loinger saying, detainees who crossed the border illegally—though what other way was there to cross these days?—were usually held at a center, sometimes for quite a while, during which time the authorities determined what should be done with them.

He hadn't mentioned any of this to Nellie or to the sisters. It would have done no good to frighten them. And they had a strong case. To be sent back to France would mean certain death for them. They weren't fleeing for the promise of more food. They were fleeing for the promise of life.

"You don't understand. I have to go and make sure they're cared for. The children are special. They need help and can't be left to fend for themselves."

"If you are dead, you will do them no good. The sooner you cooperate, the sooner you'll be able to join them. Let the doctor do his work."

What more could he do? His head was throbbing, his vision blurred, his brain scrambled like eggs in an omelet.

After an interminable wait, the doctor appeared, a smile on his face. "You are one of the fortunate few. How you managed to get out in one piece is beyond me. Or maybe I should say you got out relatively unscathed. A concussion, quite a few bad bruises, and a sprained ankle."

"I wouldn't have gotten out at all if not for that American journalist."

No doubt about it. Nellie had saved his life. He owed her everything. If only he could see her and tell her all the jumbled thoughts battering his brain.

A short time later, they had him settled in the ward. Despite the pull to see the rest of his little band once more, his weighted eyelids closed, and he drifted off to sleep.

In his dreams, Vater haunted him, chasing him over the border, crossing it himself, searching every square inch of Switzerland from the highest peaks to the verdant valleys, at last grasping Jean-Paul by the arm and pulling and pulling him away from all he loved.

"Jean-Paul? Are you waking up?"

The voice wasn't Vater's. Quite the opposite. It was soft and feminine. Tender. Each word a caress.

He flicked his eyes open. A woman's smiling face greeted him, her cheeks plumping, a curl falling across her shoulder.

"Nellie." He croaked out the word.

Her grin deepened. "Hello, sleepyhead. I've been waiting for you to wake up. Let me get you a drink." She poured some water from a pitcher beside his bed and offered it to him.

He attempted to sit, but lying still must have stiffened his muscles, leaving him too sore to move.

As she helped him up, some of the water sloshed over the glass's side.

"Trying to drown me now?" He laughed, and she joined in, her face softer than he had ever witnessed.

"How are you all doing? I'm surprised they allowed you to leave the detention center."

"We're not there."

He raised his eyebrows. "You're not? I suppose you had something to do with arranging that."

Her shoulders jerked in a silent chuckle. "I wasn't about to allow them to separate us from the children. And I insisted all three of us were needed to see to their care."

"You, Mademoiselle Wilkerson, are a most amazing woman."

"I don't know why you would underestimate me at this point."

"Believe me. I would never make the mistake of doing such a thing."

"How does it feel?"

"What do you mean?"

She crossed her legs and leaned back in the chair. "To finally be free of your father."

How did it feel? He hadn't had much of a chance to ponder the events of the past few days. So much had happened. All of his life, he had been frightened of the man. Afraid he would displease him as a child. Afraid of being caught and killed by him as an adult. "Strange. Evil is strong. It has no boundaries. Only by God's goodness and grace is it contained. But someday, it will be eliminated. Wiped away forever."

"That will be a glorious day."

"It certainly will be."

"What about your mother and your brother?"

He lay back against the pillows and stared at the white ceiling for a few minutes. "I can't honestly say. It's been so long since Mère had a relationship with Vater. They never spoke in person after he left, only corresponded through letters and telegrams. For her, I don't think it will make a difference."

"And your brother?"

"If Josef survives, I'd like to speak to him and find out why he made the choices he did. It could be that he'll have to stand trial for war crimes, depending on what his role has been. Vater never shared that information with me, so I'm not sure. But I would like the opportunity to say a few words to him at least."

"I hope you get the chance."

She stayed and they spoke for quite a while, until the hospital announced that visiting hours were over. With a great sigh, she came to her feet and tucked a stray strand of hair behind her ear. "I wish I didn't have to go."

"Me too. But the children need you. I'm sure they missed you being there to put them to bed. Go and get some rest. A good night's sleep free from the worries war brings."

"I've only had to deal with it for a few weeks, while you've been enduring it for over four years. I pray that you manage a peaceful night's sleep. You need it far more than I do." She leaned over him and brushed a fleece-soft kiss against his cheek. "I'm so very glad you're alive."

In that moment, with her so near her breath warmed his skin, he had never been more alive in his life.

---≈---

Wednesday, July 12, 1944

"You must have been one terrible patient for them to kick you out of the hospital so fast." In the morning sun, with time to study Jean-Paul's bruises as Sabine drove them to her house, Nellie couldn't believe what the Nazis had done to him. Or how he'd managed to survive.

"It's not as bad as it looks."

Had he read her mind?

"I'm too hardheaded for them to do me any real harm."

"You are blessed by God's good providence, *monsieur.*" Sabine wove her way through early-morning Geneva traffic. "To have escaped from Nazi clutches as many times as you have, you must be one very blessed man. I have heard too many stories from my brother about the horrors awaiting those who are captured."

"They are all too true, I'm afraid."

"I can see that in your face."

They bumped over an uneven strip of pavement, and Jean-Paul winced.

He wasn't fooling Nellie. "You aren't as well as you make yourself out to be."

"I couldn't stay there for another minute. I missed. . .the children."

She bit her tongue lest she ask if he missed her too, though it had been less than twelve hours since they parted. "They'll be so glad to see you. Perhaps you can get Claire to stop insisting that we play hide-and-seek."

"We'll have to teach her a new game. Maybe tag."

"And then she'll be slapping me at odd moments of the day. If only we could show her a card game or something quieter."

"I never had you pegged for the quiet sort." A half-smile lifted one side of his mouth.

Sabine turned a corner with a great deal of care. It was nice of her to not want to hurt Jean-Paul. "I will make you a wonderful breakfast when we get to my house. I have no idea how I will fit all of you around the table, but we will have a celebration feast. I've already been to the market and gotten eggs and bread and milk for the children."

"It sounds spectacular." Nellie pressed her grumbling belly. "I would sit on the floor if I had to in order to enjoy such a meal. You're such a gracious hostess."

"Some may be entertaining angels unawares." Sabine stopped at an intersection and glanced at Nellie and Jean-Paul. "Perhaps even those children."

By the time they arrived at her cottage on the city's outskirts, Jean-Paul had wilted and rested his head on Nellie's shoulder. She held him by the elbow as she led him into the tiny house. No sooner had they stepped over the threshold than Claire and Leo burst from the kitchen and barreled toward Jean-Paul.

Sabine corralled them. "You must be careful of Monsieur Breslau. He is hurt, and we must not hurt him any more. Let's see what Sister Angelica and Sister Raphael are doing." She shooed the children into the kitchen once more.

"I wish she would have let them stay." Although he spoke the words, he said them with little force or conviction.

"There will be plenty of time for that later. Right now, you need to rest. Sabine has made up a bed for you."

"But my breakfast."

"It is possible to have eggs and bacon for lunch or even dinner. It won't hurt you to wait. I'll tell Sabine not to cook anything for you until you're strong enough to sit up and eat. Right now, sleep is the best medicine for you."

He put up no further argument, and Nellie saw to it that he was tucked in. "Rest well."

"*Merci, ma chére.*" His voice trailed off.

But as she closed the door, she could have sworn he said, "*Je t'aime.*"

She leaned against the wall, her heart trembling like a poplar leaf. Had he meant to say he loved her? Or had he meant it only as a friend? A brother to a sister. Or maybe, because of the blow to his skull, he was talking out of his head.

Falling in love with a French maquisard had not been in her plans when she boarded the ship in Southampton. Not at all.

So what had happened?

A kind man who loved the unlovable and the unworthy, enough to put his own life at risk for them.

She sucked in a breath. A man who followed Jesus and His teachings, enough to give up his place on this earth for others. A man who wasn't evil.

That was what had happened. She'd met a man who wasn't evil to the core. More than that, who was a good man.

Yes, she had fallen in love with him. They hadn't known each other very long, but she'd seen enough of him in different situations to know that he was a man she could trust her heart and her life to.

Would he have her? She was stubborn and used to making her own way. Her independence had always meant a great deal to her. She refused to be ruled by a man the way her mother and many of the women in her town had been ruled by their husbands. They said nothing. They didn't speak up for the voiceless.

Jean-Paul defended those who were persecuted. And he put up with her ways.

From the other side of the door came a light snore. Jean-Paul had fallen asleep. That was good.

Where would they go from here? That was a very good question. She had a job to do. She patted the envelope of pictures once again tucked beneath her blouse. Even though the Allies were making good progress, the war was far from over. More stories remained to be told.

Was she the one to tell them?

If not her, than who? Hadn't she said something like that to Jean-Paul when they were getting ready to leave St. Roch?

Soft children's laughter floated from the kitchen, followed by a round of shushes from the women in charge of them. Right now, they were free. It was enough.

She'd leave the future to God.

≋ CHAPTER THIRTY-THREE ≋

Friday, July 14, 1944

The walls of the small cottage closed in on Jean-Paul. Sabine was more than a gracious hostess, but sharing this tiny space with four women and three children was a little more than he had bargained for. Even if it had only been a few days and the children did spend most of their time in the garden just being children.

Their happy, carefree faces lit up the house. Never again would they be forced to play hide-and-seek. They could laugh and scream in delight any time they chose.

But he had healed, at least to a degree, and he couldn't sit still. Nellie told him that in English, they called that "ants in the pants." What a strange expression, yet it fit. That was what he had.

Almost as if he had conjured her, she entered the living room where he paced in front of the stone fireplace. He turned to face her and attempted a grin, but it must have been more like a grimace because Nellie came and drew him into an embrace.

"What's wrong? This should be a happy time. You're free of your father, and we're all free of the Germans."

A terrible headache, an aftereffect of his beating in prison, picked this moment to torment him, his temples throbbing to the beat of an unheard drum. "We're not all free."

A shadow passed over her face. "I know. So many continue to suffer. Even a short distance from here."

"When we listened to the BBC last night..."

"*Oui?*" She scrunched her eyebrows. "I noticed you getting very somber at one point."

"They said, '*Sur mon balcon, je ferai pousser des volubilis.*'"

"I thought that was very strange. 'From my balcony, I shall make something grow.' I don't understand the word *volubilis.*"

"It is the purple flower Sabine has in her garden. The one that only blooms at the beginning of the day."

"Oh." She laughed, the melody lilting and soothing. "In English we call them morning glories. But what does it mean, that you're supposed to grow *volubilis* on your balcony?"

"It is a coded message. The British often use them, broadcasting them on the radio, to signal to the maquisards that they are going to make a drop of weapons and other supplies."

"So there is to be a weapons drop soon." A bit of the light fled her eyes.

"Tonight. The message always comes the evening before."

"Do you know where this one is supposed to be?"

"I've been away for too long. I don't have any idea, but it's driving me crazy. How can I sit here and do nothing when my fellow Frenchmen are fighting to free my country?"

"I understand that it's difficult. But you've done so much already. Look at how many you've saved."

"It's not enough. There are more. Everyday citizens who sit on the edge of their seats, waiting, biding their time until the Allies arrive to liberate them. But I hear that the Maquis is gaining momentum it never had in all the years of the war. Men are joining us in droves, no longer content to sit back and wait for their freedom to come to them. They aim to bring it to themselves."

"And you want to be there when they do."

"*Oui.* Do you know what today is?"

"*Quatorze Juillet. La Fête Nationale.* The day the French revolution began."

"And now another one is beginning. A fight I need to be a part of."

She bit her lip. They both longed for a future together. But how could he rest until all of his people were free? They couldn't rely solely on the Allies. It was long past time for them to rise up and fight for themselves. For their own liberty.

"I wish you wouldn't go."

"I'm torn in two. I want to be here with you and the children." How could he declare his love for her when he was about to let loose the words that tickled his tongue? "On the other hand, my people need me."

"I need you too. So do the children."

"I know. For the sake of Simone, though, and the people of Claire's village, and all those still in hiding and in bondage, I must fight. But I'll return. In the meantime, you have important work to do. You'll be so busy, you won't even miss me."

"I'll miss you every hour of every day, no matter what I'm doing."

"Get that photo to the right people. I'm doing what I can to help the cause. You have a job to help free Europe too. So go do it. When this is all over, and I pray that will be very soon, I'll come back here and find you. And then we won't have these obligations hanging over our heads. We'll be unfettered and free." Perhaps then they could make a life for themselves. If she would have him.

A single tear tracked down her ivory cheek, and he brushed it away, then drew her close to him, so close that her heart thudded against his chest. Could she feel the way his answered hers?

For a long time, they stood together, forming a bond that only death would break. *Lord, may that be many, many years in the future.*

With a light touch, she rubbed his back in small circles, soothing and promising all at the same time.

He bent over and kissed her, tentative at first. She responded in kind, stepping even closer to him, and he deepened the kiss. He savored the taste of her, the feel of her, the nearness of her.

When the children's voices rang in the kitchen behind them, he forced himself to break the kiss and step backward. He shouldn't be making promises he might not be able to keep. Claire rushed into the room, chattering about something Jean-Paul didn't understand.

Nellie swept her into her arms. The place he belonged. How long before he would be there again?

"When will you leave?"

"As soon as possible."

"But you aren't even fully healed. You still have headaches and blurry vision."

"They aren't too bad. Not troublesome enough to keep me from the battle. If you had a brother, wouldn't you urge him to fight for America?"

"I don't have one, and *non*, I would tell him to stay home."

"But he would go, and you would be proud of him."

Her shoulders drooped. "*Oui*. I would. So many of our young men are involved in this fray."

"And that is what I must do."

"How will you get across the border again? Especially with your father searching for you?"

"I'll cross at a different spot. With the Allies pressing on every side, he won't be able to keep up the search much longer. Soon he'll be forced to flee for his life."

"I'll pray for you."

"*Merci*. I'll need every one I can get."

"Don't frighten me more. And hurry back. We'll be waiting."

He would do everything in his power to fulfill her request.

Saturday, July 15, 1944

With the utmost care, Nellie rewound the last roll of film in her camera, opened the back, and pulled out the precious cylinder. Though it was small and seemed insignificant, what it held was of the highest value. That and the envelope of photographs. The world needed to know what had happened to Claire's family. To many families in that small village.

If they didn't already understand the true horror of Hitler, they soon would. And Nellie prayed the world would never forget.

She had been busy visiting Jean-Paul in the hospital and entertaining the children, but now Jean-Paul had left for France and the children had settled into Sabine's house. It was beyond time for her to put this film and those photographs into the hands of someone who could disseminate them.

She found Sister Raphael giving Albert a bottle in the tiny bedroom they shared. "I'm going to drop off the photographs and the film."

Sister Raphael nodded and smiled, never taking her gaze from the infant. "I'm so glad that photograph is getting into the right hands. I'll pray that it will change the world."

"I doubt it will do that, but perhaps it will change a few people's minds."

"You miss him, don't you?"

Nellie didn't have to ask who Sister Raphael meant. "More than I thought I would." She took a moment to sit on the edge of the bed beside her. "What if he never comes back?"

"What if he does return?"

"Then I will be the happiest woman in the world."

"Concentrate on that." Sister Raphael lifted the baby to her shoulder to burp him. "Think of all he's survived so far. He's tough, like an old rooster."

Nellie couldn't help but laugh at the comparison. To her, Jean-Paul was nothing like Old Red when Mama had finally stewed him. "What he's doing is very dangerous."

"Everything he's done to this point has been dangerous." Albert gave a big burp, and Sister Raphael rose and placed him in the little blanket nest she had made on the floor. "He survived all that. And now he has more motivation than ever to make it out alive. You'll see. It will all work out."

"You sound more and more like Sister Maria-Theresa every day. I pray you're right." Nellie rose and straightened the navy-blue skirt she had borrowed from Sabine. She couldn't walk into a newspaper office in her tattered pants and baggy jacket. She fiddled with the waistband that cut around her middle.

Sister Raphael stood in front of her and stilled her hands. "You'll do fine. As soon as they open that envelope, they'll be astonished at what they see."

"What if they don't like the photograph? What if it doesn't stir them the way it has me? All of my work will have been for nothing."

Sister Raphael cocked her head. "Do you hear those children in the yard? Were they for nothing?"

"Yes, that is true. Even if they throw the photographs back at me and refuse to develop the film, it will have been worth it. Claire is alive. She will be cared for. The Nazis didn't do away with her." Though Nellie's heart ached for Claire, never knowing the depth of her mother's love. No longer hearing that laughter or feeling that gentle kiss on her cheek.

"Get along with you now. Soon Leo and Claire will be clamoring for a treat and will never let you out of their sight."

"*Merci.*" Nellie hurried out the door, clutching the borrowed pocketbook that contained the precious pictures and the roll of film.

She had a decent walk to get to the tram that deposited her in front of the newspaper office. Ah, here was something familiar and comforting. A place where she felt at home.

She entered the lobby, showed the secretary her press credentials and her American passport, and was directed to an elevator. As the lift carried her up three floors, she couldn't help but tap her foot, praying the entire way that the people here would agree she had captured Claire standing in front of that burned-out church just right.

That her story would be one the world would hear and never forget. That they would see hope in the eyes of a child who had lost everything.

The secretary led her to a corner office and informed her the editor would be with her shortly. Left to her own devices, Nellie wandered to the window overlooking the street. The city of low buildings, many with red-tiled roofs, hugged the tip of Lac Léman, the same blue as the mountains which rose around it.

Everything so normal. The world continuing on as if this weren't an oasis of peace and calm in a desert of inhumanity.

While she'd been in London, Mama had written her about life in the States. A little bit of rationing. The boys leaving. Some of them not coming home. But there no one feared for their lives or hid in cellars or were locked in churches and burned to death.

Everyday life continued much as it always had.

When they arrived here, she had been able to get a message out to Mama. Just to let her know she was alive and well. Mama had telegraphed back her relief almost immediately.

She took a few turns about the room, the plush gray carpeting silencing her footfalls but not the pounding of her heart. If only all the world could know Claire and her story. They would fall in love with her the way Nellie had. They would want to do everything they could to end this war so children like Claire and Leo and Albert and other persecuted people could live.

Just about the time Nellie was ready to go crazy, a wiry older gentleman entered the room, shutting the door behind him with a soft click.

"*Bonjour. Je suis* Monsieur Perrot."

She shook his hand. "I'm Nellie Wilkerson from the *Chicago Tribune.*"

"Have a seat." He motioned to the leather chair across from where he settled himself. "My secretary tells me you have something I'm going to be very interested in."

"I believe so, sir. What I've brought you today and the story I have to share will shed a light on what Hitler is doing across Europe and might just spur the Allies on to a speedier victory." She gave him a brief account of the past several weeks, including the fire at the church which claimed the lives of Claire's family. Was that really all the time that had transpired? How life had changed in that short period.

Monsieur Perrot leaned back in his leather chair and puffed on his cigar. "I'd heard rumblings about the burning of that church, of course. We all have. But to have a photograph of a Mongoloid child who survived such barbarism is astounding."

"I was with a French maquisard, and we found her hiding in the hedgerows. We observed the Germans and went in as soon as they left, as soon as it was safe for us to do so. I hope you'll find the picture to be moving and stirring. I believe it tells the entire story in a single snap."

She dropped the envelope onto his tidy desk. He clutched it and peeked inside. He fingered through the first several prints, then gasped. Several interminable minutes went by before he looked up at her. "You shot this?"

"I did."

He stared at her, open mouthed.

"And. . . ?" She slid to a half-standing position. She had to restrain herself from shaking him to get him to speak.

"Sit back, Mademoiselle Wilkerson."

Oh no. This couldn't be good news. You were only ever told to sit when the news was bad.

Once she was relaxed against the chair's back, he withdrew the photograph from the envelope and pushed it across the desk toward her.

And there it was.

The precious photograph Nellie had carried across France.

Claire in front of the church that claimed so many lives, her almond-shaped eyes wide, her prominent forehead scrunched in confusion, begging for someone to help. Pleading for someone to care.

"This is remarkable. Worthy of a Pulitzer Prize."

Oh yes. From a disposable child to one who would inspire the entire world to care.

⟩ CHAPTER THIRTY-FOUR ⟨

Tuesday, August 1, 1944

Deep in the forested Alpine foothills, Jean-Paul lay on his back, staring through the thick branches at the single star he managed to pick out among the leaves. For now, the countryside lay quiet, tucked in slumber. Not a peaceful sleep but the sleep of anticipation. It was an anxious, tangled-in-the-sheets sleep because of what the next morning might bring.

That was how every night had been since he had crossed back into the Haute-Savoie region of France. Strange. It had been less than a month since he had fled for his life from this country. Switzerland had been the Promised Land. For weeks, he had dreamed of getting there. Of being safe. Of being free.

But he couldn't rest while Frenchmen, Jews, Mongoloids, and so many others still bent under Hitler's heavy hand. And so he found himself in the country that had fed and nourished him and watched him grow into the man he was.

Mère continued to live under their oppression. She had yet to draw in a breath of free air. For her, for all the others, he fought.

But he couldn't harness his thoughts or keep them from returning to that little cottage on the edge of Geneva. More specifically, to the beautiful young American woman staying there.

Nellie.

As long as her image continued to appear in front of his eyes at unbidden times, he would never sleep well. A dull ache occupied his chest most of the time. Except for when he was serving as a sniper, driving out hidden pockets of Germans from liberated villages here in Eastern France where the maquisards were the ones fighting for freedom.

What were they going to do? She was a career woman. She may not even want to settle down. But other than Mère, he had no obligations in France. At least once they had driven German boots from their blood-stained soil. He could follow Nellie around Europe. Perhaps get himself a job with a paper or a magazine. If nothing else, use his language skills as a translator.

His dream had been to rid his country of their oppressors for so long that he was left with little to strive for. He had been at university when the war broke out, studying business. He could finish his degree and get a job almost anywhere.

One thing he didn't doubt. Nellie needed to be part of his life. He would fight for her as hard as he was fighting for France. Never again would he let her go.

If he managed to return to her. If he managed to stay alive that long.

"Jean-Paul." Luc, whom he'd reconnected with since joining the fight, shook him by the shoulder.

He sat up. "Time for my watch already?"

"Afraid so. I'm going to get some sleep."

"Any activity tonight?"

"*Non*, it's been pretty quiet. Just manage to stay awake, okay?"

"Will do."

Luc lay down, rolled on his side, and was snoring before Jean-Paul had gone ten paces. He settled himself against a tree, his American-made weapon laid across his lap as he peered into the darkness. The moon had already set, so even if someone was about, he may not catch sight of them until it was too late.

That meant he had to rely on his hearing to do the job for him. Concentration. No allowing Nellie to invade his thoughts or his day-dreams now.

Every now and again, one of his fellow maquisards stirred in his sleep. Otherwise, only the hooting of an owl kept him company.

And then came the breaking of a stick. Possibly nothing more than a deer.

Lots of sticks breaking. No deer. Not even if there were two or three of them together.

Low voices cut off the owl's echoing calls. Jean-Paul straightened. Gripped his gun. Every nerve went taut.

Though he couldn't make out the words, the timbre of the language left no doubt they were speaking German. Would they skirt around the maquisards' encampment? Or run straight into it?

He took only shallow breaths, and even then, only when necessary. His hands sweated. Perspiration trickled down his face.

The voices approached. Did the Germans even know Jean-Paul and the other men were here?

He could now make out their words. "We'll slip around and catch them from behind at first light."

They marched straight toward their position. They would tramp right through camp. Sound asleep, his men would have no chance to fight back.

It was Jean-Paul against however many Germans there were. Plenty more than one, that was for sure. But he couldn't allow them to slaughter the maquisards.

He raised his gun.

Waited until they were almost on top of him.

And fired.

The enemy returned fire.

Tuesday, August 22, 1944

Whenever she wasn't busy at the newspaper, Nellie spent her time staring out the front window of the small apartment she had been able to rent with the sisters and the children. Monsieur Perrot had allowed her use of his building and equipment to do her work for the *Tribune*. That helped to keep her mind occupied.

But as soon as she left the office to walk the couple of blocks to their apartment, her mind turned to Jean-Paul. Annemasse had been liberated four days ago. He'd promised to return. So where was he?

Perhaps he had decided to stay in France until the entire country was free. At the rate the Allies were moving, that wouldn't be too much longer. Still too long for her to be apart from him, to not know what was happening to him. If he was even alive.

For now, she would stay in Geneva and wait.

She sat pressed against the window, watching the movement on the street below, praying to see a dark-haired man making his way to the building and inside to them.

But no one came.

Claire scampered across the small room, stood beside her, and pressed herself against the window in much the same way Nellie did. Nellie fiddled with Claire's braid. "And what will become of you now, little one? You have no more family." Parting from all three of the children would be the biggest heartbreak of Nellie's life.

At least she would see Velma again.

But what if. . . ?

It was a question she couldn't entertain until she had answers about Jean-Paul's whereabouts.

"Come have some supper." Sister Angelica had snuck up behind Nellie.

"I'm not very hungry."

Claire, however, ran off to the kitchen where Sister Raphael had stewed a chicken.

Angelica took Claire's place in front of the window. "Watching and wishing for him to come won't make him get here any sooner."

"I know."

"Come and have something to eat. Remember how hungry we were? Now we have plenty. We shouldn't waste it."

So she sat at the small round table, but she gave most of her portion to Claire, who gobbled it up.

After she cleared the table, she helped Sister Angelica wash the dishes. "I know you're anxious to return to St. Roch and your life there. You don't need to wait with me here. We have no idea if or when Jean-Paul will come."

"How would you care for the children? You work all day. Sabine is busy. Sister Raphael and I have discussed this. We're going to stay until he returns, and then we'll make our plans. We don't even know if our convent still stands."

It was entirely possible that it lay in ruins. Much of France must by now.

"*Merci beaucoup* for being willing to help. I could always arrange other care for the children."

Sister Angelica handed Nellie another plate from the rinse side of the sink. "They've been through too much to have yet another change in their lives. True, they are resilient, but that only goes so far. Because we're familiar to them, we'll stay."

Nellie dropped her dish towel and hugged Sister Angelica, her throat too clogged for her to form words.

As she lay in bed that night, snuggled between Claire and Leo, she prayed for Jean-Paul, for his safe return, and that it might be soon. And, hard as it was, she released her hold on him and entrusted him to God.

She must have fallen into a fitful sleep, because a banging on the door roused her. For a moment, she was disoriented, and it took a minute for her to get her bearings.

Once she did, she threw on her wrap and made her way to the entry. Sister Raphael had beat her there and had already opened it.

In strode Jean-Paul.

Nellie covered her mouth to squelch her squeal lest she wake the children. Next thing, she was in his arms, showered with his kisses all over her face, finally resting on her lips.

She reached up and hugged him by the neck, kissing him back, reveling in his nearness. Though not yet sated, she pulled back. "I'd begun to doubt you would come. I was afraid you'd forgotten about us. Or worse."

"How could I ever forget about you?" He leaned closer, his breath tickling her neck, sending a tremor down her spine. "I had to do some pretty fancy shooting, but I was determined to make it back."

She answered him with another kiss. This time, it was he who pulled away.

By then, Sister Angelica had come from her bedroom, tying the sash around her robe. "It's good to see you, Jean-Paul. Nellie was about to go crazy with worry."

Good thing the room was cast in shadows, or he might catch a glimpse of the heat rising in her cheeks. "Not crazy."

"Almost." Sister Angelica gave a rare chuckle. "So tell us what you've been doing."

"Before that, tell me about the photograph, Nellie."

She clasped his hands. "You would never believe it. It turned out better than I dared imagine. My boss at the *Tribune* was thrilled with it and published it along with the story I wrote. Since then, it's been picked up by newspapers all over the world. I can hardly believe it. And he has been allowing me to continue writing articles about my time in France, using all the photographs I took."

By this time, Sister Raphael had returned to the room with a copy of the newspaper in her hands. "Look for yourself. Your young lady is famous."

Nellie grimaced. "It's not the kind of thing I'd like to be famous for. In fact, I don't want the attention drawn to me but to the circumstances and the events occurring here."

He kissed her again.

Sister Angelica and Sister Raphael backed out of the room, and at last, she and Jean-Paul were alone. "How did it really go?" she asked him.

"Though I went through so much in the four years of the occupation, I'd never been in battle. It's so different from anything else." He shuddered. "But the important thing is that we drove the Nazis out and my people are free. At least some of them. And Paris should be liberated any day now, if it isn't already."

"That's so wonderful."

"My question for you is where do we go from here? I'm sure you're anxious to return to the States and continue working there."

"When I wasn't worrying about you, I was pondering my future." She almost said *our* instead of *my,* but didn't dare assume anything. They had no commitment, no agreement between them. "I've been in Europe for a long time, and I like it here. The only thing drawing me back to the States is Velma."

"Oh." His voice deflated.

"But I can't leave Claire behind. The sisters want to return to France and reunite Leo and Albert with their parents. I don't know what to do."

"Stay." The single word was a plea, his voice cracking.

She swiped at a tear that had leaked unbidden from her eye, even as one flowed down his cheek.

"Marry me."

Tingles raced up and down her arms. She couldn't make her mouth move to answer, so she just nodded.

After many more kisses, they parted, the apartment quiet except for the ticking of the alarm clock from Nellie's room. "Can I be bold?"

"I don't think you need my permission for that."

"I would be happy to return to France and work from there. I can take pictures anywhere in the world. But my acceptance of your proposal comes with a condition."

"Of course it does." But Jean-Paul's words were lighthearted.

"Two conditions, actually."

"At this point, I'd do almost anything to get you to marry me."

She gave him a playful swat on the arm. "The two conditions are Claire and Velma. I want them to live with us. To be ours. Forever and ever. June can't take care of her sister. From what I know, she never even visits her."

She rushed on before he could object to her terms. "I know it won't be easy taking care of two Mongoloid children. Well, Velma's not a child anymore, but you know what I mean. Most people put them in institutions. Hide them away from the world.

"But they are valuable. They have contributions to make to society. If nothing else, they have contributions to make to us. Together, we can do this. We can be a family."

He touched her lips to shush her. "Of course, *mon cœur*, of course they will live with us. I expected that, was planning on it. I would have it no other way. Just as I can't imagine my life without you, I can't imagine my life without them."

"Then we're getting married."

"The sooner the better."

"Of course. We won't have the picture-perfect family, but—"

"It will be just perfect for us."

And once again, he covered her with his kisses. He was right. The picture of their family, strange though it was, was absolutely perfect.

⧳ AUTHOR'S NOTES ⧳

What's true and what's not true? I'm often asked this of the books I write. Much comes from real life. Much comes from my mind. Sometimes the lines blur. So here's what's based on historical fact.

My physical description of Nellie Wilkerson is based on Evelyn Sharp, a real American female pilot who trained over 350 men under her and died ferrying a plane during WWII. I came across her picture with other female pilots, and she stood out to me. I knew right then and there that I had found Nellie. I like to think they had the same indomitable spirit. Evelyn was an amazing woman.

The women reporters at the beginning of the story, Martha Klein and Frances Cannes, were not actual people, but there were many intrepid and notable women working in the field of journalism at the time. Martha Gellhorn was a woman who did write a letter to military authorities after being denied permission to enter France, though she didn't address the letter to General Eisenhower. "It is necessary that I report on this war," she said. "I do not feel there is any need to beg as a favor for the right to serve as the eyes for millions of people in America who are desperately in need of seeing, but cannot see for themselves."

Most of the reporters in England at that time were staying at the Dorchester Hotel. There was a crowd of them gathered in the lobby on the morning of D-Day, listening to the radio, anticipating events they knew where happening because of the unusually high aviation activity over the city of London.

The *Prague* was a real hospital ship. Events in this section of the book are taken from the real-life story of Martha Gellhorn, and many of the descriptions of what happened are based on hers. Unlike Nellie, she did get back on the ship to England, though she did scoop many of the male correspondents, including her estranged husband, Ernest Hemingway. Finally, days after D-Day, Gellhorn and other female correspondents were given permission to go to France and cover the front lines of the war.

The photograph of the church is based on a real photograph taken after the Germans massacred 642 people in the village of Oradour-sur-Glane near Limoges on June 10, 1944. No one is exactly sure why the Germans chose this particular town. The Nazis rounded up every resident in the town square. They then took the women and children, locked them in the church, and burned it to the ground. Those who tried to escape, they shot dead. The men were taken to barns and shot.

Roger Godfrin, not quite eight years old, was among the few who survived, and the only school-aged child who did. Already a refugee from Lorraine, he knew what the Germans were capable of. His mother trained him to run away and hide if the Nazis ever came. That's just what he did on that fateful day, fleeing the village school, hiding in a garden and in a field. Oradour-sur-Glane is preserved as it was on that day as a memorial to those who lost their lives.

L'asile is a made-up town. The word means "sanctuary."

I named the fictitious convent St. Roch because he was the patron saint of invalids, among other things.

Marianne Cohn, Mila Racine, and Rolande Birgy were real people who worked as part of the French resistance, in part smuggling Jews over the border to Switzerland with the *Oeuvre de Secours aux Enfants*. So were cousins Georges Loinger and Marcel Mangel, the latter who went on to become the famous mime Marcel Marceau. He was of Jewish descent and changed his name after the war. He relied on his acting skills during his work with the resistance and taught the children to mime in order to keep them quiet.

They would dress the children as Scouts and have them pretend they were on their way to the border region for summer camp. Often they would get a soccer game going and Georges or Marcel would kick the ball over the border and then have the children cross in order to get it. They must have lost many balls this way. Another ruse they used was the one I used in the book, having the Jews climb the wall during a funeral.

Many children came alone, and they sewed their real names inside their clothing so they would be able to reunite with their families after the war. The Swiss, trying to maintain their neutrality, detained those who crossed. Some were sent back. Many were held in sterile detention centers. Some were eventually released into Switzerland.

Jean Deffaught was the mayor of Annemasse when Marianne Cohn and the children she was smuggling were detained at the Hôtel Pax in his city. He took his life into his hands and went to visit them in prison, bringing food, bandages, and blankets. Eventually, he managed to get the seventeen youngest children released and to a safe haven. Eleven children remained with Marianne. When Jean Deffaught devised a plan to break her out of prison, she refused, stating that she wanted to stay with the children.

After her murder, when he learned that the remaining children were to be made to "disappear," he arranged for their release. They were taken to the safe house with the other children. Yad Vashem recognized Jean Deffaught as Righteous Among the Nations on October 19, 1965.

I did a little finagling with Marianne Cohn's death. She was actually arrested in May 1944. Then she was taken from the Hôtel Pax with a group of prisoners and beaten to death in a forest outside of the city on July 8, 1944. If I had kept that date, it would be the day after Jean-Paul arrived there. I needed the characters to know of her death in order to show what could happen to them.

On July 31, 1944, the Maquis received a coded message on the BBC. It read, "*Sur mon balcon, je ferai pousser des volubilis,*" which translates, "On my balcony, I shall make *volubilis* (morning glories) grow." The following day, six waves of American aircraft dropped four hundred containers with more than one thousand tons of arms and explosives. This was the beginning of the popular uprising in France that aided in the liberation of the country.

Annemasse, a suburb of Geneva on the French side of the border, was a popular spot for Jews to cross into Switzerland. It is located in the state of Haute-Savoie. It was the Maquis who, with an infusion of American arms on August 1st (I took a bit of license with the actual date to make it work better with the story), fought the Germans in the state of Haute-Savoie and finally achieved the Nazis' surrender on August 19, 1944, without the support of any Allied troops.

⚎ ACKNOWLEDGMENTS ⚎

Even in the midst of a pandemic, a book isn't written in complete isolation. That is due to the help, encouragement, and prayers of many.

Thank you to the amazing team at Barbour Publishing for allowing me to write Nellie and Jean-Paul's story. It's one I've been longing to dig into for some time now, and I'm so pleased I get to share it with the world. Thank you, Becky Germany, for the great work you do in coming up with the fantastic ideas that become these amazing series. Thank you to Abbey for all you do for handling the endorsers and taking care of much of the day-to-day stuff. Thank you also to Shalyn and your hard work on the marketing end of things.

A huge shout-out goes to Ellen Tarver, my fabulous editor. You have this way of taking the lump of clay I send you and helping me form it into a worthy vessel. I don't take you or your hard work for granted. This story would be nothing without your insight.

Much thanks to the Pencildancer team—Angie, Diana, Jen, and Jenny, who run it along with me, and the readers who cheer for us, support us, and spread the word about us. You all are a terrific asset. You keep me from losing my mind.

Thank you to all my readers. Without you, there wouldn't be books. What a sad world that would be. Even in these crazy times, you have continued to buy books, enjoy them, and spread the word about them. On behalf of all authors, thank you for helping us to weather this storm.

This book wouldn't have been possible without the prayers of many. I can't list all of you, for there are so many who have stood with me; but Janet, you know how special you are to me and how much I treasure our time together, even if it's had to be on the phone. God has been gracious in helping me to craft this story.

Merci beaucoup to my family. My husband, Doug, you are my rock and my safe landing place. You picked up so much of the slack at home while I was writing this, all without my even having to ask. I'm so grateful for you and the support you've been to me over the years. I couldn't do this without you. Brian, Alyssa, and Jonalyn, my precious children, you remind me that author isn't the only job I have. Even though you're not at home anymore, Brian and Alyssa, you are never far from my thoughts or prayers.

My precious Jonalyn, you inspired Claire. You have the same resilience she does, coming at age five to a strange country with strange people who spoke a strange language. How scary that must have been for you, especially since you didn't understand what was happening. Yet you have thrived. You trusted us with your life, just as Claire trusted hers to Nellie and Jean-Paul. You have brought so much joy to us. We cannot imagine life without you. You are as worthy as any Nobel laureate. I will never allow the world to believe otherwise.

Above everything else, all glory be to God for His saving, sustaining grace. Someday, evil will be put away forever. Come quickly, Lord Jesus.

LIZ TOLSMA is the author of several WWII novels, romantic suspense novels, prairie romance novellas, and an Amish romance. She is a popular speaker and an editor and resides next to a Wisconsin farm field with her husband and their youngest daughter. Her son is a US Marine, and her oldest daughter is a college student. Liz enjoys reading, walking, working in her large perennial garden, kayaking, and camping. Please visit her website at www.liztolsma.com and follow her on Facebook, Twitter (@LizTolsma), Instagram, YouTube, and Pinterest. She is also the host of the Christian Historical Fiction Talk podcast.

HEROINES OF WWII

They went above the call of duty and expectations to aid the Ally's war efforts and save the oppressed. Full of intrigue, adventure, and romance, this new series celebrates the unsung heroes—the heroines of WWII.

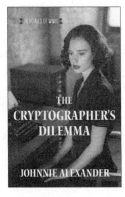

The Cryptographer's Dilemma
By Johnnie Alexander

FBI cryptographer Eloise Marshall is grieving the death of her brother, who died during the attack on Pearl Harbor, when she is assigned to investigate a seemingly innocent letter about dolls. Agent Phillip Clayton is ready to enlist and head oversees when asked to work one more FBI job. A case of coded defense coordinates related to dolls should be easy, but not so when hearts get entangled and Phillip goes missing. Can Eloise risk loving and losing again?

Paperback / 978-1-64352-951-6 / $14.99

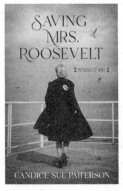

Saving Mrs. Roosevelt
By Candice Sue Patterson

Shirley Davenport is as much a patriot as her four brothers. She, too, wants to aid her country in the war efforts and joins a new branch of the Coast Guard for single women called SPARs. At the end of basic training, Captain Webber commissions her back home in Maine under the ruse of a dishonorable discharge to help uncover a plot against the First Lady. Shirley soon discovers nothing is as it seems. Why do people she loves want to harm the First Lady?

Paperback / 978-1-63609-089-4 / $14.99